T0266360

Orange
HORSES

Orange
HORSES

MAEVE KELLY

With an introduction by
Simon Workman

TRAMPPRESS

Previous publications: 'Amnesty', *New Irish Writing*, Irish Press, 1973; 'Journey Home', *New Irish Writing*, 1972; 'Morning at My Window', *New Irish Writing*, 1972; 'Orange Horses', *Wildish Things*, Attic Press, 1989; 'Love', Poolbeg Press, 1976; 'The Sentimentalist', *New Irish Writing*, 1976; 'Cause and Effect', *New Irish Writing*, 1981; 'Parasites', Poolbeg Press, 1976; 'The Last Campaign', *New Irish Writing*, 1971; 'The Vain Woman', Poolbeg Press, 1976; 'Pilgrim's Tale', *New Irish Writing*, 1981; 'The Fortress', Poolbeg Press, 1976; 'A Life of Her Own', *New Irish Writing*, 1981; 'The False God', Poolbeg Press, 1976; 'The Tattooed', *New Irish Writing*, 1971; 'Queen', *Best Irish Short Stories 2*, Elek Books Ltd, 1977; 'Ruth', *New Irish Writing*, 1978; 'Day at the Sea', *New Irish Writing*, 1974.

Some stories previously published together in the collection *A Life of Her Own*, Poolbeg Press, 1976.

This collection published in 2016 by Tramp Press
First published by Michael Joseph Limited
Copyright Maeve Kelly, 1990
Introduction copyright Simon Workman, 2016
All rights reserved

www.tramppress.com

10 9 8 7 6 5 4 3 2 1

Tramp Press gratefully acknowledges the financial assistance of the Arts Council.

ISBN 9780993459207

Thank you for supporting independent publishing.

Set in 11pt on 15pt Sabon by Marsha Swan.
Printed by ScandBook, Sweden.

A Life of One's Own

by Simon Workman

In her review of *Orange Horses* in 1991, the writer Aisling Maguire described Maeve Kelly as a 'late bloomer in the literary field' owing to the fact that Kelly did not publish her first collection of short stories, *A Life of Her Own* (1976), until well into her forties. Rather than any reflection on the evolution of Kelly's talent, this late flowering points to the limited opportunities for writing and publication during her early lifetime and reveals much about the cultural climate in which she began her career. Though the number of published Irish women writers increased in the 1970s and early 1980s, only one in ten Irish books printed during this period were authored by women, and this ratio drops to one in fifty when considering mainstream, non-women-oriented presses. The relative paucity of women's writing in these years is bound up with how women writers were received critically, and the subtle bias evident among some reviewers who tended to read women's books in terms of the gender of the author. Kelly was alert to such prejudice, and in her first novel *Necessary Treasons* (1985) the main character Eve articulates her frustration at how certain critics analyse women's writing:

> ... she could not account for the irritation she had recently felt on reading a review of a woman's collection of poetry which the reviewer described as verse, the work of a minor poet – too self-absorbed, as was the work of so many women. Only two weeks earlier another critic had described a woman's first novel as lacking an obsessive voice. The weight of prejudice against women seemed at times beyond endurance, yet it was difficult to pin down and classify.

As evidence for this form of critical inequity Kelly could justly point to certain initial reviews of *A Life of Her Own* (all stories of which are contained in *Orange Horses*). Though the book received strong praise in a number of contemporary journals and newspapers, the critic J.B. Kilfeather was disparaging of the collection, arguing:

> Women do not have an easy time in Ireland but surely this writer is piling on the agony. ... there are the stories of sickness of girls and women. And miscarriages and loutish husbands. ... All of which I can well believe and even feel a certain degree of sympathy with the protagonists of the stories, but Maeve Kelly does go on rather much about it.

Following a similar line, the writer Tom MacIntyre argues that though the book is articulating an important theme in addressing 'the subject position of women in Ireland', Kelly fails to express this topic adequately because 'the melodramatic is an obdurate element in her sensibility' and she's 'not above piling it on'. Particularly insidious here is the way the argument openly acknowledges the difficulties facing Irish women while tacitly perpetuating the prejudices which degrade and delimit their daily lives. Facile phrases such as 'piling on the agony' and 'does go on rather much' complacently dismiss as histrionics and hyperbole the profound distress and trauma experienced by many women in Ireland at this time.

The twenty stories within *Orange Horses* are part of Kelly's lifelong struggle to dispel such complacency and bring marginalised, particularly female, forms of experience into the larger national consciousness. It is a sign of Kelly's deftness of touch as a writer that this larger intention does not overwhelm the integrity of her fictional worlds. Key to Kelly's work is her scrupulous attentiveness to the strange complexities of human behaviour and her precision in rendering the intricate and conflicted inner lives of her characters. In *Orange Horses* Kelly displays a remarkable palette of tones; she is capable of crafting scenes of gentle humour or chill tragedy as well as generating moments of lyrical intensity bordering on the visionary. The collection's narratives also move across time and space: stories range from islands on the far west of Ireland to dingy student accommodation in the centre of London, from the War of Independence to the IRA letter-bombing campaign of England in the 1970s, and from the impoverished life of rural farmers to the heady world of successful young female writers and passionate artists. In charting these worlds, Kelly pivots from a quality of deep humanity reminiscent of Mary Lavin to a pitch of bleak incisiveness evocative of the early work of Edna O'Brien. Yet as the critic Isabel Quigly argues: 'Kelly's voice is very much her own, neat, unflashy, often funny, often sad.'

Born in Ennis, Co. Clare in 1930, Kelly was educated in Dundalk before moving to St Andrew's Hospital in London to qualify in General Nursing. Though she pursued post-graduate theatre nursing in Oxford, Kelly had to give up her profession when she contracted TB. After finishing her work in England, she subsequently returned to Clare where she lived and farmed with her husband Gerard O'Brien Kelly with whom she had two children, Joseph and Oona. Her first story to appear in print was in the *Irish Press* 'New Irish Writing' page in 1971, and the following year another story won the Hennessy Literary Award. After moving to Limerick, Kelly became involved in the Irish Women's Movement which, at that time, was largely focused on issues such as equality of opportunity in employment and education, the availability of contraception, and the plight of abused women, single mothers, widows, and deserted wives. Evidently energised by these matters, Kelly co-founded both the Limerick Federation of Women's Organisations and the Limerick Refuge for Battered Wives in 1974. She was administrator of the latter organisation, now called Adapt House, for fifteen years. Her sense of the vulnerability of victimised women can be gauged by a letter published by *The Irish Times* in 1975 in which she laments that victims of domestic abuse are 'the most cruelly treated of our citizens' and that many of the husbands of beaten women 'regard the legal system as upholding their right to abuse and neglect their wives as they see fit.' The lack of legal support for abused women was a function of the prevailing moral ideology of the political and ecclesiastical authorities which tended not to interfere too deeply into what they considered the private domain of the family. In mid-century Ireland this led to a veil of silence around the physical, sexual and psychological abuse of women in the home, and it was not until the 1970s that feminist activists such as Kelly brought these issues to the public attention and pushed for changes in the law. As well as legal reform there was also a pressing need for research into the nature and extent of domestic violence. Kelly made an important contribution in this regard by initiating a major study on violence towards women entitled *Breaking the Silence* (1992) which used testimony from women who had accessed Adapt House services.

As with authors such as Edna O'Brien, Leland Bardwell, Bernard MacLaverty, and Eavan Boland, Kelly also helped to break down powerful taboos surrounding violence in the home by making it the subject of her writing. Her extensive experience of working with abused women in Adapt House informs *Necessary Treasons*, which sensitively engages with the issue of domestic violence as well as offering a history and rationale of the women's refuge movement and its struggles. Her most striking representation of this theme, however, is the title story of this collection, 'Orange Horses', in which a young Traveller woman lives under constant physical threat from her husband Fonsie. By setting her story within the Travelling community, Kelly was giving vital exposure to a class of people who had been largely invisible in Irish short fiction. Indeed, in a review of *Orange Horses* in 1993, the writer Celia de Fréine praised Kelly's focus on Traveller life noting that: 'until recently (with few exceptions) the only time we read of Travellers was in media reports.'

'Orange Horses' initially appeared in Ailbhe Smyth's anthology, *Wildish Things* (1989), and in his review of the book John A. Wiseman praised the story as displaying 'writing which is powerful and irradicable.' This potency of expression is evident in the narrative's opening scene which begins:

> Elsie Martin's husband beat her unconscious because she called him twice for dinner while he was talking to his brother. To be fair, she did not simply call him. She blew the horn of the Hiace van to summon him.

The bleakly ironic tone and blunt-edged horror of this passage are sharply reflective of the terrifying arbitrariness and warped internal logic of Fonsie's savagery. His violent attack causes Elsie to miscarry her five-month-old baby, whom she believes to be a boy, and leaves her with a wired jaw and various other gashes to her head and elsewhere. In the days after, she grieves not only because she has lost a child but because he 'might have been the one to protect her' unlike her other sons who she knows will 'hit their wives to control them'.

Despite the viciously patriarchal nature of her family, Elsie refuses to accept her oppression and, despite grave threats of beatings, she is able to get 'her dole money split so that she got her own share and the share for half the children.' Elsie also buries the money she gets from begging and the horde becomes a 'secret like a flame to be kept alive'. The story revolves around her desperation to avoid 'watching her history being repeated'. This pertains most directly to her eleven-year-old daughter Brigid, whose rebellious desire to ride her brother's ponies bespeaks her mother's unvoiced spirit of resistance. Brigid, however, believes that her independent streak is rooted in the paternal: 'I'm not like you, Mama. I'm like Dada and no one will bate me into the ground. You shouldn't let Dada hit you.' As Elsie is bitterly aware, Brigid's boasts of defiance are perilously and tragically fantastical. Her romanticised version of reality is implied at the level of image when she refuses to accept that the orange colour of a horse she has ridden is simply a trick of the light. However, according to critic Heather Ingman, Brigid is significantly named: 'In both of her manifestations as pagan goddess and fifth-century Christian saint, Brigit is associated with imagery of fire and sun, and the imagery of fire recurring throughout Kelly's story points to a submerged woman's world under Brigit's protection, which will offer Elsie a way to survive.'

The tale ends in disaster as Elsie's caravan burns down leaving no remnant of her or her daughter. The reader is left in a state of profound ambiguity about the fate of these two characters: have they died a terrible death? Have they escaped with the money Elsie has been saving? Or does Kelly intend us to read the ending as a form of mythic transformation in which daughter and mother are conveyed into an ideal realm augured by the 'orange horse that never was' which 'could be the greatest secret of all?' Kelly's radical refusal to offer narrative closure unlocks her main characters from the exigencies of plot while also reflecting their aspiration to defy or surpass the restraints of their current existence.

Elsie's fight for survival in 'Orange Horses' points to one of the overarching themes in the volume: namely the gritty struggle for territory – whether material, political, psychic, or spiritual – which permits the self to survive and evolve. Several stories in *Orange Horses* address this process in terms of women's vulnerability within patrilineal systems of land inheritance. In 'Journey Home', Maura engages in a battle of wits with her brother Sean for control of the family farm after he returns home from Africa with his family. Similarly in 'The False God', four sisters, who have selflessly abandoned romantic and educational opportunities for their mother and their farm, dispute their brother's entitlement to their home on his return from America. In 'A Life of Her Own' a young narrator is devastated when her aunt Brigid marries and moves out of the home she shares with her brother Jack. Brigid explains to her niece that her motivation to marry is based on securing her future: 'I have no life of my own with your uncle. The farm is his, the house is his. If he should marry, what would become of me? Can you imagine me a governess in Spain for instance, or a housekeeper to a parish priest?' Though seemingly content within her new marriage, Brigid dies in childbirth; a death made more probable by the fact that 'she was not young and the risks were greater in those days'. Despite her tragic end, Brigid has had a profound impact on the narrator who has given a sworn promise to her aunt that she will secure a profession and not 'let them give all the education to your brothers'. As with 'Orange Horses' the name Brigid becomes associated with a means to survive beyond the role of 'mother figure or wife figure or whatever a "good woman" should be.'

Female access to education is a recurrent concern in *Orange Horses* and is addressed most directly in 'Cause and Effect' in which a highly intelligent, retired science teacher, Miss Melican, mediates on 'her life and its silences.' In her youth she had been a 'rare phenomenon with a Masters in mathematics and physics' and had harboured ambitions to go on to do further scientific study. Yet she had also been 'extremely sensible' and concluded that she 'would probably have remained assistant to some man, her discoveries absorbed in his, her ideas credited to him.' Though this attitude could be characterised as excessively cynical, the projected future Miss Melican describes echoes that of Northern Irish scientist Jocelyn Bell Burnell who, fourteen years before the story was published, detected the first radio pulsar, a form of neutron star, while working as part of a graduate research project at Cambridge University. Though her findings directly resulted in a Nobel Prize in Physics in 1974, the award went to Anthony Hewish – Bell Burnell's supervisor – and another Cambridge scientist Martin Ryle. 'Cause and Effect' is a salutary depiction of how such failures in the recognition of female achievement at the highest levels of education not only check women's ambition but deprive humanity of scientists who could potentially change our understanding of the universe.

'The Sentimentalist' also engages with the problem of female access to education and shifts focus from science to the male-dominated discipline of philosophy. The story is narrated by a rather sceptical, yet spirited, older woman whose ambition is to become a prominent female Irish philosopher. Her 'life's work' is a book she is writing which she hopes will stand alongside the theories of the greatest male philosophers. She lives a largely hermetic existence and recognises this as 'the price I must pay for independence'. Her ironic, detached attitude stands as a foil to her cousin Liza, who is a committed romantic nationalist who had passionately supported the Gaelic Revival as well as becoming a member of Cumann na mBan. Despite her intimate involvement with the struggle for independence, Liza finds that there is 'no place for her among the new policymakers'. She realises too late that her 'gods were all false' and that she 'should have looked for political power'. Just as the elderly narrator is alienated within the predominantly male field of philosophy, so Liza becomes marginalised within the political affairs of the new nation. Liza's story functions as a microcosm of the larger history of women in post-independence Ireland and starkly reflects their side-lining within the new state.

Despite the provision of equal rights for women in both the 1916 Proclamation and the 1922 Free State Constitution, the decades after independence saw a steady diminution of women's liberties as the political and ecclesiastical establishment began to define women's role as properly within the private, domestic sphere. Limitations, including marriage bars, were placed on their career in the civil service and there were also restrictions in industrial employment. In 1934 the

Criminal Law Amendment Bill banned the importation or sale of contraceptives and, in 1937, the new Constitution of Ireland forbade laws granting dissolution of marriages. Article 41.2 of the latter document explicitly demarcated women's natural area of activity as in the home, working as mothers and housekeepers. The consequences of the nation's valorisation of women's vocation as homemaker, wife and mother are explored most piquantly in Kelly's 'The Vain Woman'. The story focuses on Mary Murphy, a socially atomised housewife, who has had fifteen pregnancies, ten full terms births and has six surviving children, five boys and one daughter. Exhausted from her role as primary carer to six children, and disconnected from her chauvinistic, hard-drinking husband, Mary suffers an existential crisis concluding that: 'Nothing mattered. There was no meaning to anything'.

Mary's sense of meaninglessness is partly the result of the collapse of her Catholic faith. She no longer respects the institutions of Catholicism and has ceased attending mass after being told to receive a blessing to be purified after the birth of her first son. Her break with the Church further vitiates her sense of identity and self as she wonders: 'Who am I? Who is me? What is me?' In pursuing these questions, and much to the chagrin of her husband, she develops an interest in philosophy, psychology, and sociology and surprises herself in her comprehension of 'the most complex and abstract of ideas.' Her life changes dramatically when an artist named Patrick Murphy moves in next door. The two develop a strong bond and he eventually asks if he can paint her. Rather than simply acceding to the role of passive muse, Mary brokers a deal that if Patrick is to paint her in the nude, then she must also be allowed to paint him naked. This parity of artistic agency might usefully be compared to the relationship outlined in Kelly's 'Parasites', in which a young female writer and an aspiring male poet fall for one another. The romance ends when the woman realises that the poet would have 'destroyed' her if she had let herself wholly become his muse. In contrast, the mutually constructive artistic relationship between Mary and Patrick provides a deeper form of connection and is the context for a passionate love affair in which Mary's dormant sexual desire is reawakened. Their affair is abruptly ended when Mary's husband discovers her infidelity and locks her out of the house, implicitly using the children as a weapon. Unable to get divorced and with the full weight of the Church and the ire of the local community pressing down upon her, Mary is forced to convince her husband to allow her to return. Patrick, realising the impossibility of their love, promptly leaves.

As with other stories in *Orange Horses*, 'The Vain Woman' displays Kelly's skill in charting the often occluded experience of women in the domestic sphere. However, as Virginia Woolf argues, a writer's focus on such subject matter can sometimes lead to an underestimation of the quality of their writing. In *A Room of One's Own* (1929) which exerts a pervasive influence across many, if not all, stories in *Orange Horses*, Woolf complains of the trivialisation of 'feminine' values in literature: 'This is an important book, the critic assumes, because it deals with war. This is an insignificant book because it deals with the feelings of women in a drawing-room'. Such perspectives have persisted in the critical discourse and may partly explain why Kelly has been relatively neglected as a writer.

Another contributing factor in this regard may be the specific formal and thematic qualities of Kelly's short fiction and how they deviate from previously established aesthetic norms of the genre. Frank O'Connor, one of the most influential theorists (and practitioners) in this field, famously suggested in *The Lonely Voice* (1962) that the short story is typically characterised by its treatment of 'submerged population groups' which are generally 'outlawed figures wandering about the fringes of society'. At its most characteristic, according to O'Connor, the form is shot through with an 'intense awareness of human loneliness' with the result that it is inherently 'romantic, individualistic, intransigent'. Though O'Connor's theorisation of the short story has proved remarkably enduring and robust, especially within the Irish literary sphere, it may have acted more as procrustean standard than enabling model for Kelly. It is certainly true that she often depicts lonely figures straining against society's strictures and adrift from its moral certitudes, yet these individuals tend to be less romantically iconic than the 'outlawed figures' listed in *The Lonely Voice*. Whereas O'Connor sees types such as 'tramps, lonely idealists, dreamers, and spoiled priests' as at the heart of the short story tradition, Kelly focuses on exhausted student nurses, late mothers, disinherited spinsters, and middle-aged chess-playing widows pursuing men ten years their junior.

In a slightly larger context, Kelly's understated nonconformity is also evident in her subtle divergence, in several stories, from the fatalist timbre of much mid-twentieth century naturalist Irish fiction. She depicts characters who find a way to transcend the determining dynamics of an oppressive social order or set of historical, cultural or biological forces. In 'The Last Campaign', Martha and Joe, whose hopes for children have been frustrated by fertility problems, experience a crushing disappointment when all the cattle on their farm become diseased and are taken to slaughter. Despite Joe's inherent taciturnity, borne of his socialisation into a traditionally Irish form of masculinity, the catastrophe prompts a profoundly cathartic and seemingly enduring emotional rapprochement between husband and wife. In 'Pilgrim's Tale', a fifty-year-old devout, former missionary nun suffering from cancer travels to a religious shrine with her niece. While there, an 'unrecognised ember of rebellion' takes 'fire within her' and she rejects her religion while simultaneously feeling a new and 'real kinship with her sister and their dead free-thinking mother.' Rather than prayer or religious ritual, it is this recognition of female solidarity with her 'humanistic feminist' sister which gives her a measure of comfort for the future. In 'The Fortress' a sickly child's recovery from illness mirrors her strengthening relationship with her mother whose kindness and stoicism she comes to understand as a self-willed aspect of her individual humanity rather than a quality of a universal maternal type. Kelly's concentration on the connection between daughter and mother in this tale accorded with a new emphasis on the mother-daughter relationship in Irish fiction during this period and challenged the prevalent focus on the father-son relationship in Irish writing.

Kelly's most radical formal departure from the naturalist mode is 'Morning at My Window' which is narrated by an Irish migrant nurse and relates her experience working in post-war London. This world is reprised in Kelly's second novel *Florrie's Girls* (1989) which depicts the difficulties faced by a young woman named Cos who emigrates to London to train as nurse in the early 1950s. The story of post-war Irish women's migration to Britain has been largely absent from the historical record until recently and both *Florrie's Girls* and 'Morning at My Window' are important contributions to the larger social history of post-war Irish female migration, as well as vivid portraits of migration's effects on the nature and evolution of Irish identity and nationality. The title of the latter text is an allusion to T.S. Eliot's poem 'Morning at the Window', and a section of the poem is quoted as epigraph in the story. Kelly's substitution of the possessive adjective 'my' for the definite article reveals a larger perspectival contrast between the two texts. In 'Morning at the Window', the narrator gazes out his window and becomes 'aware of the damp souls of housemaids / Sprouting despondently at area gates.' In 'Morning at My Window', Kelly shifts the dynamic from the female as 'object' and observed to 'subject' and observing. While Eliot asks the reader to sympathise with downcast housemaids from afar, Kelly offers an insider's view of the life of working nurses and invokes an empathetic engagement with their plight. Though changing the narrative point of view of Eliot's poem, Kelly echoes the poet's modernist style by deploying a stream-of-consciousness technique. The spirit-stifling discipline demanded of the young nurses is evinced by the narrator who ventriloquizes the voices of those in authority and their pestering rules and dicta:

> Remember to say please and thank you in case they think you're being above yourself. Avoid conflict between staff. Rules of the road. Avoid head-on collision, confrontation, making an issue. Bedpan round. Mrs. B needs a laxative. Miss D, poor old Miss D, is incontinent and so ashamed she pretends to be cross.

The prose throughout is vividly impressionistic and restlessly polyphonic. Spoken and unspoken instructions, complaints, and rebukes punctuate affective vignettes of dying patients and the narrator's internalised struggle to reintegrate her increasingly disintegrating psyche. Her mind, she tells us, is not 'routine' and 'must have chaos for creating'. Her story is testament to the subterranean, anarchic fragments of self which productively disrupt imposed identities borne of moribund orthodoxies; in a larger sense, the narrative reflects the disruptive energies released by Kelly's own writing and its relation to the dominant structures of thought within Irish culture and politics.

The stories contained in *Orange Horses* were published over the course of almost two decades, the first appearing in 1971 and the last in 1989. Broadly speaking, this was a period of liberalization in Ireland, particularly with regards to the rights of women. Kelly was a notable voice in pressing for these changes. In a review of recent fiction by Irish women in 1984, the writer Susan McKay noted of Kelly that she is 'one of the writers of today who has made a consistent stand "against the conventions of her times" and for the "ennoblement of womankind". She does so with a sense of comedy which characterises all of the most sure-footed of our writers.' McKay's commentary foregrounds two of Kelly's greatest strengths as a writer: her technical mastery and her unfailing condemnation of what the writer Juanita Casey terms the 'immaculate misconceptions' governing Irish women's lives.

Kelly, of course, is not unique in combining her skill as a writer with a thoroughgoing feminism and is one among a number of Irish writers whose output led to progressive and profound changes to the predicament of Irish women in the last fifty years. What makes her career more unusual, however, is the manner in which she combined writing with political activism and her equal commitment to both activities; Kelly not only brought new social problems to the franchise of Irish fiction, she doggedly and pragmatically campaigned for their amelioration. While her writing has sought to dismantle the repressive cultural ideals pervading Ireland's political and legal systems, her activism fostered a more direct challenge to the institutions which enacted and buttressed the prejudices linked to such beliefs. In 'The Last Campaign' when Martha's husband implies that there is nothing meaningful left of life, she counters by stating simply: 'There's fight'. Kelly's life and writing have embodied this knowledge. Across half a century, she has tenaciously campaigned for those who have been silenced, battered, bullied, and abandoned. She has fought to dispel entrenched notions of family, sexuality, identity and gender and prepared the ground for the more equable, progressive and heterogeneous Ireland of the new century. *Orange Horses* was fundamental to that fight and bears its scars. It is the culmination of Kelly's achievement in short fiction and represents a vital contribution to Irish writing of the twentieth century as well as to the history of women in post-war Ireland.

MAEVE KELLY, an Irish novelist, short-story writer and poet, was born in Ennis, Co. Clare and educated in Dundalk. She qualified in General Nursing in St Andrews Hospital, London and did postgraduate theatre nursing in Oxford before returning to Ireland. She spent many years farming in Co. Clare with her husband Gerard O'Brien Kelly and their two children, Joseph and Oona. After moving to Limerick she was a founding member of Limerick Federation of Women's Organisations and the Limerick Refuge for Battered Wives, now call Adapt House, where she was an administrator for fifteen years. In 1972 she won the Hennessy Literary Award. She is the author of two short story collections, *A Life of Her Own* (1976) and *Orange Horses* (1989), a satirical fairytale, *Alice in Thunderland* (1993), two novels, *Necessary Treasons* (1985) and *Florrie's Girls* (1989), and two collections of poetry, *Resolution* (1986) and *Lament for Oona* (2005). Kelly's work has been translated into several European languages and has been broadcast on RTÉ and BBC. Kelly's *A Last Loving: Collected Poems* (2016) was recently published by the Irish publisher Arlen House.

Contents

Amnesty

Every June when the peel were running, the sister was at the boat slip before seven in the morning. She moored the flat-bottomed craft to the one rotting post at the pier. The brother heaved out the sacks of fish, and rowed back to the island. She waited for the 7.15 bus. When it pulled up beside her the bus conductor said, 'Good catch?' and she either nodded or shook her head crossly. Not one word did she utter on the journey to town and the Fish Merchant. Nobody knew that the grimness of her silence was simply a necessary part of her life. It was her preparation for the tussle over pennies per pound with the Fish Merchant. This way she stored her mental energies, drew on her strength of will so that he might not 'best' her. In the old days when calves were sold at the street fairs she had gone into training in the same way. The steely core of her will was not to be softened by pleasant talk of weather or crops or children. People who knew her were wise enough to leave her alone. They said, tolerantly, that after all what could you expect from a poor creature whose every day was spent in the company of a deaf mute? The brother had been born that way. Still, others said, it wouldn't hurt her to bid you the time of day at least. And how was it that on the way back from town she was all beams and friendly talk, like a long-playing record? You couldn't stop her. It was true. The bus conductor on the return journey could vouch for that.

'And wouldn't we all smile and talk,' he said, 'if we had the same bagful of money?' And that only a fraction of what had been left in the bank.

Over the years, the mainlanders, by conjecture and rumour, built up a picture for themselves of a woman who smiled only when she had money in her fist, of two strange islanders whose days were passed in silence and incomprehension. The mainlanders were not hostile to the sister. They pitied her and had regard for the way she cared for the dependent brother. They admired her energy and diligence in work. But who could be warmly friendly with such odd people? At times a farmer counting his cattle along the estuary shore would hear the sister's voice amplified by the water between them, as she talked to herself. It was strange to hear the words floating across, disembodied, and it was hard to put sense or meaning to them. She was once heard singing the Agnus Dei on a Sunday morning, although it was many years since either the brother or herself had been to Mass. 'Lamb of God, Who takest away the sins of the world, have mercy on us: Lamb of God, Who takest away the sins of the world, have mercy on us; Lamb of God, Who takest away the sins of the world, grant us peace.' It was quite likely she sang it as a hymn of praise to her own flock of sheep. No one could imagine the sister petitioning God or man for anything, not even for peace.

When the peel were running they fished at the turn of the tide, she handling the boat, he watching the currents, signalling sharply with his arms when she was to turn, throwing out the great empty net. When it was too heavy for him, they both hauled in the shimmering young salmon, baulked of their urge to spawn, and emptied them on to the bottom of the boat. Some seasons the results were poor. That meant less fertiliser for the stony island, less carrying power for its cattle and sheep. The island parched easily. In dry summers it showed brown and singed when the mainland farms kept their glossy green. They never ventured out in rough weather, although they were occasionally caught by a storm. When that happened they hauled in the nets, fish or no fish, and headed for the nearest landing place. Where they fished, the river widened into the estuary and the cross winds were treacherous.

Several foolhardy sailing boats were capsized or had their occupants thrown into the water by a suddenly swinging boom. But the brother and sister knew the river well. He in particular knew all its secret recesses, where the swans nested, where the mallard came to feed. In hard winters, when the mud was frozen to silver and the river reflected the lavender and pink of evening skies, he would lie on his stomach in ditch or reedy bank, watching his breath vaporise as he waited for the wild geese to come in and feed.

Although he could not hear their haunting lamenting cry, his heart would pound with excitement when they arrowed in and he felt the crack of his gun in the tissues of his own body. The sister was proud of his hunting skill, and would clap him on the back when he brought home two rabbits and pointed his forefinger triumphantly to tell her he'd got them with the one shot. His hunting was an expression of his masculinity but at the same time he had his sister's thrifty soul and he always killed for the pot. He never brought back a bird or beast disintegrating with the blast of pellets, so torn that the feathers could not be plucked neatly. And he would not do what tourists did – massacre birds when the weather had been bad for so long that they were starved into docility. He spat in contempt at the sight of such meanness.

The beauty of the island sometimes made the sister's eyes dreamy with wonder. Unlike people who are peasants by nature even if they are bred in the heart of a city, she took time to look at the shapes and colours of stones, at the rock plants adorning their hosts with varying hues of leaf and flower for each season, at the wild roses wreathing their way through love-locked hedges. Visitors came from the continent or England or America, with romantic notions of island life. She had once been offered big money for the island. If the bidder had tried to seduce her, she could not have been more offended. 'The cheek of it,' she declared. 'A stranger! The nerve of it. Looking to take the island off me. They can buy the whole country, but they won't buy my island.' And she became even more possessive of it, appreciating its shape, the way it turned its cliff face to the rising sun so that the rocks sparkled in the morning, the way the hedges threw giant shadows on to the fields in early autumn evenings.

There was an ancient burial mound on the island, rising hump-backed near their house. Archaeologists came on a

Sunday expedition with a group of town enthusiasts to look at it and make notes. She discouraged a repetition of the visit. It didn't matter if the mound was the property of the nation. It was on her island. No curiosity boxes would come peeking at her house, oohing and aahing at it, saying 'How quaint. How charming. How adorable.' She had to hide the brother from them. He had a habit of grinning foolishly at everyone so that they thought he was an idiot and treated him accordingly. That she would not allow. She scolded him for acting that way, but he grinned at her, screwing his finger into his forehead in mock madness, and laughed in his giggling, hiccoughing way. There were other times when he resented being frowned on and he scowled back at the mouth making angry shapes at him. Then he would go to the mound, picking at its protruding stones, grunting angrily. 'Complaining about me to the dead,' she thought. But if it gave him comfort, what of it? The ghosts of a thousand years could have no sting left. Maybe they liked being complained to. It was better than nothing. If the dead are not invoked they are deader than dead. A strange thought came to her. Was that why he was born? To be a companion to the forgotten dead? And why was I born? To care for the companion to the forgotten dead? It was no more futile than any other occupation, she thought. For all occupations not geared to immediate need seemed futile to the sister. She had little more than contempt for the busload of mainlanders, gossiping their way to the town shops. Spending their money on foolish dispensibles. Clothes. She had the same coat for thirty years. Her skirts were made by a tailor in the town who also made the rough tweed suits the brother wore. In warm weather she sported a suit of the same material with a pink cotton blouse, her one concession to colour.

The peel were running hard this year. Prices came down

because of the glut, but the full sacks gave her a feeling of accomplishment. The Fish Merchant's man was waiting at the bus stop near the shop, ready to lift off the bulging sacks. The Fish Merchant himself came out to greet her, rubbing his hands together to control his greed or to clear off the sweat between the two palms or to erase the smell of gutted fish before he took hers. She allowed him this brief familiarity but withdrew her hand from his at the first quick touch. His money will do me. Let him keep his handshaking for others like himself who value money for its own sake, never for the new net it might buy, or the maiden heifer or the sack of flour against the winter's greed. They began to haggle immediately.

'Can't sell them. No sale. No sale. Too many altogether,' he told her.

'You can put them in that big freezing place you have,' she said, 'and keep them for the Christmas parties your swanky customers give.'

'Listen,' he said. 'The people who buy young salmon are just like you and me. They look for good value.'

'And you'll give it to them, I suppose,' she sniffed.

'Who else? Who else?' He spread his hands wide, showing how vulnerably honest he was.

I know you, she thought. Full of town cunning. You'd take the eye out of my head and come back for the other one.

'Six shillings a pound,' she said firmly.

'Six shillings! Six shillings!' He was shocked at her avarice. 'Thirty pence for a pound. That's £2.40 for an eight-pounder.'

'Don't try conning me with that new money. I can multiply with the best of them.'

He grinned to himself. She looked suspiciously at him. He had a greasy fishmonger's mind. He caught the look and seized his slight advantage. 'Why don't you go and buy yourself a new hat today? Or one of those nice new dresses the ladies all wear now.'

Is he mocking me? She peered at his two big sleepy grey eyes. New customers were codded into thinking their blankness meant innocence and were afraid to hurt his feelings by watching the scales when he threw the fish in. 'Lovely day, missus.' His smile was a lure away from the quick deceiving hands. The smile and the eyes were of heaven. But not the voice, thought the sister. The voice has the gravelly meanness of your soul.

'Three shillings. Fifteen pence. That's all I can do for you now. Bring them somewhere else if you like.' He turned his back on her. And she was caught. Filled with an old and terrible humiliation.

She was a young girl again, sent in to market with the new potatoes, her mother's bitter warning ringing in her ears. 'Not a penny less than that, mind. Don't come back with less.' It was the year of the war, 1939. The end of the hungry thirties when Dev had tried not to pay the British the land annuities on the repossession of Irish farms and the British put an embargo on Irish cattle. At least the island could use the resources of the river, which was more than the mainlanders could do, but they all suffered the poverty of the time. Nineteen hundred and thirty-nine was the end of everything and the beginning of everything. It was the year her father and eldest brother were drowned.

At the market there was soft talk and grinning men, hands stretching hungrily for a good bargain. 'You're a lovely girsha, God bless you. And are you the only one at home? You should have a pretty dress to wear.' The market full – sweat, smells, laughing, teasing, arguing. 'You should have a pretty dress to wear.' Tinker talk. Was he a tinker? White teeth in a brown face and blue eyes laughing like the river on a sky blue day. 'New potatoes. New potatoes,' she called faintly, hoping he wouldn't hear, hoping he was deaf like her brother. But no. Not deaf and dumb. For then he'd never be able to say nice things to her. 'You're a lovely girl.' All the old women. 'Ah go on, love. Give us a bargain now. Such a lovely girl you are. Throw in a few for luck. There, good girl. Good girl. God bless you.' Turning his back on her. Whistling between his teeth, laughing at her clumsy selling, laughing at the way she was cajoled out of her potatoes and paid little more than the price of the seed.

'Why don't you buy yourself a nice dress? A pretty girl like you should wear pretty clothes.' Oh the madness of a June day, the last year of the hungry thirties. She took his hand and fell into the clamour of the town. In another world was the quiet island and the threatening river, and the plaintive curlew. But the town received the river. It swallowed up the river, wrapped itself around her, cosseted her with bridges, arched in loveliness. It twisted round her curves, locked her into canals, buried her in slobland. It taunted her with garbage, sent the gulls screaming while they scavenged. It used her and abused her, then turned its back upon her when angry and swollen she beat at its doors.

It was late that mad June day, when the sister rode out of town on her bicycle, her cheeks the colour of the new pink dress, her eyes blazing with memories of a squandered day, her pockets and baskets empty. Her mouth still tasted the ice cream and the kisses, the kisses and the ice cream, the ginger ale and kisses, the kisses and the ginger ale. Her heart fluttered like a pigeon caught between her ribs. At the pier the brother was waiting anxiously with the boat. He mouthed at her fussily, but she laughed and showed him her new dress. He touched it delightedly, rubbed the material between his fingers, traced with his small finger the pattern of butterflies and flowers, the lace edging on the collar and bodice. He let his breath out in wonder, then counted on his fingers, gesticulating at her to know how much money she had brought home. She shrugged. Ooh. He sucked in his breath and clapped a hand over his mouth. Only then did she understand the calamity. Not once in the whole lovely day had she anticipated her homecoming. Wearily she climbed into the boat and let him drag the bicycle in after her. The tide was ebbing and she let him push the boat by himself, over the mud, until it eased into the water. Mumbling angrily, he took the oars.

The sister never forgave her mother for the stinging slap on her face and for the name she called her. She forgave her the ranting and wailing and mourning over the wasted day, the baskets of new potatoes gone and nothing to replace them. But she never forgave the slap or the word. She never forgave the priest's visit and his soft but accusing questioning. And she never forgot the mother's hard looks at her in the months that followed, or the relief in her eyes when the flesh fell off her and she grew thin. Flat as a board she had remained for the rest of her life. The brother, although he rescued the dress and coaxed her, imploring her with big eyes and hands to wear it for him, could not soften the humiliation. That was the birth of her steel core.

To the Fish Merchant's back she said, 'I'll take my fish and I'll empty them into the dock.' He turned and she deliberately began to drag the first sack along the pavement.

A boy came up. 'Sell us a fish, missus?'

'I'll give you one,' she said, 'if you run around town and let everyone know I'm selling salmon at fifty pence apiece.'

'Stop, stop,' shouted the Fish Merchant. 'I was only joking. I'll give you five bob.' She ignored him. 'Six. Six. I'll give you the six.'

'You're too late,' she said, 'you're too late.'

'I'll have the Guards on you,' he frothed. 'It's not legal.'

'You do that,' she glared, 'and you'll never get another of my salmon.'

'There are others,' he said. 'You're not the only crazy eejit fishing on the river.'

'I know the others,' she answered. 'Some nights when the peel are running they'll be slopping pints in a public house and you'll be waiting a long time for your silver kings.'

'Isn't seven enough for you so?' He was pathetic in defeat.

But she needed him too. 'You can afford it,' she said. 'And remember not to drive me too hard the next time. I'll take seven today and we'll start afresh tomorrow. Or will you want them tomorrow?'

'Bring them in as usual,' he said sourly, turning away from the blazing eyes. One day, he thought in satisfaction, the old hag will kill herself with work.

The sister was exhausted. She had come straight in off the river. They had started fishing at four. She smiled grimly. It had been a profitable night. She crossed the street to the bank, ignoring the frantic horns and infuriated drivers. At the bank she stopped for a fraction of a second before hurrying by. She walked past the country shop where they sold boots and thick trousers and check shirts. At Regina's boutique she stood and gazed in at the mannequins who stared haughtily over her head with their plastic eyes, their nylon hair brightly blonde or seductively red, their slender limbs thrown elegantly forward, their hands curving in a gesture of disdain. A faint smile dimmed the fire in her eyes. A faint hungry tenderness warmed her. She hurried inside. The salesgirls looked at her, sure she would turn around when she realised she was in the wrong shop.

'I want a pink dress,' she said, 'with flowers and things on it.'

'Is it for yourself?' one of them asked, coolly surprised.

'Who else?' she replied. 'Myself of course. One of those maxis if you please. I don't hold with people showing off their ugly knees and thighs. And mine,' she glared defiantly at their exposed legs, 'are no worse than most.' That'll stop their sniggering, she thought.

'Lady Muck come to town,' muttered one, but the kinder of the two came forward.

'Let me help you.' The rails of dresses were dazzling.

'Lovely, aren't they?' smiled the girl.

'Lovely, lovely, lovely,' said the sister. 'Have you e'er a one with butterflies on it?'

'I don't think so,' said the girl. They searched in vain.

'Butterflies and flowers I want,' said the sister.

The girl thought for a moment. 'Why don't you buy a butterfly brooch and wear it with a flower dress? Would that do?'

'It's an idea. You're a clever one to think it. I'll take that dress if it's the right size.'

'Well it's my size,' the girl said doubtfully. The sister looked at her round limbs and curving breasts and sighed.

'I used to be that size once, and that shape. And I'd say my size is the same.'

The girl put the dress into a white bag with the word 'REGINA' printed in blue and a silver crown over the 'R'. At a knick-knack shop the sister bought a plastic butterfly which she placed in the bag with the dress. She had a cup of coffee in the hotel before doing the rest of her shopping and caught the bus home at midday.

The brother was waiting as usual. His eyes gleamed with excitement when he saw the bag. 'A new dress I got. For myself.' He giggled and pointed to himself, shaking his head. He could read her lips but a lot of the time she didn't bother facing him or was in too much of a hurry. 'It's a pink one.

And look.' She brought out the butterfly brooch. He held it in his palm as if it was a real one ready to lift its wings for flight. His eyes grew sad. She knew he was remembering the June day. She gave him a new pipe and some dainty cut tobacco in a box. He pulled at the oars joyously and they turned for the island. Turf smoke was rising from the chimney straight up to the blue sky. The river was like a looking glass, cut easily by oars. The island was an emerald rising from its blue setting. The brother was making his happy noise sounds. His singing. On the upland fields the sheep were scattered like white beetles. In the meadow the grass was almost seeding.

The sister knew only the one kind of defeat and that had nothing to do with ideas. If she was a country woman conquered by town, she did not know it. If she was provincial conquered by Dublin she did not know that either. If she was old Gael defeated by foreign money and foreign customs she knew nothing at all of that. Defeat was ill health, hunger, the loss of the island, death. Yet she had smelled defeat at the turn of the Fish Merchant's back. The pink dress was not now a rent flag thrown on a burial mound. It was a song of triumph, a declaration of peace. 'I'll wear it to Mass on Sunday,' she said. 'And I'll pray for Ma's soul.'

Forgiveness was a sweetness that smoothed out lines and quenched burning looks. It eased her drying bones and lifted the corners of her mouth.

Journey Home

The day they arrived, it rained. Sean smiled sardonically when he said, 'We thought we'd left the rainy season behind us.' Somehow, when Sean smiled it was always sardonically. Josie looked approvingly at him, and agreed.

Their two children were hideous. As she packed their things into the boot of her car, Maura thought that she loathed her brother and his wife almost more than she loathed their ghastly children, Nigel and June. It was incredible that her brother, the grandson of a Fenian, could have christened his children so ineptly. But then when you looked at his wife, nothing was incredible. The children whinged and wrangled all the way from the airport. 'Don't like this car. It's old and dirty.' Little brats. I'd love to whack their bottoms with a thorny cudgel. Her vicious desires surprised even herself.

'Shush dears.' Their mother had affected her best colonial accent but could not quite conceal the cockney twang acquired from too long living in lower London society. 'You mustn't be naughty now, darlings. We're going to have a lovely holiday and we're all very thankful to Nana that she lets us stay in her lovely old farmhouse.'

'Nana!' Maura crashed the car into third gear as she passed an articulated lorry.

Sean's knuckles whitened as he gripped the front ledge. 'I see you're as good a driver as ever, Morrie.'

'Morrie,' she snarled silently. 'Nana' makes you want to puke. A Sheanin Ui Duibhir, how much did you sell it for?

Next thing he'd be calling himself John Dwyer.

'Morrie, how's Nana?'

Nana! Et tu, Brute. 'Ma,' she said deliberately in her flattest accent, 'is fine, thank God.' Nigel sniggered.

'I say,' gurgled Josie, 'I just love your brogue. People are always telling me I have a lovely brogue, but when I come home here, I know I'm only trottttting awfter yoooo.'

'That right?' said Maura briefly, glancing into the mirror to see if any male driver behind her was about to take advantage of the safe sixty feet she'd left between herself and the oil tanker in front. A fiend with a bald head and a red-headed companion had obvious intentions of doing same. She swung out to the middle line, indicator flashing a violent warning. Keep back, you old buzzard, for I'm not about to be pushed off the road.

'Aye downt loike Awntie Morrie much,' said June. 'She dwives awfully fawst.'

That's right, thought Maura, you pronounce your labials and dentals and you'll do. But not here, by Christ. Not on my bloody farm. My farm, my farm, my farm. Mine it should be, for I've paid for it in sweat and tears. There's my receipt. She shuddered away from the sight of herself in the driving mirror – a grizzly old woman at forty-five. And himself beside her, smooth as a banana skin and almost the same shade now after eight years of tropical living.

'You mustn't say that.' Josie's reproof was in a tone which, by a subtle cadence on the word 'say', suggested that the child was right not to like her Auntie Maura or her driving, but wrong to express so direct an opinion.

'Let her speech away,' said Maura. 'Honest opinions are hard to come by these days.' Josie was determined to agree with everyone. She had a hard time balancing between two stools all the time. A crash on her rump will come sooner or later. Better sooner than later. Oh God, make it soon. Oh Maura, don't appeal to God, that father figure with a beard benignly beaming through rosy clouds, that ascetic man carrying his cross up a hill, that dove fluttering its spirit somewhere else. Oh Lord above send down a dove, with wings as sharp as razors, to cut the throats of those English dogs, who shot our brave Sinn Feiners. Visitors mean more work. Who'll help me milk the cows? Who'll muck out the yard, scour the churns, feed the calves? Well, Josie can take over Mother for a while. Lift her on to the wheelchair with Sean lending a gentlemanly hand. Rub her back to prevent bed sores, clean her toes. Not that I mind doing it, God knows I don't. She's my mother after all. Why do I keep bringing God into it? What was it they used to say up North while we visited great-uncle Tom? 'The dear knows.' Very safe, that.

No religious undertones, no expressions of traditional faith. She slammed on the brakes as a lorry pulled out of the side road ahead. She pulled down her window and snarled out at him as he passed, 'Bloody nit. You shouldn't be let out on the road.'

Sean tut-tutted beside her. 'I really don't think you should use such rough language. It's very unbecoming.' It becomes me, you nit. Would you prefer louse? Coarse language for coarse people. Me, I'm coarse. Always was. Such a rough child, Mother said. Gets it from her father, God rest him. Sean takes after my side, of course. The Hartigans had gentle breeding. Oh Sean won't have any of that pulling and dragging to do. I'll see to that. He'll have a good education and a good job.

I was slow, of course. I don't know why. Not stupid. Slow. Slow to think, slow to act, slow to react. But not any more. Not any more. I'm quick, quick, quick. My thoughts are quickened by venom. They corrode my mind. They'll burn me away some day, and I'll be led off cursing and people will say I'm a megalomaniac and they'll lock me up. But I'm locked up already. Chained by duty and lack of education to miserable living on rocky Galway land.

'Did you get the flush toilet in yet, Morrie?' Josie's question hung in the drone of the car, dreading the answer 'no' but hoping for 'yes'.

'No,' said Maura with satisfaction. 'Th'auld dry toilet works grand. Thanks be to God,' she added for good measure.

Sean was displeased. 'I especially meant that money to be used for that purpose. Did you spend it?'

Oh, on liquor and wild living, brother. 'Yes, I spent it. The black Kerry cow got stuck in a drain and died. The money came in handy. Bought a fine strong Friesian heifer. Calved down last month.' A lovely calf she had. A beauty.

Snow white legs on chequerboard body and a little pink nose where the white hair hadn't grown on the glaze. No trouble to her. Calved out in the paddock there, with the sun shining and the birds singing. Proper order. That's the way things should be. Birth in the sunshine of the day. Death in the sleep of the night.

'Well, that's fine. I'm glad the money was useful. But you do need the other thing too.' It surprised her again. His refinement. It was so excessive. He couldn't bring himself to say the word. Josie wasn't that bad after all.

'I dunno. Mother has to use the chair in the room, and I –'

Sean broke in sternly, exercising his great white-master authority, 'Morrie, remember the children.' What children? Those adult midgets behind me? Call them children? They could buy and sell me. Couldn't buy or sell a good bullock, though. Wouldn't know the difference between a blackface ewe and a mountain goat.

'When I'm gone' – Mother had meant dead, of course – 'the farm must go to Sean. It's really his place, you know, dear. When he was only a little fellow before your father died, his grandfather put his hand on his head – he had lovely hair too, a mass of black curls, and he said, "This place is to be for this boy." I always respect the wishes of the dead. I know, dear, that you've worked hard here. But Mick Meany wants to marry you this long time back, and he could give you a good home – when I'm gone, of course – and I'll leave you money for a dowry so you won't go empty-handed to him.'

'Yes, Ma.' Mick Meany. Bald-headed old coot. As hard as his stony land. One hundred and twenty years old if he's a day. Think I'd lie in that fellow's bed? I'm not that badly off for a man. Oh for some brawny fellow wider than myself, who could wrap me around with two big strong arms and pull the plough on a windy day, and no bother to him. A fellow who could whistle while he worked, and would gulp his food down in a hurry to be out to his fields. That's the sort of fellow I'd like. Coarse, maybe, but strong. As strong as a horse, and able to tell me bawdy stories that I could laugh at without being ashamed. They don't make fellows like that any more. Dirty old divils, or sniggery slithers they make in plenty but nothing in between. And who'd have me anyway? A fellow like Da. He'd suit me alright. Oh but he was great sport. The jokes he used to tell, and the stories when we'd be bringing up the cows together. Sean inside doing his homework. Da said I was the farmer. He meant me to have the farm. And have it I will, if I have to kill you all for it.

It was twenty miles from the airport to home. Every two years Maura took the car on the same journey. Every two years, during the past eight, Sean came home from British East Africa. Only now it wasn't B.E. Africa. There were new states, new names, new people. Not long down from the trees, Sean said once, emanating his aura of civilised behaviour. Maura's fury groped for words in defence of the dignity of man but her educational lack left her inarticulate and twice as angry. Sean was an accountant with an industrial firm. They had a luxury bungalow, their own swimming pool, a car each, a garden boy, and a girl in the house. Josie was always complaining about her domestic help. Every few months she found them so unstable, unreliable and ineducable (all her favourite words) that she dismissed them and hopefully employed more. Ma loved to hear them talk of their life. Casual references to the time they went on safari, boring colour slides, showing elephants, trunk view and rump view, antelopes in dainty poses, lions majestical perched on rocks, thrilled her to pride. It seemed a vindication of some sort that a photograph of her son, an Irishman, posing in khaki shorts, a camera slung over his shoulder in lieu of a gun, to a backdrop of flamingos, could stand on the mantleshelf in the parlour, underneath the pike-head his grandfather had rammed into position many years before. The incongruity of it escaped her completely.

The ancient Irish castle now in the hands of an ancient Irish-American hotelier lay behind them. The rolling green of East Clare changed to the small stone-scattered fields of Galway. Maura swung the car off the main road for the last lap home.

Behind her, Josie was ecstatic. 'Oh, the fuchsia. How lovely it is. And the elderflower is out. Oh and look at the honeysuckle. Let's stop and admire it all.'

Grudgingly Maura pulled into the scented hedge. The visitors got out, the children grumbling that they were hungry. Maura was impatient. She paced up and down for a few minutes, looked at her watch, then climbed pointedly back into the driving seat. 'Cows have to be milked at five,' she said.

Sean was apologetic. 'Sorry, Morrie.'

'Watch the lorry,' she said, turning on the ignition key.

The children chanted it excruciatingly the rest of the way. 'Sorry, Morrie, watch the lorry, sorry, Morrie, watch the lorry.'

'They're quite clever, aren't they?' Sean said amusedly.

Oh quite clever. Like you. Clever. Clever. A clever little bastard. Coming in for the visitors in dung-splashed trousers and boots, smiling cheerfully. Isn't he the great little man? He must be a comfort to you now, Mrs O'Dwyer, now that himself is gone. Oh a boy is great on the farm. And he's so good-looking. Look at the head on him, a fine lad. The image of your own father, ma'am. The O'Dwyers were always plain, God help them. Good hardworking people, but not blessed with good looks, you might say. The girl there now, she's an O'Dwyer surely. She has the stamp of them on her. And who but herself with the stamp of an O'Dwyer on her could have milked cows, fed calves, watched the sows farrow all those long years while clever Sean studied? Who but herself with the white fog from the lake thick over the fields could have pulled the calf from the boghole, fixed the slates on the roof, trammed the hay with the help of neighbours? Who but a coarse, rough woman could have lifted and hauled till her muscles bulged and her neck settled into her shoulders?

Who but a woman of no breeding could have let tawny hair turn grizzled and dry and white skin run to furrows like a ploughed field?

'I have a letter in my pocket from the convent.' She announced the information in the same voice as she would use to say the hens are laying well lately, or the weather is mixed middling. That's the way it is. Thinking about it doesn't change it.

'Oh,' Sean laughed. 'Thinking of taking the veil?'

'Yes,' said Maura. 'Next month with the help of God.'

Even the children were silenced. 'You're not serious of course.' Sean had never known whether to take Maura seriously or not.

Maura disdained to reply.

'You couldn't leave Mother now,' said Sean.

'Why not?' asked Maura sensibly. 'She has yourself and Josie to care for her.' In the seat behind, Josie swallowed a gasp.

'Well, I know one thing,' Sean laughed again, determined to treat it all as a merry joke, 'you'll never leave the farm.'

'Why not?' Maura repeated herself. 'It's not my farm. Never has been. I'm only the hired hand. Unpaid. It's time I lived my own life.'

'Have you discussed it with Mother?' asked Sean.

'No. Nothing to discuss. I'll leave that to you and Josie. You're the big talker, Sean. You'll be able to put it all into nice convenient words.'

'But you were never very religious,' Josie poked in the ludicrous understatement as a plea for good sense. 'You'd be miserable in a convent.'

'No more miserable than I am now,' said Maura. 'I've nothing to gain, maybe, but nothing to lose either. Besides, they say a change is as good as a rest.'

'It's a funny sort of vocation,' said Josie cattily. Maura was pleased. Scratch the veneer ever so slightly and underneath is the same old feline ready to claw to survive. How would she survive on Lough an Eala? She smiled, picturing the crumbling of that polished façade. Sean's banana skin wouldn't stand up to much either. She had them. She had them both. They'd be glad to sign over the place to her. And then let them come home on holidays if they pleased, but she wouldn't be able to take time off from *her* farm to meet them at the airport.

Sean, Josie and the children were quiet for the next few miles. When Sean spoke it was in the cool tones of a great brain coming out with a carefully considered and irrefutable solution. 'As a matter of fact, I'm glad you've decided to live your own life. As you say, it hasn't been much fun for you. And it is, after all, *my* farm. I can't expect you to run it any more. I'll get a good manager in. I can afford one now. Modern methods will do a lot to improve that land. Farmers must be educated now. We can get someone to look after Mother. Then when I retire, I can come back myself to Lough an Eala. Josie always loves it. Don't you, Josie? You go into your convent, Morrie, and with God's grace you'll be very happy.'

They were coming into the corkscrew road, four miles of humps and hollows, twists and S-bends – as if the road had diligently followed the crazy tracks of a warble-chased calf two hundred years before. Maura put her foot down on the accelerator. A red rage consumed her. She'd never been a match for his cunning and she wasn't now. The old car leapt forward. She was oblivious of Sean's cry, 'For God's sake, take it easy,' the children whimpering and cowering in the back, Josie's hysterical scream as hedges, grassy banks came flying for them. Her arms ached from wrenching the steering wheel to right and left. She took fierce delight in the screech of brakes as she two-wheeled around the sharpest bends. She blew on the horn ferociously – clear the way everyone – Morrie the great is coming, watch out accursed world, the killer is on the rampage. She sang loudly and happily –

Is iomaí slí sin do bhíos ag daoine
Ag cruinniú pinghinne is ag déanamh stóir

The rowdy drinking song added to the terror of the drive. At last she stopped outside their farm gate. She turned off the ignition key and looked at Sean.

His face was contorted. 'You're mad,' he said. 'I always knew you were crazy.' The whimpering of the children and the quiet sobbing of Josie formed a fitting background to his words. 'I don't know how Mother has survived all these years with you. God knows what she's had to put up with. Josie will care for her from now on.'

Maura got out of the car and walked through the side gate to the lake. The sheep dog stopped his excited barking and raced after her. Her mother was calling from the house. 'Is that you, Maura dear? Are they here? Did they come? Sean. Sean. Sean. Josie. Are you coming? What's keeping you?' The old querulous voice faded as she neared the lake. The swans were on it. Their grace and beauty made her smile. And they had cold hearts to match. She turned her grizzled head to the field where the cows grazed. Come on, Shep. Hup there, hup there, bring 'em up, bring 'em up.

Josie, she thought. Josie's my trump card. Josie will crack first.

Morning at My Window

They are rattling breakfast plates in basement kitchens,
And along the trampled edges of the street
I am aware of the damp souls of housemaids
Sprouting despondently at area gates.
'Morning at the Window', T.S. Eliot

Mr Eliot was aware of the damp souls of housemaids, sprouting despondently at area gates. What a pity, said I to myself, that he was not aware of the damp souls of student nurses drenched in despondency, drowned in their own misery and asphyxiated by the sadness of others. I soon shall have no soul left, or if I have it will be so narrowed and cicatriced by the scarifying experiences of my days that it will not be worth a passing thought, a line of doggerel, or a verse from a poem.

We used to chant at school a cruelly unimaginative introduction to the native tongue which still echoes down the hallowed, hollowed halls of my memory. I just adore succinct
prose. I cannot abide adjective-slinging writers. Where was
I in my succinct prose?

The Gaelic chant. It went like this. *Eirighim ar a hocht
a clog gach maidin.* I arise at eight o'clock each morning.
Mind the CHs. Chchchchch. Catch it at the back of your
throat. *Nighim m'aghaidh agus mo lamha.* I wash my face
and hands. *Chuirim orm mo chuid eadaigh.* I put on my
clothes. And for some reason, every morning when I stagger
out of bed and splash my eyes open with the water on the
rocks shared by my sister lamplighters I think of that plain
chant. And it isn't iron that enters my damp but narrowing
soul. It's gall and wormwood, vinegar and bitter aloes, and
the taste of bile in my mouth regurgitating therefrom.

Oh soul. Hold tight to yourself now, or the little bit of
you that's left, and clothe your body with clean uniform,
white starched apron, clean collars and cuffs, white starched
cap. Clothe your face also with a smile for it's all you're
allowed. Five minutes to dress, five to tear across the windy
grounds to the main block and five to gulp a cup of tea
and soggy toast. And a few aspirations on the way up the
stairs, for the lift is either on its way up or down or sunk in
between with some frenzied prisoners crying faintly for help.

And it's a quarter past seven and I'm just in time to
report to night nurse. Good morning nurse. Smile. Did you
have a quiet night? Smile. Bleak response from the pallid
face. Oh have you a damp soul too, sister in distress? Or is
twelve hours of caring for thirty ailing bodies all by yourself too much for you, you frail creature, you weaker sex.
Pull yourself together. Prop up your sagging chin with a
smile and deliver your report. Did I ever tell you the story

of the Bugandan student nurse who had a Celtic flair for words? The first night she wrote in graphic but succinct (of course) prose, Mrs X is sinking. Next night, Mrs X is sinking fast. Next night, she is sunk. Anyone sunk tonight, nurse? You're twenty years old, nurse. Twenty whole years. How many boats have you rocked to sleep? How many life rafts thrown? How many Mrs Xs have sunk before your eyes? Why do you keep thinking of your friends in office jobs, grumbling about the boss's habits, nine-to-fivers and tennis on summer evenings and boyfriends into the bargain. Such mundane considerations are not worthy of you and your high calling. You serve others who cannot serve themselves. Dry your dripping soul and do your stuff.

Breakfasts first. Porridge for Mrs P. None for Mrs B. Mrs Y likes it thin. Mrs D likes it thick. Mrs M wants cornflakes. Sister says what the hell does she think this is, the Ritz? Boiled egg and toast for Mrs J. Mrs O'L is a diabetic. Where's her chart? What's she on today? Hurry up, hurry up. Mrs G's an ulcer. Never, ever describe a patient by her disease. Oh, sister, you hard-boiled old thing you. Don't you know that? Each patient is a person. A real live person with an IQ, an ID and a unique fingerprint. With ten children or no children, a husband who brings her flowers and sits and holds her hands, or one who rushes in at the last minute because the babysitter never came, or a husband who never comes except on Sunday during pub closing time because he's a genuine gilt-edged prize of an Irish bachelor who took a bedmate and an unpaid housekeeper for life and it's very inconvenient of her to be sick.

Breakfast over. Help the wardsmaids clear up. Mind you don't spill anything on the floor or they'll be on strike. Remember to say please and thank you in case they think you're being above yourself. Avoid conflict between staff.

Rules of the road. Avoid head-on collision, confrontation, making an issue. Bedpan round. Mrs B needs a laxative. Miss D, poor old Miss D, is incontinent and so ashamed she pretends to be cross. Poor old Miss D. The body is an encumbrance. How it weighs down the soul, even clothes it in false colours, gives it a wrong public image. Who but my soul and I know what hides under my blonde hair and gooey bluey eyes. Pink cheeks too. I inherited them from my mother. Where did you come from oh soul? Passionate brunette. Deep down maelstrom of rebellious thought and I don't believe a word of it and it's all bozamba and codswallop and the world is a mess.

Stand for a second while sister isn't looking and refresh yourself by breathing in those tangy bronzy chrysanthemums grown in somebody's back garden. I hate the big hothouse ones.

Pussy-faced, over-ripe, over-fed. Sr Damien says they make her feel she wants to squash them. Like she wants to pinch me and she's always clutching and holding and getting upset when I break another syringe and says she'll stop it from my pay. My allowance. Student nurses are not paid. They are given a training allowance. Note the subtlety of that. All student nurses must be in by 10PM and lights out by 10.30. Must feed well and sleep well in order to be of value and give of their best. Who wants to be out after 10? Not I. No hairy he-man, no blue-suited Irishman at the Galteemore, no sleek, polished Englishman, slightly amused by Irish quaintness of which he gets full measure, since he seems to expect it, can lure me from my well-earned rest. Work-and-bed-work-and-bed-work-and-bed. You Irish girls never get up for morning Mass. There's half past six Mass every morning in the convent chapel and only the faithful few attend, besides the community of course. Now girls, any questions? Yes Mother we don't like the food and we think it should be improved.

O the insolence. O the daring. O the effrontery.

Who do you think you are! (My soul, my weeping soul, who do you think you are?) Ah well. Conflict should be avoided at all costs. Yes Mother, sorry Mother, Matron, Mother. Which is it? Supposing I said yes Mammy. O the daring. Shut up soul. Keep quiet and survive. Speak out and die dog.

Bedpan round over. Test the specimens. Mrs O'L's insulin must be increased. Hate the smell of boiled pee. Why did I say that? We always call it urine. Lie down soul. Your scars have set you mad. We always call it wee wee at home. Mammy I want to do my wee wee. Well do it love. You don't have to make a public pronouncement. Just thought I'd let you know. All right love.

Love. Oh Mother, oh Father, oh brothers and sisters, how I miss you all. Love at home, green fields, wet-smelling streets, the castle at the end of the road, the kettle hopping off the range. Oh look at that, the new patient's full of albumen and she's due for op tomorrow. Label all the specimens. Put away test tubes. Hurry, hurry, hurry. Remake all beds in surgical annexe already made by night staff. Go along ward kicking in castors. Change water glasses, flowers. Oh Miss P. Of course I will. Don't worry. It happens to the best of us. Platitude No. 896740. Poor Miss P. Tidy up sluice, wash out sinks, baths, toilets. Time for ten o'clock coffee. Please sister, may I go to coffee? Always thinking of our stomachs, aren't we nurse? Oh, go on. Be back on time. It's Mr Psshawwolfenstow's round this morning. Mr Hopalongg Cassidy and his underling Twinkletoes. Go for coffee. Where are my fags? Puff, inhale, whooooo. Puff, inhale, whooooo. Home sister. You girls smoke too much. Filthy habits. And you didn't leave your laundry out this morning. And clear away all that rubbish from your dressing table. Nurses are not allowed do-das and knick-knacks. Have some consideration for the domestic staff who have to dust your rooms. But sister I always dust my own. Of course, of course, you always have an answer. *You* know it all!

Soul, do you know it all? Why did you weep soul in your blank bleak corner of yourself when Mr Brownlow died five minutes after you had given him an injection of heroin? Nurses are so hard. Nurses are so callous. Do nurses have souls? Do souls have nurses? How fortunate I shall be if in my last extremity – dee dum dee dee I could put it to music – I had somebody as kind and loving as me to look after me.

Was it murder to give heroin to a dying man gasping and praying for it, to persuade night sister he needed it so badly he had to have it? Was it his pain or my pain I couldn't bear? Is the equation compassion equals self-pity verifiable? Another fag for God's sake. Give us an old butt then. Stupid to put it on a pin and try to smoke it. Stupid but try it. It's a shade better than poor old Wigglesworth dipping into the amphetamines. Buckle on the harness. Gird the loins. Back to the fray. On duty, sister. Mmmm. Yes. Do the dressings and bad backs with Nurse Super Efficient and try and learn something. And don't drop a receiver on the floor. Sigh. You know how Mr Psshawwolfenstow likes quiet on his rounds. Yes sister, thank you sister. Thank you for letting me breathe, sister, for the privilege of sharing your rarified air. Mr Psshawwolfenstow hates noise. Why does he throw the ribs on the floor when he's doing a resection up in Theatre 3 so that I have to grovel around on the floor and pick them up? My ears scream at the sound. Does he not hear the sound? The roots of heaven being pulled out and paradise and memories of sunny evenings crashing about my head.

And mutilated bodies running away from their souls. Death and destruction, butchery. Healing hands how are you. Yes blank, no blank. Can't bring myself to say sir. Can't call you sir, sir. Really sorry about that, just can't do it. You're not a sir to me, sir. I was only relieving someone else that day on chest unit. Run rabbit, run rabbit, run, run, run. More swabs, more sterile water. DON'T TOUCH ME, NURSE. Blast it, have to change my gloves. Haven't you ever been taught aseptic technique? Where do you get these girls nowadays, sister? Scraping the barrel a bit, isn't it?

Oh the dregs, that's me all right. Funny how I did that. Knew it was stupid but I did it. Got all mixed up with sterile non-touch asepsis and carried a full basin of boiling water from the sterilising unit using two cheatles forceps. *Conticuere omnes* as old stodge Aeneas would have put it. Deathly silence everywhere. All activity suspended, anaesthetist waiting in stupefaction, sister's eyes tilting over her mask. His and all sundry assistants' likewise popping. But I made it. Right to the stand. No crash, no first-degree burns and thanks be to God for it.

Do you think sister, is she mentally retarded?

O sir, I don't think you're a sir at all, sir. Do your plumbing and tailoring and leave me and my soul to lick our wounds.

Well here he comes and underling Twinkletoes. All set for promotion and keep those pretty little Irish nurses at a distance. Can't afford to get involved there, ha, ha. No bogtrotters and broad brogues in Harley Street. Oh, Twinkletoes, why don't you blow your nose, or smell like a rose. If I were Herod's daughter I really wouldn't have you on a saucer. But little Fatty Hall, aged sixty, I'd let him marry me mother if she weren't already spoken for since twenty-five years ago. All behind the times and all behind, says old Twinkletoes, whinnying into his coffee. I'd like to drown you in it and refuse you artificial respiration. Old Fatty Hall talks to patients, even the poor ones. No flashing of gold-filled teeth in private rooms and whistle-stop tours of public wards with open discussion of signs, symptoms and prognosis, whether grave or not, at the foot of the bed. Ah, no. Old Fatty Hall, 5ft 5in and 13 stone, knows his onions. I never lay out many of his mistakes. Never close the eyes of an internal haemorrhage of his.

Sister Gemma is taking temperatures. Sweet, sweet, sweet. Face like a madonna under the blue veil. Heart like a madonna's too. Detached, enraptured, constant private adoration. Hard to make beds with a madonna. The lily-like hands slip from the blankets, leaving corners untidy. Perhaps she's doing all this for the good of her soul – her nice round whole white soul. Pure and ready for the Lord's hand to write on. How the Jewish women love her, which strikes me as paradoxical, so practical and earthly themselves. Her gentleness sedates them, their anxieties, their fluttering nerves, their worries about their families. I hope to God she doesn't sneak off to meditate in the middle of ops this afternoon. Mary has chosen the better part. Nonsense. She did not. She opted out, backed away, shut her eyes and drifted along. Lazy loafer. Ah but sweet and gentle and elegant. Watch how she shakes the thermometer, long fingers flick from the wrist. Never blots the temperature chart either. Exquisitely neat.

How are you this morning, Mrs K? Oh lovey, I'm fine, much better, thank you. You're looking great, Mrs K. No. You're not. Don't die, Mrs K. You look terrible and your wound is breaking down again. Did I ever tell you the story, Mrs K? Oh, nurse, don't make me laugh. It does me good but it hurts. Whisper, oh nurse, I love you. Don't let them change you to another ward. I need you. No. Mrs K. Of course not. Nurse Super Efficient don't frown. Allow me the luxury of a little love and gratitude.

Nurses do not establish relationships with patients, nor have special feelings for one more than another. Well that's fair. Trainee nurses are called probationers. Why are we on probation? For being young, for being healthy, for daring the harrowing world of sickness to touch us. For having the arrogance to take other people's burdens on our backs and hope to bear them. For the crime of foolishness, naiveté, innocence.

BOYFRIEND: Ha, ha, so you're a nurse. Nurses know a lot.

ME: Like what?

B.F: Ha, ha. Don't act the innocent.

ME: You're only a little boy and you're no friend of mine.

EX B.F. What did I say? What's the matter?

Insensitive brute, buckethead, muttonhead. I'm a thousand years old and I'll never be young again. All the world's a hospital and all the men and women merely patients. How my back aches, how my heart aches. How my soul weeps.

PATIENT: How do you manage to be so serene and happy all the time?

I wear a mask with a smile on it.

Luncheon's up from the kitchen. Put away dressing trolley. Scrub hands. Give out trays, napkins, cutlery. Feed the helpless, encourage with small talk. Just a little or sister will say I'm spending all my time chatting. I skate precariously on the thin line between dutifulness and loving.

Sister has a thing about Mr Psshawwhat'shisname. She blushes at him. Feeds his vanity. Maybe he needs it. I feel magnanimous and charitable. Maybe it's good for his ego. Maybe underneath that polished exterior lurks an unfinished lonely soul cringing away from past errors. Maybe he wears a mask too. *Absolvo te.* For your penance pick up the ribs yourself.

Go to feed my own self. Excuse me please, on entering dining-room door. Stony stare from staff nurse at head of table. Another unfinished soul. Or unborn, or stillborn. A blank page doomed never to be written on. No label for you, lady. *Ego te absolve* also. Who will absolve you, oh soul, my soul, my self, my me. I am who am. *Je suis l'église.* Oh for the luxury of such stupidity. Never to have the tiger of pity gnawing at your innards.

Protein-enriched cardboard for dinner. Frogs' spawn for dessert. If it gets swallowed quickly it doesn't have time to insult the tastebuds. And very likely it's just as nourishing as roast pheasant washed down with cherry brandy.

Contemplate for five minutes in order to preserve identity. Examination of conscience. I (*mea culpa, mea culpa*) have an unroutine mind. Can't get used to routine. Routine spares the body but kills the soul. Routine is for physiological functions. The mind must have chaos for creating. Out of disorder comes order. Out of order comes routine. Out of routine comes stagnation, out of stagnation comes corruption, out of corruption comes death. DON'T THINK, NURSE. NURSES ARE NOT MEANT TO THINK, ONLY TO OBEY. RULE OF THE ROAD NUMBER 6,542.

Wish I didn't think I had just eaten horse. Why is it more cannibalistic to eat horse in these islands than to eat a poor docile pampered Hereford bullock? The steed bit his master, how came this to pass? He heard the good pastor cry, 'All flesh is grass.' Irrelevance number 10001.

Luncheon hour over and it is six hours since I opened my eyes this morning. Mr Eliot, what were you doing wasting your time at area gates?

Orange Horses

Elsie Martin's husband beat her unconscious because she called him twice for his dinner while he was talking to his brother. To be fair, she did not simply call him. She blew the horn of the Hiace van to summon him.

He had never beaten her unconscious before. He was surprised and a little frightened when she lay down and did not get up. He was a small man but she was even smaller, weighing barely seven stone, and she was further handicapped by being five months pregnant. Afterwards his mother said that if Elsie had fed herself better instead of wasting good money on them fags she'd have been able to take the few wallops and get over them the way any normal woman would.

'He didn't mean nothin',' the elder Mrs Martin said. 'He got a bit ahead of himself. But she shouldn't have blown the horn at him that way. A man won't take that kind of treatment from any woman and I wouldn't expect him to. He has his pride.'

She leaned on the caravan door while she spoke, staring out at the twisted remains of a bicycle, a rusty milk churn, a variety of plastic containers, three goats, two piebald ponies all tethered to an iron stake, and a scattering of clothes hanging on the fence which separated her domain from the town dump. Behind her, Elsie lay stretched. Her jaw had been wired in the hospital and was still aching. The bruises on her legs were fading and the cut in her head had been stitched and was healing nicely now, thank God.

'You'll be grand again, with the help of God,' her mother-in-law said, watching the ponies reach for a fresh bit of grass on the long acre. 'Grand,' she repeated with satisfaction as if by saying the word she made it happen, God's help being instantly available to her. 'You're grand. I'll be off now and I'll cook him a bit myself. I'll get one of the young ones to bring you over a sangwich. You could manage a sangwich.'

Elsie closed her eyes, trying to squeeze out the pain. Her stomach had not shrunk back to normal. The baby was only gone a week. She folded her hands over the place where he had been. She was sure he had been a boy, the way he kicked. She grieved quietly for him, for his little wasted life that never got the chance to be more than a few small kicks and turns inside her body. But she was sorry for herself too, because she had had a feeling about him, that he would be good to her. He might have been the one to protect her when the others were married with their own wives. She could tell by the older boys that they would hit their wives to control them. She wouldn't interfere but she would not stay around to watch her history being repeated. She had planned a life for herself with this baby. The plan would have to be changed.

Brigid, her eldest daughter, stepped lightly into the caravan and stood beside her. 'Nana says would you like a drink of tay with your sangwich.'

'Shut the door,' Elsie said crossly. 'You're letting the wind in. And sweep out the place. Didn't I tell you to do it this morning? Do you ever do anything you're told?'

'I did it. Them childer have it destroyed on me.'

'Who's minding them? Are they all at your Nana's? Where's Mary Ellen? Where's your father?'

'I dunno.' The child took the sweeping brush and began to sweep the floor. Her sullen expression annoyed her mother almost more than the careless way she swept the bits of food through the caravan door and out on to the green. A dog poked hopefully through the crumbs, then looked up expectantly at Brigid. She said, 'Geraway outa that,' without enough conviction for him to move. He placed a paw on the step. She pushed it off and stared maliciously at him. 'I'll tell my daddy on you, you little hoor,' she whispered and then, a living image of her grandmother, leaned on the brush handle surveying the scene.

'Look, Mama,' she called. 'The sky is orange. Why is it orange?'

Elsie lay back, floating between waves of pain, bathing herself in its persistence. She tried anticipating its peaks, the way she had been learning to anticipate the peaks in labour pains for the baby who was born dead. For the first time in her sixteen years of childbearing she had attended an antenatal class. It had all come to nothing. She should have known better. Her husband hadn't wanted her to go. He had been persuaded by the social worker to let her try it. But he had grumbled a lot after her visits and told her she was getting too smart. Baby or no baby, he said, you're due a beating. Keeping in with the country people isn't going to do you any good. And they don't care for you anyway. You're only a tinker to them.

She turned her head to see what Brigid was up to. The child had dropped the brush and was standing very still staring at something. 'What are you staring at?' the mother called.

'The pony is orange too,' Brigid said softly. 'The pony is orange.' She had cross eyes of a strange pale grey and the glow of the sunset lit them and changed their colour to a near yellow. One of the ponies suddenly tossed his head and flicked a quick look in her direction before turning his attention back to his patient grazing. Brigid wondered what it would be like to ride him. She was never allowed to try. If she did, her brothers knocked her off. She was beginning to think that she didn't want to ride. She would soon forget that she had ever had such a desire. Her brothers rode like feudal lords, galloping through wastelands and even through the crowded streets, proud and defiant. Brigid fixed her sombre gaze on the pony's back. It must be like the wind, she thought. It would be like racing the wind. That's why her brothers were so proud and cocky. They could race the wind, and she couldn't. Her father did it once. Her mother never did it. Her mother got beaten and had babies and complained. Her mother was useless.

Elsie called out, 'What are you sulking about now? Would you take that look off your face? If you can't do anything for me would you go away and leave me in peace.'

When she was gone, Elsie wanted her back. Brigid, she cried hopelessly, Brigid. It was a pity she wasn't lovable so that Elsie could cuddle her and tell her she was sorry for being cross. But what was the point? Brigid was eleven years of age and she should be doing things for her mother. What did she do all day? Gave them their breakfast in the morning and pushed the small ones in the buggy but beyond that – nothing. She spent most of the day moping around, listening to the gossip in the other caravans.

The caravans were arranged in a circle around the small caravan owned by Hannah, Elsie's mother-in-law. When her children married and had their own caravans they took their place in the circle whenever they came for a gathering. Their father was dead. There were nine surviving sons and seven daughters. When the father was sixty he stopped beating Hannah and got religion very bad. He paid frequent visits to the holy nun in the convent who could cure everything but death. He died peacefully, like a baby asleep, and had a huge funeral. From England and Scotland and all over Ireland the relations came to bury him. The casualty department in the hospital was kept going for two days with the results of their mourning. Hannah was very proud, though she wept for weeks, being supported by all her daughters and all but two of her daughters-in-law, Elsie and Margaret Anne.

Elsie remembered Margaret Anne, the way she used to drink the bottles of tawny wine so that she wouldn't feel the beatings. One night she drank a full bottle of vodka and choked on her own vomit. She was twenty-three. There were no fights after her funeral. There was no public lamentation. Her children cried and her husband cried and took the pledge for six months. Two years later he married her youngest sister and they went away t'England. There were plenty of sites in London for them. They would simply break down a gate, pull the caravan in and stay put until they were evicted. England, Elsie's youngest sister said, was a grand place. They had been put up in the best hotels for months because they were homeless.

Elsie often thought of staying in the best hotels too. Her husband called it one of her notions. His sisters said, 'That one has too many notions.' She had notions about not wanting to do the houses with them, about not wanting to stay home, night after night, while her husband went drinking with his brothers. The worst notion of all was when she arranged to get her dole money split so that she got her own share and the share for half the children. The welfare officer gave her dire warnings that if she changed her mind again, as she had done before, she would be left with nothing. Her husband coaxed, threatened and beat her but she would not surrender.

She had notions about Fonsie when she met him at the horse fair in Spancel Hill. Her parents had pulled their caravan into a by-road a few miles from the village. It was a scorching day when she saw Fonsie tussling with a colt, backing him up, jerking his head to show his teeth, running his hands down his fetlocks, slapping his flanks. The animal reared and bucked and frightened bystanders.

'Aisy, aisy,' a farmer said, 'you'll never sell him that way.'

'I'm not asking you to buy him,' Fonsie said smartly.

'You're not, for I wouldn't,' said the man. 'I never saw any good come from a tinker.'

'You wouldn't have the price of him,' Fonsie said and turned his head and winked at Elsie. His red hair was like a mad halo and his eyes were a blazing blue. She was like a rabbit hypnotised by a weasel. She followed him everywhere. She badgered her parents until they consented to the wedding. She was fifteen. She ignored all their warnings about his bad blood. He was the middle of the brothers and above and below him they were all the same. Always drinking. Always in trouble. Always dodging the law, frequently in jail or facing the judge and getting some smart solicitor to get them off on a technicality.

Fonsie never went to jail. He was too smart. But he didn't want her to be too smart. Smart women annoy me, he said. So be smart and stay stupid. One night when she was three months pregnant, he hit her because she was too smart by half, an ugly bitch who gave him the eye at Spancel Hill and was probably after being with someone else and the child could be anyone's.

There were different notions in her head then when she picked herself up from the floor and cried for her own people who were travelling up North. Through one of her sisters-in-law she got word to her own sisters. One of them travelled to see her and give her advice.

'Don't be saying anything to him when he is drunk.'

'I didn't say anything,' Elsie said.

'Well maybe you should have. Did you look at him? A man can hate a hard look. He'll take it as an insult.'

'I looked at the floor,' Elsie said. 'I was afraid to look at him.'

'Well, there you are then. That's how it happened,' her sister said triumphantly. 'You didn't spake to him and you didn't look at him. Sure that explains it.'

'He says the child isn't his.'

'An old whim he has. His brothers putting him up to it. They're too much together. They should be at home with their wives instead of always in each other's company. They're terrible stuck on each other.'

Elsie knew that was the trouble. A man was all right on his own with a woman but put him in with the herd of men, especially the herd of his own family, and he lost his senses.

Her sisters had always given her plenty of advice. Don't get too fat or you won't be able to run away when he wants to bate you. Learn the houses that are good to the Travellers. Don't try them too often. Don't look for too much the first time. Always bring a baby with you. If you haven't one, borrow one. Keep half of the money for yourself. Her mother gave her one piece of advice. Keep silent and never show a man the contempt you feel for him. It is like spitting in the face of God.

It was good advice, especially the bit about the money. Her sisters had not told her how to keep the money, where to hide it, what to do with it. For them that was the simplest part. They could thrust their hands down into the recess between their breasts and pull up a wad of notes worth a couple of hundred pounds. When a caravan was needed their men would call on them as others would call on a banker. Their interest rates were negotiable and were never paid in kind but in behaviour or favours granted. Her sisters knew how to control their husbands but they were simple men and not as cute as hers. He always seemed to know when she had money accumulated and usually managed to beat it out of her. His spies were everywhere, his sisters and mother always prying and asking questions of the children. She stopped bringing the small children on her rounds. In spite of warnings it was easy for them to let out important information, like where she had been for the few hours of her absence. Elsie knew that she was one of the best of the Travellers for getting money from the settled people. They liked her because she was polite and handsome and clean. She didn't whine and she didn't exaggerate. Pride and a certain loyalty to her own people wouldn't allow her to tell the truth about her husband's drinking and beatings. For some of her regulars it wasn't necessary. Her black eyes and bruises were enough.

The latest accumulation was lying under a stone in the mud bank, twenty paces from her caravan. £353.00 in twenty-pound notes and ten-pound notes and five-pound notes and one-pound notes. She had counted it lovingly, feeling the notes, smoothing them out, folding them into twenty-pound bundles held in place by elastic bands, the whole lot wrapped in a plastic supermarket bag. If her husband moved the caravan her treasure was still measurable. It was thirty-five paces from the third cement pole, holding the last section of fencing around the dump. If someone moved the poles it was a hundred paces from the bend in the new road. If the country people decided to change the road, as she knew from experience was a likely occurrence, it was two hundred paces from the last brick house on the estate. If that went then it was straight under the last rays of the setting sun on 23 September. If there was no sun on 23 September she would dig the bank from dump to road in the middle of the night until she found it. If there was no bank – If someone came with a bulldozer – She sat up suddenly. She wanted to rush out to claw at the clay, scrabbling like a dog crazy for his buried bone, in the mud and bare-rooted trees.

She lay down again, her secret like a flame to be kept alive but not so alive that it would leap up and consume her. At long last she had learned discipline. At long last she had learned her mother's secret of silence. When she used the Hiace horn she almost broke the secret. The sound of the horn had its own words and her husband understood them. Only that morning he had looked at her and said, 'You're due a beating and when I have time I'll give it to you.' She should have been there waiting for him, dinner ready, whenever he turned up. She should always wait around the caravan, never farther away from his mother's or his sisters' vans. He didn't like her going to his brothers' vans where she might gossip or plot treason with their wives, or worse, be unfaithful with one of the brothers.

Once only had Elsie and the sisters-in-law plotted. The great idea came to them that they would run away together and leave all the children to Hannah. There were forty-three children under the age of twelve. They sat contemplating the idea in wonder on a sunny morning when the men had gone to collect their dole money and the sisters were gossiping with Hannah. The idea had been thrown out by Mary Teresa and when the magic of it had been chewed over and gloried in it was Mary Teresa who began to destroy it. She said my Danny would never be able to look after himself. After that it was a landslide of surrender. Kathleen said her two boys were wild already and if she left them to their father, no knowing what would become of them. They'd end up in trouble with the law. Bridie said her fellow wouldn't take a bite from anyone only herself. Eileen said mine are all at school. He'd never bother sending them and they'd lose all the schooling they had. And she'd never mind them – meaning Hannah. She's all talk. When it comes down to it she won't look after another woman's children even if they are her grandchildren. All talk, that's all she is. Elsie thought uncomfortably of Brigid and how she hadn't got around to giving her all the loving she should have done and how her father had eyed her a few times but she couldn't put that thought into words. She said I'd be worried about Brigid. Then suddenly all the women remembered their daughters in surprise and confusion and began to name them off, one by one, picturing each child, pretty or plain, cross-eyed or red-haired, loving or defiant, as if naming them became their remembrance.

Elsie lay thinking about all of this as the sunset deepened into a scarlet glow, filling the caravan with its radiance, bouncing off her brass ornaments and mirrors, turning her faded blanket into a brilliant rug, a kaleidoscope of purest wonder. She dozed for a while, soothed by the sun's strange lullaby. She was disturbed by shouts and the thunder of hooves around the caravan. She twitched the curtain to peer out. The magic had gone out of the sky but over the town the pale shape of a crescent moon could just be seen. The pickers were beginning to set fire to the dump and its acrid-smelling smoke drifted in a long low swathe towards the housing estate. The cries of children at a last game before bedtime reached her and above them came the shouts of her two eldest sons who waved their arms and ran after one of the piebald ponies. As Elsie peered through the window she could see the animal tearing away into the distance, towards the high church steeple, with its rider hanging on for dear life.

More trouble, Elsie thought. Someone had stolen the pony.

Then the door was pushed in and Johnny and Danny burst upon her, pulling at her blankets, crying, 'Get up, get up, Brigid has taken the pony.'

Fonsie was after them, face red with rage, shouting, 'That's your rearing for you, the little bitch has gone off riding like a tinker on the piebald.'

Well then, thought Elsie, stroking her wired-up jaw, here's a right how do ye do. The little bitch is up on a pony and away like the wind.

'Wait till I lay hands on the little rap,' Fonsie said bitterly. 'Bringing disgrace unto the whole family. She's your daughter all right. But is she mine? Answer me that will you?'

'She is yours,' Elsie said. 'She didn't get that wild blood from me. Did you ever see one of my sisters up on a pony? Have any of my family got red hair? Every one of us has brown eyes. 'Twasn't from the wind she got the blue eyes and the hair.'

'She could be Danny's. From day one he was hanging around you. From the minute I brought you back.'

'He was twelve then,' Elsie said, wearily playing the chorus to an old tune.

'What has that got to do with it? You were fifteen. Brigid's near twelve now. She's not like a girl at all. There could be something wrong with her. When your jaw is better let you see to it and when she gets back here I'll give her a lesson she won't forget. Don't give me any of your old guff.'

'Supposing she doesn't come back?' Elsie had started to say, but he didn't want to hear it and he jumped off the step and joined his brothers who had gathered to grin at his discomfiture. Elsie watched them, a few thrusts of fists, a few raised voices, another soothing voice and they climbed into Danny's van and drove away.

One of the pickers stopped by her window, his sack full of bits of copper and aluminium, the wheel of a bicycle hanging like a huge medallion down his back.

'You've got a bold one there,' he said. 'And to look at her you'd think butter wouldn't melt in her mouth, cross eyes and all. Have they gone to fetch her?'

'Gone to Old Mac's,' Hannah joined in, leaning her large behind against the caravan, looking the picker up and down. 'Did you get much today? That's a miserable old wheel you got. I'll take it off your hands for 50p.'

'Go back to your knitting, old woman,' he said scornfully. 'I have a buyer for this. A proper bicycle dealer.'

'Well that shifted him,' Hannah said, as he heaved his load up on his bicycle and wobbled away down the road, disappearing like a ghost in the fog of burning plastic bags and litter. 'Poking his nose in where he isn't wanted. I hope you told him nothing.'

Elsie turned her face to the wall and groaned.

'Hurts you, does it?' Hannah asked. 'You shouldn't have let that black doctor put the wire in. I wouldn't let a black doctor next or near me. Nor one of them women doctors either. But you were always the one with notions. I'll go away now and look after your poor childer for you. They're crying with the hunger, I expect, if they're not watching the telly.'

The blessed peace when she had gone flowed over Elsie, better than any painkiller. The second pony munched near her window, stretched the full length of his tether. Brigid could have fallen off by now. She could be lying on the road with a broken arm or leg. In the distance the siren of an ambulance screamed hysterically. That's probably her, Elsie thought. They have picked her broken little body up and brought her to hospital. She's unconscious or maybe dead. I'll never see her again.

The dark closed in on the caravan. Elsie listened for the voices of her children as they made their different ways to their aunts' caravans. If Brigid were here she would come and say goodnight to her. She would cuddle up against her and she would not push her away impatiently. Brigid, Brigid, she groaned aloud.

'I'm here, Mama.' Brigid was beside her, hopping up and down on the bed. 'Did you see me? I never fell off once. Did Dada see me?'

Exasperation filled every inch of Elsie's body. It took charge of the pain. She wanted to sit up and shake Brigid till her teeth rattled. She opened her mouth to say our father'll kill you and good enough for you when Brigid said, 'I wouldn't have done it if he hadn't turned orange. The sun turned him orange and I wanted to ride him while he was that colour.'

'He wasn't that colour at all,' Elsie said. 'You only thought he was that colour.'

'He was. I saw him,' Brigid insisted, her crossed eyes glinting with temper. 'Can I cuddle into you, Mama? Can I sleep here with you?' What was the use of anything, thought Elsie. The child was safe and sound and wanting to sleep beside her and she didn't want anyone in the bed with her. She wanted to toss and turn and groan in privacy.

'I might keep you awake.'

'You won't, Mama. And I'll get you anything you want. Will I make you a sup of tay? Did the fellas see me? What did they say?'

Elsie began to laugh. 'Oh my God,' she groaned, 'don't make me laugh. My jaw aches. They were raging. They'll kill you when they get their hands on you.'

'I don't care,' Brigid said. 'It was worth it. I'll kick them and I'll ride the pony again and again. I've him tethered now. I fell off loads of times but I got up again. It's easy. I'll practise. If they see I'm good, they'll let me do it. I'm not like you, Mama. I'm like my Dada and no one will bate me into the ground. You shouldn't let Dada hit you.'

Oh Mary, Mother of God, intercede for me at the throne of mercy, prayed Elsie silently. Give me patience. Help me to say the right thing. She said nothing. She thought of the money wrapped tightly under the stone waiting to liberate her.

Brigid was almost asleep. She flung an arm across Elsie's stomach and said, 'I'll make money for you when I'm big and you'll be able to buy anything you like.'

'Won't you want to buy things for yourself? Maybe your own pony?'

'When I'm big I won't care about the pony,' Brigid said. 'When I'm big.' She was already asleep. Elsie looked down at her pale freckled skin and carroty eyelashes and she smiled. An orange sun and an orange horse and orange hair. She looked with love at Brigid and she understood her world. For a moment she had a glimpse of some meaning beyond the caravan and the dump and the pile of money buried under the bank. Was it heaven that she was thinking about? Some place up there, way beyond the sky where you could go to bed and rest easy, a place like the Dallas off the telly without the fighting and arguing. All the arguing would wear you out. You either got worn out or as fat as a pig like some of her sisters-in-law who stuffed themselves even when they weren't hungry. It was the opposite with her. Her stomach couldn't take food when the arguing and shouting was going on. After a beating she couldn't eat for weeks.

An orange horse was like a flame, she thought. It would burn the air up as it raced by your window. It would warm your heart but never singe your soul. It could fly up to the clouds and down again. It could give you more notions than anyone would ever know. You could touch it and not feel it. You could feel it and not touch it. It could have a meaning that you might never understand but knowing it was there would change your life. It would help you find a way to spend the money you saved. It would save your life if you let it. It would make your jaw ache less. It was better than the holy nun, God forgive her for thinking such a thing. If Margaret Anne had seen it she might never have choked on her own vomit. An orange horse that never was could be the greatest secret of all. She stroked Brigid's hair and fell asleep.

People in the town said afterwards that the flames of the fire turned the sky the maddest orange they had ever seen. Three of the caravans went up together but the only casualties were a mother and daughter. Their caravan went up first. The heat was so intense it was a wonder the whole lot of them didn't go up. A gas cylinder exploded. The police were questioning a man who had thrown a can of petrol into the first caravan and set it alight. He was drunk. He didn't know what he was doing. There were screams from the caravan, terrible screams that those who heard them would never forget. But the firemen found nothing.

It was the heat, they said. It was an incinerator. A Hiace van was burned and left a carcass of twisted metal. A pony died and left a charred body but in the caravan there was nothing. Nothing.

The Sentimentalist

The Americans say that eccentricity is the norm in Ireland. I wish they were right. What after all is normality? Can it simply be equated with dullness? I ask the question because the only people I find interesting are those whom the dull people of my acquaintance call odd. And I am certain that behind my back I am called odd, with accompanying shakings of the head, which frequent shakings may account for the displacement of the few brains my charitable analysts possess. It does not worry me at all. But then I am not a lover of people. I find children irritating, the old irritable and the middle-aged merely opinionated. And the young are so incredibly gauche. It pains me to have to acknowledge their familiarity. I do not care for animals, except for cows, who combine supreme usefulness with a rustic kind of beauty. I do not consider myself a misanthropist, but on the whole I find women silly and demanding, and men stupid and aggressive. Most people are dishonest. Worse, their dishonesty is contagious so that even I am occasionally infected and I find myself accepting their outrageous statements out of a false sense of good manners. Besides, it is wearying to be in disagreement all the time, and I confess I am a little lazy, which is why I live by myself in this three-roomed cottage in the middle of Martin Leahy's farm. I rent the house very cheaply because it has none of the inconveniences of so-called civilised living. Its chief attraction for me is the lack of a roadway to my door and whenever my relations or acquaintances feel obliged to visit me they must do so on foot, along a muddy track of about three miles. I have an old ship's spyglass in my sitting-room and I occasionally scan the horizon to make sure I am not caught unawares. I cannot understand my relatives' need to visit me. I am sure they do not enjoy it, but they seem to take it on themselves as a painful duty and I am too considerate to deprive them of their sense of responsibility.

One visitor I welcomed was my cousin Liza. We knew each other since we were young girls. Her father and mother committed suicide in a romantic pact in 1915. They were pacifists, living in England, and refused, they said, to be embroiled in the folly of war. So they left their only child to the care of my parents, who, I think, fulfilled their obligation admirably. They gave her, and us, as much affection as was necessary for our survival. Very quickly Liza became one of the family. We loved her English accent and tried our best to copy her, with laughable results. Even more laughable were her attempts at acquiring Gaelic, which we were then just beginning to learn. It was quite beyond me. I have no flair for languages. Since English has been imposed on us, for historical reasons, I accept it and consider it adequate for my needs, a vehicle for communicating thought. I concede that I may have lost something, subtleties of expression more in keeping with my cultural background, not to mention the heritage of tradition which is difficult to translate adequately. However, I have always been a pragmatist and I accept the reality of conquest. The new nationalist fervour associated with the revival of the language was boring to me. I despise passion, wasted emotions. But not so Liza. Typical of the convert, she threw herself totally into the Gaelic revival. She joined the Gaelic League, attended the Abbey plays and became a member of Cumann na mBan. I could not approve. It has always seemed to me that organised groups, military or civilian or religious, are death to the individual and therefore retard human development. It can be argued that for the apathetic mass such groups are necessary, but I believe that one strong-minded individual can achieve more on her own if she is prepared to sacrifice her life for her cause. I do not mean by that the futile sacrifice of death, which simply perpetuates myths and has no logical value. Martyrdom is the ultimate folly, the self-indulgence of the sentimental. I mean that one person, standing alone, against the convention of her times, must, if she applies herself, learn wisdom, fortitude and knowledge, and provide the vital link between the generations which must lead to the ennoblement of all womankind. I use the term loosely to include men.

Liza was impulsive and sentimental in that charming way of the English. She scurried around the countryside in those early years waving flags and crying slogans. It saddened me to see her in her ridiculous uniform, allowing the uniformly foolish ideas of her group to take over. I do not deny that the history of this country has been a tragic one, but the worst tragedy of all has been the number and variety of its saviours – most of them with foreign or English blood – which it has attracted. Liza saw herself as one of those saviours.

In the course of her missionary work she married a young man from Waterford, a timid ordinary fellow whom she tried to indoctrinate. It was useless. She wept over his 'dreadful tolerance' as she called it. He admitted the savagery of men, the injustices his countrymen had suffered, but he constantly saw the other side, and constantly made allowances. 'I love him for it,' she told me. 'He is so gentle and kind, he can see no evil in anyone. I hate him for it too. He will not fight for anything. I know *you* won't fight, but somehow that is different. And Father and Mother were different too. They were committed and so are you. He is not committed to anything. He loves everyone.' It was shocking that he died, shot down at their front door by the Black and Tans, before her eyes, probably because of her reputation as a nationalist. To me, it had a poetic justice, but I did not tell her what I thought.

I hoped the futility of his death could cure her. But no. She kept his hat and coat on the hall stand, left the bullet holes in the door and walls and the blood-stained rug where he fell, and carried on. But she was not political, not ambitious, not scheming, and she was not a man. So there was no place for her among the new policymakers born out of his blood and others like him. 'I cannot give up my dream now,' she said. 'Poor Willie died for it. My house, his house, will be a memorial to him. It will be the glory of Ireland.' Her grief and her innocence moved me. Against my better judgement I helped her to organise the house for students. It became the only summer school of its kind, open from April until September for young people from all over the world and from all over Ireland who came to imbibe the old Gaelic culture and learn the language. For fifty years she kept the school going. For fifty years she took only Irish-produced food and wore only Irish-made clothes. She allowed herself tea and coffee, confessing it a weakness, but grew her own vegetables and fruit. She refused on principle to eat oranges or bananas because, she said, they were the product of slave labour. She was always available for picket duty, ban the bomb, anti-apartheid, women's rights. When the farmers were imprisoned after their marches she picketed the jail and was booed by the town population. A city woman herself, she believed in the nobility of working the land and declared the farmers were the guardians of the country's traditions. Dedication of that sort is truly admirable, and how rarely one finds it. But oh, the folly of it all. The folly of living one's life for a useless dream.

Liza's house was in the centre of a spreading suburb. All around her walled gardens, hundreds of semi-detached homes sprouted the inevitable television aerials. The view of the river which she used to enjoy from her bedroom window became swallowed up in the new hollow block landscape. When at the age of seventy she closed her school, she was unprotected during the vulnerable months of fruiting and had to fight to keep her apples growing. Hordes of boys challenged each other to climb her walls and rob her orchard, encouraged to do so perhaps by the silliest of all aphorisms, 'Boys will be boys'. The bravery of these young fellows is typical of the spirit of our time. One old lady became a formidable enemy to be challenged and defeated. To the socialists she was a property owner, a *fíor Gael* crank to the Language Freedom Movement, a rock in the path of progress to the speculators who viewed her two acres with hungry eyes. Worst of all, she was an embarrassing reminder to the few old nationalist members of the government.

I visited her last autumn when the paths were slippy with the rotting leaves of her chestnut trees and the stone house seemed to fade into the grey day. While we sat by the fire over tea I asked her would she not think of settling in the Gaeltacht now that her work in the school was over.

'I am Gall to them,' she said. Vinegary was not an adjective I would have applied to Liza and I suppose I looked bewildered. 'I mean Gall as opposed to Gael,' she sighed. 'Foreigner.'

'Well, I suppose you are,' I agreed.

'Not because I am half English,' she said a little tartly. '*You* might be even more foreign to them.'

I had to admit that I felt foreign whenever I visited such places. 'Don't you think they are a little chauvinist in their separatism lately?' I asked.

'You don't understand,' she said. 'I don't mean to be harsh, but really Jo, have you ever felt deeply about anything? Have you no values at all? Don't you care what has happened to this country, or what is happening? What do you do with your life?'

'I think,' I said. 'What else is there to do?'

'You sit in that hut, reading and thinking. Is that a way to spend a life?'

'It's the only way for me,' I said.

'But such a waste,' she cried. 'Don't you feel you have wasted your life?'

It seemed a strange thing for her to say.

But although she is only six months younger than me, she always seems much younger and I tend to indulge her. I did not tell her about my book, my life's work, which will, I hope, put all those foreign male philosophers to shame. It is time we had an Irish philosopher who does not come out of Maynooth tarred with the Roman brush, and it is past time we had a woman philosopher. But I could not discuss that with Liza. I am too old now to start exchanging confidences. It makes my life somewhat lonely, especially at my age, but I recognise that as being part of the price I must pay for my independence. Liza always said I was a cynic, but that was because she was a sentimentalist and only saw her own truth.

Last spring she visited me and accused me of deliberately torturing her by living in my isolated kingdom. 'It is cruel to expect me to walk that distance to see you. Some day I will not come, and I suppose you will not care.'

'But you know it is my only defence,' I protested. 'It's as good as a moat around a castle. Otherwise I would never have any peace. I am always glad to see you, Liza. But not too often. Not even you.'

'Oh your hard heart,' she sighed. 'I don't know why I bother with you.'

I could not reply. Silence on these occasions seems the best policy and is often more reproachful than words. And then she said, 'Forgive me dear. What would I have done without you all these years? You so sensible, I with my foolish, foolish dreams. Such folly.'

I was horrified. Here was a threat to my own integrity. If Liza became a cynic anything was possible. I might end my days guarding her orchard with her.

'Gaelic Ireland is dead,' she announced, as if she had just unveiled truth. 'I and others like me prop up its corpse and pretend we are keeping it alive.'

I was forced to lie. 'Nonsense,' I said. 'You know you have lived your life in the fullest sense, believing in what you did. And you were right.'

'My gods were all false,' she said. 'You knew it. I should have looked for political power. That's obvious to me now.'

'Politics would have destroyed you,' I said.

'I am destroyed anyway. They are going to knock down my house and build sixteen houses where I have kept my summer school.'

'Be precise.' I had to be stern in order to hide my fear. 'Whom do you mean by "they"?'

'The Corporation has compulsorily acquired my house. They are right of course. I am taking up far too much space. I am old. There are young people with children waiting for houses. Think of all the children who could grow up in my two acres.'

What could I do but fight for her, poor sentimental Liza. I left my book unfinished and marched with her, up and down the path in front of the house, armed with placards of protest. Of course we made wonderful headlines. The cub reporters made their names with us. 'Two indomitable eighty-year-olds fight for their home. A husband's young blood spilled here for Ireland. Is the Corporation the new oppressor?' I expected some salvos from the *Socialist* magazine, but age, I suppose, still arouses pity, if not respect. Liza's old pupils rallied. She became the heroine of the day, the integrity of the past standing against the hollow men of the present. They flocked around her, middle-aged and young, grandparents and parents. There were some emotional scenes in the garden last summer when after the success of our campaign, a hundred or so of her pupils came to cheer her. She stood in the centre crying happily. 'You dear people, you dear wonderful people.'

I attended her funeral when she died a few weeks later. I owed her that much. It amused me to watch the performance, since it finally vindicated my lifestyle. Everyone spoke in

Irish. I suppose they praised her work, her dedication. When I passed her house yesterday I saw the demolition notice on the wall. Beside it was a brass memorial plaque with an inscription in Irish. Fortunately I could not understand it. I have never had a flair for languages.

Love

Mary Deasy was forty-five
when she married Jimmy
Burke. He was just turned
fifty. It seemed an unlikely
match and her relations were
disapproving. She lived in
one of those neat labourer's
cottages you can see scattered between the towns of
Ireland. Her father had been
a farm labourer in the days
when a man would walk fifty
miles for a good farm job and
be glad of thirty shillings a
week, with whatever perks of
free milk or cast-off clothes
the farmer chose to give him.

On the acre attached to the cottage they kept a cow, a sow with her bonhams, a half dozen hens, and they grew the soft fruits which the thrifty mother turned into jams to be sold in the village. There were two apple trees – one for cooking apples and one for eating – and there was a small tilled patch with a few drills of potatoes, turnips, cabbages, carrots and onions. Mary Deasy's father was a skilled worker, much appreciated by his employer, and the family was well thought of in the village. When the old people died all the sons and daughters had left to improve themselves in the big town. Mary stayed on, keeping the house and little plot of ground as neat as it had been in her parents' day.

It was therefore a surprise when she married Jimmy Burke, who worked off and on – and more off than on – as a labourer with the county council. She had first met him when he was trimming the hawthorn hedge across the road from her cottage and he sang out pleasantries to her about the fragrance of May and the delight he took in his work. He seemed like a wandering poet to her then, a man like O'Carolan of the East or Raferty of the West with a song for every occasion. He seemed less of a poet after their marriage when he lay around the house, his legs getting in her way as she brushed and dusted; but he was agreeable and even-tempered. He made a bad fist of milking the cow or tending the garden but he was company and she had been lonely. He was not always idle. When the weather suited him he poked in the garden because it was pleasant to do so and he milked the cow in the heat of the summer evening when the scent of the orange-blossom tree drowned the subtler scents of the fields near by. For three years this idyllic existence continued until Mary became pregnant.

It created a sensation among her brothers and sisters, one of whom coarsely said that it must have been more by good luck than good management. Mary was a mixture of fear and delight at the unlooked-for event. Jimmy and herself had assumed she was too old for children, and since he was as easy going about sex as he was about everything else, the likelihood of children coming on the scene had never occurred to her. Jimmy took the winks and nods and nudges with good humour and even began to take pride in himself at his newly acquired status.

Their son was born on a day when the crooked branches of the apple trees were bared to the east wind shrilling through them. The winter cabbages huddled in rows and the potato pit had the remnants of the night's frost on top of its straw covering. As naked as the new-born baby the fields lay open to the sky. The cow humped her back at the hedge where a few evergreens gave her shelter and the hens shook their feathers angrily at the cruelty of the day.

A fortnight later Mary was home with the infant. He was a placid baby. He lay in his cot, taking food when it was offered him, and slept through the nights from midnight until morning. Mary's sisters told her how blessed she was, comparing her good fortune with their own sleepless nights and the villainous behaviour of their offspring. Mary said little but privately thanked God for His care of her in giving her so perfect a baby. Jimmy took an interest in his son and would rock him to sleep or poke his finger at him until the little fellow closed his fist around it. He was very good about minding the baby – which was just as well, since it was sowing time and Mary had to be out in the garden digging and manuring and planting.

Her small savings were almost used up by summertime and she was glad when Jimmy got his annual work from the county council. She began to make plans for the future of their son and worked out ways of earning money for his education. She put down strawberry beds and planted pear trees along the sunny wall of the cottage. She started knitting Aran sweaters, her fingers flying through the intricate patterns. But by winter when Jimmy was out of work again she had to dip into her hoard to keep them going. Her family scolded her for being so soft with him. Lazy, good-for-nothing they called him. But she rebuked them and said he was a good man, easy to live with and always in such fine humour.

'And no wonder,' they said. 'He's had a soft landing right enough. Why should he worry about anything? You do all the worrying.'

'I don't worry,' Mary replied. 'God is good. Look at the beautiful baby He sent us. He's so quiet.'

They agreed, but whispered between themselves that perhaps he was a bit too quiet. That it wasn't natural. And why wasn't he sitting up, or chewing an old crust, or getting his first tooth? But eventually the baby did all these things, although later than other children of his age. 'He'll come,' Mary would say, if the subject were ever brought up. 'He'll come. He's slow. But he'll come. God is good.' When he walked with his knees knocking and his toes turned in, she said, 'He's just finding his feet, the creature. But he'll come.' And when at four his speech was slurred and hesitant, she said, 'He's just feeling his way. He's taking it handy, like his father.' His father, however, shook his head, and spent less time with the boy and went out to work more often, but brought less money home in the pay packet. The time went by, and the little boy went to school when he was five.

Mary brought him to school on the carrier of her bicycle. She explained to the teacher about his being a little slow and how you needed to have patience with him but that he was so good and loving she knew he would not give the least trouble. The teacher looked thoughtfully at him and said he'd be fine and that she wasn't to worry. He gazed with big eyes at the two of them and stared bewilderedly after his mother when she cycled away, her head low over the handlebars so that the tears running down her cheeks might not be seen. In the garden she hoed more vigorously than usual. She kept remembering how he loved to do the weeding with her, or how he chased the white butterflies through the rows of beans, or how he pursed his lips to whistle back at the birds. She looked at the clock every half hour and long before school was over she was waiting outside for him, leaning on her bicycle.

When the doors opened the children came out hesitantly at first and then in a great gush of excitement. Their mothers greeted them with exclamations of joy. Mary felt out of place among so many young women, most of them half her age. Her heart began to pound until at last he came out alone, looking around him dazedly.

'I'm here, Tom,' she called softly. 'I'm over here.' He ran to her, flinging his arms about her, burying his face in her skirt, laughing and crying. 'Shush,' she said. 'You'll make a holy show of us. How did you get on?'

''Twas OK,' he said, climbing on to the carrier of the bicycle. 'Did you bake me curranty bread?'

'I did,' she said. 'And I put a T for Tommy on it. You'll be able to write your whole name soon.'

'I ruthered be home wi' you,' he said.

'And you will too. School is only a little part of each day, and a little part of our lives.'

When they got home he ran around the house looking at everything as if he had been away for a whole year, touching the tablecloth, poking the fire, climbing up to feel the hands of the clock, hugging the dog and the cat, racing out to the cow, tumbling head over heels in the grass until she called to him to stop or he'd make himself sick. They had their dinner together, beaming at one another out of their great love.

That night she told Jimmy about it all and hardly noticed when he made no response, she was so busy knitting and smiling and remembering.

The seasons were swallowed up in the great mouth of the year and the years slid into the maturing century. The little boy grew bulky and towered above his schoolmates. His feet still turned out and his knees hit each other as he ran after butterfly or ball. His speech became more careful. It was only when he was excited that the words tumbled over one another. His mother had long since stopped saying, 'He'll come,' or 'He's slow.' She might say instead, 'Take it easy, Tommy. You've your life before you. Take your time.' The teachers gave up bothering with him and let him through each class as a matter of course, putting him in the back row, where he could gaze out of the window without disturbing the other pupils. Sometimes he would annoy a little girl in front of him by stroking her hair or chewing absentmindedly on her ribbon and he would have to sit at the back of the room until he got control of himself. The boys were often rough and cruel to him so he played with the girls. Their teasing did not annoy him for they were soft, like his mother. When they called him 'old gomme' he laughed and shouted 'Gomme yerselves.' He was always handy for holding a skip-ping rope or climbing up on a roof after a ball and he loved to be useful. At home he busied himself with a thousand tasks, delighting in his mother's praise, 'Well I don't know what I'd do without you.' When he broke something she would say, 'If you looked at that old thing it would break,' and when he weeded the young seedlings out of the ground by mistake she would say, 'Ah, they were too crowded anyway. A thinning will do them no harm.'

His father was a shadowy figure to the boy, flitting in and out of their lives as if he had no substance. It did not seem very important when he left one morning with his coat thrown over his shoulder like a travelling man. It made no impression when he did not return that evening or any other evening afterwards. Mary wove the threads of their existence together as usual and the pattern of their days remained unchanged. She wondered sometimes about Jimmy's whereabouts, fancying him trimming the hedgerows of the world and calling cheerfully to passersby. In winter her concern for him made her visualise him with his toes turned to the open fire in some widow's house. She forgot his idle ways and thought of him making himself useful in a farmyard like other travelling men whose need for freedom was greater than their need for comfort. Now and again a fearful picture came to her mind of Jimmy lying in bed in one of the county homes for the poor and abandoned. She became so obsessed with the idea that she once made an excuse to visit their local infirmary and stared along the rows of blank old faces, dreading to recognise his among them. Her family told her she was better off without him, that he had surely found a cosy hearth for himself, but the thought no longer cheered her.

Tommy grew big and awkward and left school at fourteen. He could write his name and read a few simple words and he could count up to twenty. The people of the village became accustomed to the little elderly woman and her hulking big son. They said what a great job she had made of him and what an example of real love they were. On Sundays they sat in the front row of the church, he with his face scrubbed pink, his hair carefully parted, his nails clean, she with her smiling, unquestioning face beside him. Whenever he wriggled or tried to look behind him she would place a hand gently on his and he would be quiet.

He was twenty when she became ill. Her sisters came to visit and fuss over her, pushing him out of the way when he tried to talk to her. For one terrible week she was in hospital and he cried with joy when she came back. But she lay in bed, not able to move and barely able to talk to him, and her face had a yellowy tinge. There were secretive talks between his aunts and wondering looks in his direction. He sat by her bed, staring at her face the way he used to stare at the books he could not read at school. One day when they were alone, she whispered to him that she had something for him. 'If I go away again, and I don't come back – like your father – you are to take this medicine.' She handed him a screwtop jar with a white liquid in it. He looked blankly at it and her face twisted with anxiety. 'You've got to remember it, Tommy,' she said. 'It's medicine, for you to take if I go away and don't come back.' He could not understand her insistence, but to please her he nodded and said he would take the medicine. Relieved, she sank back on the pillow. 'You're a good boy, Tommy,' she said. 'You've always been such a good boy.' He put the medicine on the top shelf of the dresser.

A few weeks later, she died. Her sisters brushed him up for the funeral. At the graveside he stared around him at the sad faces and gaped at the coffin holding his mother. When he looked up at the sky it seemed to whirl around him and there were noises inside his head that he had never heard before. His hand was shaken and his shoulder patted and people said, 'What will become of the poor fellow?' At home he tidied up and went out to the garden. One of his aunts told him she would call to see him next day and she went off to have a family consultation about him.

The thought kept bothering him that there was something he must do. He pounded his head angrily with his fists because he could not remember. He carried on as best he could for a few days and his aunts noticed with relief that he was better than they expected. With a little assistance from them he would be able to manage. One afternoon he found the screwtop jar at the top of the dresser and he remembered his mother's words to him. He sighed with relief. He sat down and took a sip. It was bitter. He spat it out quickly. But it was medicine. He tried again, and again spat it out. He groaned, recalling his mother's words. 'Wilful waste makes woeful want,' she used to say to him when he didn't take what she had prepared for him. But he needn't waste it. He smiled in triumph at his own cleverness. Carefully he divided the mixture into two portions. He poured one half into the cat's dish of milk, the other half he stirred into the dog's dinner. 'Here, puss, puss, puss,' he called. 'Here, Rex, boy,' until they came and took their food obediently. The cow had to be milked, he remembered, and he went to do it. When he came back a half hour later, the cat and the dog were dead.

Then Tommy Burke understood the terrible thing his mother had done but not the terrible love that made her do it. He beat his chest and his head and howled his pain through the empty house. The noises inside him grew louder and the skies over him more turbulent. That night he slept on the floor beside the dead animals. Next morning he buried them in the garden. He crossed off the days on the calendar as he had been taught and when it was Sunday he went to Mass. He stared around him and fidgeted, unchecked. He followed the girls down the village street, gaping at them, with his mouth open. Sometimes he reached out to them with a plucking movement of his hands and they pulled away from him in horror. Little by little, and one by one, in the days that followed, they rejected him. The easy-going 'old gomme' was replaced by 'Yugh. Isn't he awful?' Exclamations of disgust followed him. They began to call him 'old Yuk Yuk'. Here comes old Yuk Yuk. When he climbed into the seat beside them at Mass, they moved out the other end. They crossed to the other side of the street if they chanced to see him coming towards them. He forgot to milk the cow and she got mastitis and was sick. The eggs lay ungathered and the hens began to peck them and eat them. The weeds choked the vegetable patch and the mice invaded the house for the stale bread he left lying around on floors and tables. His aunts were appalled at his habits and refused to clean up after him. One day the social worker visited him and explained to him how much better off he would be in a place where people could care for him. His words had got so mixed up he could not answer her. The sounds came out thick and frightening to him and the saliva ran out of his mouth. Within a week he was in the county home.

His speech came back a little better. He had jobs to do helping the gardener or working in the kitchen. Some of the nurses were kind to him. One whom he had known at school called him 'old gomme' affectionately. 'Old gomme yourself,' he called delightedly back. He had a room to himself high up in the building. The window was barred but it did not block out the sky. At night he would lie in bed gazing up at it when the stars polka-dotted it with light. He asked the cook to bake him curranty bread and she did. He took it easy. He took his time. He stopped wondering about the nagging ache in the back of his mind.

Cause and Effect

At the corner adjoining Wolfe Tone Street and Pearse Place, Mr O'Farrell raised his cloth cap to Miss Barlow. She met his gesture with a simper. Across the road, Miss Melican observed the meeting from behind her lace curtains and pondered on its significance. She had plenty of time for pondering on such things as she sat on her genuine Hepplewhite chair, not period, she assured her nieces when they paid their self-imposed, obligatory visits to her. All her chairs were made by the

Master himself. Her own mother had told her so, and her own mother was an expert on those matters. 'My mother,' Miss Melican was fond of saying, 'was a collector of things.'

Her nieces, she knew, eyed her chairs hungrily, as they eyed everything in her house hungrily. She viewed their lusts with satisfaction, occasionally a little sympathy. Their angled modern houses cried out for even a few of the lush carved objects with which all her rooms were filled. Miss Melican knew by hints let fall that her nieces felt her possessions were wasted on her because she did not love them. They were right. She loved only one thing in life, her ginger cat, and she was very fond of three people, Miss Barlow and Mr O'Farrell now meeting across the road, and the Canon who was already on his way to visit her. Anything stronger than affection for other people was potentially destructive. Human emotions were so often the product of simple greed and Miss Melican had little patience with the hungers associated with greed. She rarely hungered after anything.

Thirst was a familiar discomfort. It was not a physical thirst, although there were times when it seemed physical in origin, so dry and bitter was it. All her life she had thirsted after pure beauty, abstract unalterable truth, unknown, unknowable god. Had she been a poet or a prophet she would have chanted a litany of names to describe the object of her desire. A friend had long ago said that all she needed was a man, but Miss Melican could do without friends of that sort and told her so. Even in old age the remark came back to haunt her and she faced it, examined it, harried it, turned it inside out with her sharp intelligence and each time discarded it as unworthy.

She had a fellow-feeling for hermits and anchorites. She read the Psalms regularly and exulted equally with the desolation of Job and the love songs of Solomon. The harsh desert fathers would have understood her thirst as she understood how they must have groaned, not merely for water and bodily survival, but for the green opulence of hills, the daring imagery of tree-clad slopes. No wonder the desert nomads cherished the carpets woven by their daughters, the colours of gardens and precious stones imprisoned forever so that their burnt eyes might feast on them and recover lost brilliance.

For long hours at a time Miss Melican reflected on all these things as she sat on her Hepplewhite chair behind the heavy lace curtains. She meditated on the passing parade, on her own life and its silences, on other lives and their silences. Her cat, a large ginger tom, kept silence with her. He had been spayed as a kitten and seemed to have lost his appetite for conversation, with his other appetites. His vantage point was a large sagging armchair. There he lay sleeping or observing the world outside, in between meals and forays into the garden. Once he killed a thrush and Miss Melican scolded him but was secretly pleased at his initiative.

'Mice, mice are what you should be after, you bold thing,' she said, pointing a quivering finger. He stood on his hind legs and placed a penitential paw on her knee. 'If you would only get rid of the mice, you would be the greatest treasure.' She knew he was unlikely to be capable of such effort. She had, after all, without his consent, exchanged his hunting instincts, with their other undesirable side-effects, for a gentle domestic nature. He made a pleasant companion, but the mice nested in the blankets, left their stools in the porridge oats and wore hob-nailed boots while they ranged above the ceiling of her bedroom. One paid a price for everything but occasionally she wondered if in this instance the price was too high. She did not like mice. Their scampering and scuttling were signs of their other disorderly habits. Their movements lacked rhythm, their squeaks were high, uncoordinated exclamations.

There was a certain order, she believed, a formula by which one's life could be lived without reducing it to rigidly applied rules. She was not without imagination. In fact it was her imagination which made her so impressive in her speciality, mathematics. In her youth she had been a rare phenomenon with a Masters in mathematics and physics. She would have liked to have been a scientist working in a laboratory attached to some university. But she was not only highly intelligent, she was also extremely sensible and recognised that her femaleness, especially since she was a very pretty young woman, would have worked against her. She would probably have remained assistant to some man, her discoveries absorbed in his, her ideas credited to him. So she settled for education. She taught in the same school for forty-two years until, in the end, she became an institution in her own right.

Her pupils, especially those who shared her gift for mathematics, were grateful. Without her they would have suffered the divided attention of the higher maths teacher from the boy's school, or contented themselves with mere passes in the subject. Their school was blatantly geared for exams and results. Any pupil who did not accept it on those terms found herself treated as second class, deprived of the fringe benefits. Those included trips abroad, evenings at the ballet, skiing holidays at the best Swiss resorts, exotic weekends in Paris, all experiences intended to round off personalities which might otherwise become too sharpened by intellectual activity. The school produced many fine scientists, chemists and doctors, and even a sprinkling of politicians, but not one writer or painter, a fact in which Miss Melican took much pride. A country which produced the self-absorbed and the self-aware in such monumental numbers needed the clear logic, the unemotional examination of evidence which were normally the province of the scientist. When some parents, usually the fathers, complained that their daughters would waste all that education by getting married before they could harvest any of its fruits, she would get angry.

'The mind,' she said once, tartly, 'is not a rubbish bin and education is not a disposable package.'

'Of what use is the theory of relativity,' said a frustrated father whose genius of a daughter had married at twenty and had a baby five months later, 'for feeding a baby or changing a nappy? Why didn't you teach them to handle their emotions?'

'Why don't you learn to handle your own?' she replied to his fury. 'And remember that babies grow. Up and away. And babies are great educators in themselves. As long as there aren't too many, of course.'

'Oh,' he had raged. 'What percentage do you think is permissible? What fraction of baby-minding time can be allowed to offset its other disadvantages?'

Parents were notoriously hard to satisfy. All problems, Miss Melican believed, were soluble, given the proper application and proper assessment of the unknown variable. And that was where the *soupçon* of imagination came in. No more than that. Any more would bring one into the realm of poetry and religious belief. When she was accused of being a dyed-in-the-wool behaviourist she took it as a compliment, not because it was strictly true, since she recognised that all discovery was a creative leap in the dark made scientific only by its verification. But her contention that Ireland had too many leapers and too few verifiers gave her a nice complacent feeling of being among the elite.

Living in a quiet part of town, directly opposite the park, was a further source of satisfaction. The terraces of red-brick houses had not yet been discovered by trade and commerce looking for cheap offices. Her neighbours never succumbed to the lure of suburban semi-detached with their badly proportioned windows and their minuscule gardens. The undertaker, Miss Melican would drily remark, was the only furniture remover allowed into the Avenue. Death paid its visitations in little rushes, so that two or three of the residents died at intervals of only a few months, leaving longer intervals of years between the next batches. When she was taken by her nieces to see their new houses she could not imagine an undertaker ever calling there. But in the Avenue, his black-suited figure was an acceptable reminder of the inevitable. Out in the suburbs the myriad births and baptisms were signs of a false optimism, as if all was future and the past a non-entity. Miss Melican knew that since all problems were solvable, so all things came to their final solution. It was her good fortune to live where these solutions were reached by the logical steps of disease and decline and, when the body's decay required it, pain.

The only thing Miss Melican ever feared was a diminution of her mental powers. Her mother had lived to be ninety and until her last breath her mind had been clear as a bell. Miss Melican hoped for as much consideration from whatever power ruled the universe. In her moments of prayer she hinted to this Unknown that she had lived a good life, that her scepticism had been an indispensable part of her search for truth and in no way an act of rebellion. She knew herself to be a deeply religious woman in the real meaning of that word and, while not looking for favours, expected the Unknown to take account of it. Her stroke, some months back, had been a shock. But it was only a small one and the slight slurring of her speech and the shake in her hand had soon passed.

Each day, viewed from the chair behind her window, was a muted passing of time. Outside in the street the figures of Miss Barlow and Mr O'Farrell were illumined by their importance to her. Their meeting at the electricity pole at the corner opposite gave her day a special value. She recognised that value, assessed it and allowed it to give her pleasure. In the same deliberate way she erased from her memory, as if drawing a pencil mark across a faulty answer, the antics of her two nieces. Their calculated pursuit of eligible husbands had been as painful to her in old age as their mother's, her only sister, had been in her youth. Such planning, such careful arrangements of timetables, such elaborate dressing-up and determinedly bright chatter, in order to procure for a mate the most ordinary of specimens, seemed to her a gross distortion of the finest of human emotions. Love should be beyond calculation – a spontaneous combustion, an explosive fusion of two opposite elements in the flurry and disorder of casual life, the result of an accidental meeting in a railway carriage or at a bus stop. Of such happy chance love would be born. She had chosen to plan her life around her intellect and had taken the consequences, but to plan it while exploiting emotions, whether one's own or someone else's, was dishonourable.

Mr O'Farrell and Miss Barlow made no plans. They grew out of the town and the hilly countryside around it and were harmoniously at ease with themselves and their surroundings. Miss Barlow had survived the torture of an earlier religious mania and could come to terms with anything. Mr O'Farrell, who was as wise and instinctive as his cats, learned from everything.

He was an expert on cats. He assisted the vet on Tuesdays and Thursdays at the domestic pets clinic. He bred pedigree Persian Blue and Siamese as well as the English tabby in all its varieties.

'The ginger,' he told Miss Melican, 'is always the male of the litter.'

'Surely not,' Miss Melican said in surprise.

'Have you ever seen a female ginger? Of course not. They don't exist. In all my years of breeding and judging I have never come across one.'

Mr O'Farrell was a pleasant man, well behaved, and after all what did the little matter of the cloth cap signify? Other people's failings should be forgiven even if one could not forgive one's own. He lived a useful life without too much expectation. The day is sufficient for itself, he was fond of saying. Look at the lilies of the field. They labour not, neither do they spin. Miss Melican often wondered if the wearing of the cloth cap and repeated references to unemployed lilies was deliberate irony.

Miss Barlow was allergic to cats so could be excused for not liking them. It was bad luck to be allergic to anything, but a great deprivation to be allergic to cats. Miss Barlow used to find her companionship in the Church. The Blessed Saints were the most wonderful company. At one time she had been quite odd about them. She had a mania for rubbing the fingers and toes of the statues and trailed around the church aisles during Mass or evening devotions, disturbing the faithful and the celebrant. The Canon tried to offer her ramblings up in a spirit of sacrifice. But once when she rattled her rosary beads loudly and, it seemed, contemptuously, right in the middle of one of his most lyrical sermons, he forgot to be self-sacrificing.

A week of arduous ceremonies had come to an end. The days of Holy Week were the culmination of all the Church believed in and hoped for. The Canon understood the need for both mourning and celebration, and brought curates from the outer reaches of his parish to make the week a memorable one. Yet all through the great, dramatic unfolding of the sufferings and death of Christ, he was aware of

Miss Barlow tripping around the church, making the stations of the cross, with whispers so powerfully sibilant his ears squeaked in pain. Through the chanting of the Psalms at Tenebrae, even through the choir's responses to his own mellifluous baritone, her clattering, rattling and whispering went on. When the choir banged their prayer books with deliberate artistry, signifying the death of Christ and the rolling of the stone over the tomb door and that final thunderous moment of release from pain and mortality, Miss Barlow rattled the crucifix of her rosary beads over the fretwork of a confessional box. The Canon had a boil on the back of his neck which he offered up with sublime patience, but the pain of Miss Barlow's presence was infinitely harder to bear. How many of the congregation guessed at his endurance it is hard to say, but Miss Melican and Mr O'Farrell were among those who did. If he knew that he had been judged and forgiven, he did not show it any more than they did. For Easter morning, which is the joyful celebration, the singing ecstatic renewal of the Christian life, should have been unmarred by reminders of the trivial. The painful fact of death, which has a clear finality about it, however sad, was bearable, but that mushy, unreasoning sentimentality which Miss Barlow displayed was, in the Canon's opinion, an obscenity in the face of God, an insult to the Creator of life.

'For the love of God, woman,' he roared at the top of his voice, 'there won't be a finger or toe left in the parish if you do not cease. They aren't made of cast iron, you know.'

Miss Barlow shuffled down to the back seat and waited for the next passage, which called for a silence so delicate even the snorers held their grunts. At just the right moment, when the hush seemed to suspend the congregation like hang-gliders over a great valley, Miss Barlow's leather-thonged prayer book thumped to the floor, followed by her bag containing a pot of raspberry jam and a tin of stewed steak.

It was an historic moment, a fraction of time frozen for ever in the memory of its witnesses. It found echoes for years in dinner talk, pub chatter and butcher's-stall gossip. No one who witnessed the advance on Miss Barlow from the pulpit could ever forget the solemnity with which the Canon lifted her by the coat collar and escorted her – she squawking protests, he silent but grimly authoritative – to the church door.

'This house,' he said, having regained his pulpit, 'is a house of prayer and a place where the word of God must be heard with respect. If you cannot have that respect, get up off your knees and go home.'

Until that moment few people had cared for the Canon and even fewer for Miss Barlow. But having entered into the annals of anecdote, they proved without possibility of dispute that they did exist and were not like the mass of people, condemned to be unrecorded and therefore insubstantial. For such heroism the rewards are great. The Canon droned on Sunday after Sunday and no one complained. Miss Barlow's reward was even greater. Recognition brought her sanity, a gift few would have begrudged her. Christ's resurrection from the tomb was more dramatic but hardly more miraculous.

All of that Miss Melican knew and recalled as she watched her friends converse at the kerbstone. It was a source of pleasant satisfaction to her that both she and Mr O'Farrell were linked by their interest in Miss Barlow as much as by their interest in cats, or more specifically (at least in her case) by a ginger eunuch. Between them they formed a neat mathematical construction, a right-angled triangle. Mr O'Farrell and herself were the two sides forming the main angle and Miss Barlow the third side linking them. But what were the acute angles? The Canon and the Church? She doodled with her pen on the letter pad. An obtuse angle would have been a more suitable play on words for the church institutional.

Since her stroke Miss Melican had been unable to go to Mass regularly. Each Friday the Canon called to give her Holy Communion. She told him she wasn't sure if she believed in everything or even anything.

'We all have difficulties,' he said, 'but you must decide for yourself if you feel worthy to receive.'

'I sometimes feel uncharitable to my nieces. It may be that I envy them their youth. They flaunt it brazenly and yet don't value it. Always worrying about things; their mother, my sister, was a little like that. I always felt she wasted her good life.'

'Youth is wasted on the young,' he quoted.

'Who today has the grace and wisdom of G.B.S.?'

'The age of elegance was diminished by the great war and destroyed by the greater war.'

'I suppose you mean literary elegance?'

The question of unbelief was left delicately unexplored. But it bothered Miss Melican and when Miss Barlow called to see her she brought up the subject again.

'It's still a mystery,' Miss Barlow said with a great sigh which expressed the boundlessness of human ignorance. Miss Melican sighed also, but faintly, with restrained exasperation. For all her newly acquired sanity, or perhaps because of it, Miss Barlow was something of a trial. It sometimes seemed to Miss Melican that the time when she had rampaged through the church aisle was a golden age of innocence. She repressed a feeling of annoyance at the Canon's intervention. After all, if a man of the cloth could not control himself, what hope was there for less dedicated mortals? In retrospect Miss Barlow's madness had been a divine folly, adding a bright lunacy to ceremonies which had become ordinary through repetition. And here she was saying smugly: 'It's all a great mystery.' In those other days, thought Miss Melican sourly, she would have known all the answers. She would not have revealed them, of course, but hugged her secrets to herself with the selfishness of a saint who had an invisible ladder to God on which he practised levitation. Such selfishness was both necessary and admirable. If every genius revealed himself, the world would long ago have been destroyed.

The Canon was late; Miss Barlow anxiously awaited his car. She told Mr O'Farrell earnestly that poor Miss Melican was suffering from spiritual aridity. 'At her time of life and in her state of health, that's a sad thing.' Mr O'Farrell agreed. 'I'll stay here till he comes,' Miss Barlow said loyally. 'I don't want to bother her in the house. I've paid her my little visit for the day. You can tire old people out very easily, you know.'

Mr O'Farrell, who knew exactly how many years Miss Barlow had been drawing the old-age pension, agreed. He angled his body to the wall with the aid of his left arm and began to talk on the need for inoculation against cat flu and dysentery. He mused on the animal's grace, speed, the lightning swiftness of a paw as it claimed butterfly or bumblebee. Watching his own animals stalk their prey through the long grasses of summer urged him to winged prose. He extolled their virtues again to Miss Barlow.

'Cats should be protected and cherished. They possess all the inherited savagery and innocence, co-ordination of movement, of their jungle ancestors. And we don't appreciate them. We take them for granted. They are not selfish, only independent. They are the most beautiful, the most elegant, the most intelligent of animals and, as the Egyptians knew, the most godlike.'

Miss Barlow sneezed and he apologised, reaching into his breast pocket for a tissue. Miss Barlow blew her nose. Across the road, behind the lace curtains. Miss Melican, tiring of the contrived mechanics of the triangle, progressed to pyramids and circles. Round and round her pen wove, interlocking or isolating the eternal ring. Intent upon her drawing, she did not see the ginger cat pause at the half-open window and did not miss him when he leaped on to the pavement outside.

Miss Barlow saw him as he crossed the road and she sneezed so violently that the cat stopped, startled, in the centre of the road. At that moment the Canon's car turned the corner and, relying more heavily than usual on its brakes, skidded towards it. The cat leaped, the car swerved, and Miss Melican, jerked from her doodling by the commotion, witnessed as in slow motion the final shattering of the angles and triangles which had been so poetic a conceit of hers. As the back wheels went over the cat, she was filled in her chest cavity with an eruption of pain which lasted long enough for her to see through its haze the car continue on its journey to the corner wall, through Mr O'Farrell and Miss Barlow. There it ended and, as the Canon's head made its final terrible impact, her pen froze on her fingers at the beginning of another circle.

Parasites

Fame had come early to her. There had been no slow, painful maturing of a talent, no years of disappointment and despair crowned by a late glory of success. Her first book had been unashamedly autobiographical. It had simply poured out, almost without effort. All the fears and dreams of adolescence, which she had before confined to her private diary, she hurled at her readers in her sometimes crisp, sometimes melancholy style. To the publisher who accepted her manuscript, her talent was unmistakable. That uncanny gift for evoking the sensualities of life was not to be denied. That unerring eye for the idiosyncrasies and frailties of humanity deserved to be acclaimed. In an earlier decade her youth might have been a disadvantage. In this one, where middle age symbolised dullness, and old age senility, youth was an asset, a quick-selling advertisement, and her round beguiling face with its touch of promiscuity lured many to the bookshops.

Her second, third and fourth books were variations on a theme. The differences of character and location were so slight as to be hardly noticeable. The same bleak, Irish land-scape harboured the same sad, drifting, fuddled, yet curiously comic people. Her compassion and her malice alternated as before, switchbacking her readers from a state of pity to an angry contempt. Her people were real people, and she bared their souls as dispassionately as a surgeon exposing a tumour for the enlightenment of medical students. Whether the metaphor could have been carried further to include the welfare of the patient is a matter for conjecture. The people she wrote about were her own people, yet she could write about them, and about herself, with absolute detachment. Years of sensitive and imaginative observation were put to good use each time she staccatoed at the typewriter.

When she first emigrated to the other and more power-ful island, she went simply to escape from boredom. The small village pub on the west coast was like a prison to her, and her father drawing the pints to slake the endless thirst of the community was her jailer. Her mother would some-times intervene for her when she was out late at night and her father abused her and called her a streel or a slut. But mostly her mother simply said, 'Your father knows best,' or 'Your father's right.' They weren't harsh parents, she knew that. Even in her most self-pitying moments she understood their concern for her. But she sometimes felt excluded from the love they still had for each other. Her father and mother had never lost their earlier vision of one another. Her brothers and sisters could joke about it, and call them Romeo and Juliet, or Antony and Cleopatra, or Orlando and Rosalind, knowing it was always safe to quote from Shakespeare. She never saw the humour in it.

They were all avid readers, and during the long winter nights, when they could hear the Atlantic breakers crashing off the rocks below the village, they lost themselves between the covers of their secondhand books. They were reared on nineteenth-century literature. Tom and Maggie Tulliver were as real to them as David Copperfield and Peggotty, or poor Sally Cavanagh in *Knocknagow,* or Nollaig in *Glenanaar.* Sometimes their father would recite ballads for his customers, and they would peep through the chink of the door dividing the pub from the kitchen, and watch as the lean wrinkled faces of his audience cracked into smiles, or their eyes clouded with tears before they rubbed their hands across their noses or pulled out large check handkerchiefs to blow vigorously. Her brothers and sisters would join in the tears and the smiles, and her mother would sigh and shake her head and say, 'Wisha, wisha, he never lost it.' But *she* felt uncomfortable before such displays of emotion and she would turn into the fire and imagine herself far away from the smell of stout and burning peat and the incessant sound of the drumbeat waves.

In the other island the freedom to be herself was a stimulating joy. She cast off all her family and home ties and reacted to the release as a child does who has been cooped up in a house on a rainy day and is let loose for a last hour of sunshine. Everything was a wonder and a delight. The smell of the Underground stations, the crush of people, the bad manners and the elbowing at rush hour, the queues waiting to be fed at the restaurants, the excitement of booking a ticket to a play or a concert were all riches of experience beyond anything she could have imagined. To be alive, she began to think, was to know paradise. To be alive was the only paradise.

She worked in a bank during the day and spent most evenings in her shared bedsitter, reading, or browsing in the library nearby. On Sundays she walked in the park and visited the art galleries and museums. The girl who shared her room brought her to an Irish club dance one night, but she was miserable. The men drank too much and talked too loudly and sweated too profusely. She said she had never seen such men, not even in the pub at home on fair day. Her friend laughed and said they were just lonely boys, and was pushed around the floor on one bear-like arm after another. She went to a big dance hall another night and was asked to dance by a coloured man. Her friend nudged her to refuse, but she couldn't. He was quiet and well behaved and she enjoyed talking to him. But her friend was furious with her when she came back to her seat. 'They'll all be over now, asking us to dance with them.' She was a little afraid then, and when she saw another coloured man coming across the floor to her she ran to the cloakroom and stayed there until she could pluck up enough courage to go home. Her friend gave her a lecture on sticking to her own kind, and was cross when she replied, 'I haven't found my own kind yet.'

She began to write her first book about this time. Each evening she wrote from eight o'clock until ten. On Saturday she wrote for four hours. On Sundays she revised and thought and rested. They were the happiest few months of her life. Never again was she to know such absolute content-ment. She became a creator and knew the bliss of creation.

She gave life to the village that had heard her first wailing cry. From the slime of buried memories she brought forth the people of the village. Her father kept his autocratic hold on the household described in her book and her mother drifted through the pages untidily and inefficiently. The ten children, who had been the fruit of their love, alone remained undisturbed in the limbo of her memory.

When the book was published it was quickly successful. She was delighted to discover that it was also making money. The critics praised her freshness of approach, her originality of style, her unique talent. Another writer has emerged from the bogs of Ireland, they said. A warm west wind has disturbed the doldrums of the literary scene. She was flattered and excited. She moved to a new flat and began her second book.

By this time she was having an affair with an Indian Sikh. He was so handsome and charming she felt she could have worshipped him simply for his beauty and good manners. She would never have described herself as being in love with him. Love was a word somehow entangled with the noisy family and the shabby house and the craggy faces in the pub. She never thought of them outside her writing. Once she happened to remember her youngest brother's birthday and she sent him a card with a picture of donkeys on it. Afterwards she thought how foolish it was of her not to remember that donkeys were part of the scenery for her little brother, and she sent him a postcard view of the city.

In her second book she wrote more intimately about her sexual experiences. It was all part of life, and no relationship, however personal, could escape her probing, dissecting talent. Each successive book developed the subject a little further. The critics noted a new maturity, a deepening of experience. And still the background characters were much the same. Only the central character, who was always a woman, seemed to change. Her books sold well and she was able to live in moderate luxury. She left the Indian Sikh when she began to notice a waning of his interest. She gave away the fine saris she had worn when in his company and forgot about him. Her men friends were more sophisticated and better read than before and they would swop quotations in a spirit of intellectual one-upmanship. She was reasonably content.

One spring she fell in love with the poet. They had met at a poetry reading which she had been asked to grace. She thought his poetry marvellously perceptive and perfectly constructed and she had enough confidence in her own judgement to be able to tell him so. He was pleased and a little amused at her earnestness. He had no money and worked only when it became an absolute necessity, as when he wanted to buy some expensive book and his social welfare payments wouldn't allow him to fill both his stomach and his brain at the expense of the tax-paying public. When she knew him better she was a little shocked at his irresponsibility, and told him so. His warm brown eyes glinted into coldness and he said that he never questioned the morality of *her* methods of earning a living. She was outraged, but since she did love him, she let it pass.

He moved into her flat so that he could work in peace at his writing and she introduced him to her literary friends. Her publisher was waiting for her next book and she made a half-hearted attempt at it. However, she became so absorbed in the epic the poet was composing that she lost interest in everything but that. She would sit quietly while he struggled and groaned. He would tell her that he didn't want her in the room but she said she wouldn't twitch an eyelash. She just wanted to help him. She just wanted to be near him. He became a little irritated by her devotion and began to use her to fetch and carry books of reference, dictionaries, meals on a tray, a clean pair of socks. One rainy day in the autumn he swore at her to get out of his sight and she ran into the sodden streets without a coat. There was a church nearby and without thinking she went into it for shelter. There were a few old people inside and two small girls lighting candles. She rested for a while, staring up at the altar from the seat at the back. Comfort me, her mind said. Comfort me. But she just felt cold and alone.

The poet looked at her when she came in the door of the flat. He didn't apologise.

She leaned against the wall and said musingly, 'I love you.'

He was startled and looked at her with apprehension.

'I love you,' she said again, 'and I would have let you destroy me. I almost became your muse. Lady Gregory to your Yeats, and you wouldn't even have noticed.'

He recovered his composure. 'Where have you been? There was no need to run out into the rain, for God's sake. Where were you?'

'I went into a church.'

His eyes narrowed into speculation. 'What did you pray for? Patience? Forgiveness? What about all this brave new freedom of yours? Have you taken to the opium of the people again?'

'Don't be silly. I went in to shelter from the rain.'

'By God,' he put his head back and laughed. 'But you take the bloody cake. Is that all it meant to you? An ornamental, outsize bloody shelter from the bloody elements.'

'Stop swearing,' she said. 'Just stop it. You're a parasite, a boor, and you're vulgar, vulgar, vulgar.'

'Listen to the noble peasantry,' he said.

There was violence mixed with the mockery in his voice,

but she didn't flinch. 'For all your toffee accent and your Oxford degree, you'd never be an aristocrat in a thousand years. But I was born one. And bred one.'

'Some aristocrat,' he said bitterly. 'Oh what a noble nature that is. You disown everything that made you what you are, home, family, country, faith. You. The worst kind of traitor, the worst kind of renegade. You threw out the baby with the bathwater, and you were too stupid and too, too –' he searched ferociously for a word and came out triumphantly with – 'ignoble to understand what you had lost. You won't make that up in a million years. And I don't want your love. It's like being loved by a machine computerised for passion. I don't want your bread and butter either.' He tore up the page he had been working on all day and flung the pieces in her face.

'You are behaving like a child,' she said calmly, feeling the strength of her own self-control.

'You aren't even listening,' he said. 'You never listen, of course. You suck in sensation and burp it out again into your ghastly novels. Have you ever had a truly original thought in your head? Or ever said a truly original thing? Do you know what you are going to do? Like a lot of other lousy women writers you're going to eat yourself up. You'll devour yourself, bones and all, until there's nothing left. Nothing but a collection of novelettes for women's magazines. Your contribution to posterity.'

She was stung to fury and a terrible grief which she feared might choke her voice to a whisper. But when she spoke she was as clear and precise as ever. 'You're annoyed because I said you were a parasite, and you know it's true.'

'I *am* a parasite, and I *am* annoyed, and I *know* it's true, but you're a parasite too. I feed on the body. You feed on the spirit.'

'I've given something back.' Her voice shook a little. 'What have you given back?'

They had gone too far. They both knew it. He packed his papers carefully into his briefcase. 'I live in hope,' he said sadly, 'and you know there are some people who like my stuff.' It sounded childish. He suddenly looked childish, slightly crumpled, slightly pathetic. She was filled with pity for him as she watched him leave.

She moved about the room tidying up his mess. Then she had a cup of instant coffee. She smoked two cigarettes, one after another, relishing each inhaled breath. She got out her typewriter and inserted foolscap. It would be a new story.

The Last Campaign

Martha opened the back door, blinking hurtfully at the brightness of the day. The milking machine was still humming. She felt guilty because she hadn't heard Joe groaning out of bed. Sleep never seemed to ease out the exhaustion of the previous day. All the accumulated weariness was now showing in the hollows of his face. His cheekbones, jutting eyebrows, chin, were gaunt promontories under the thatch of his hair. He could do with a haircut, too.

She sat on the step and

pulled on her wellingtons, then went to the outhouse for the buckets and layers' mash. In the henhouse, the flock, grumbling and clucking to themselves, heard the sound of their breakfast being prepared and set up their morning cacophony. 'Hens,' she said to herself, flicking her eyeballs upward, 'hens are the end. Who could love hens?' She filled two buckets with the layers' mash and staggered to their door, bracing herself for the attack when she entered. A few fistfuls of dry mash thrown around distracted them while she emptied the buckets in the troughs. Joe had improvised cleverly to make the feeding troughs. He had used old rusted milk churns as centrepieces and worn car tyres, cut open, encircled them. It was into the tyres she poured the dry food. The hens ate quickly, their narrow heads taking up little room in the circle. She sniffed. The deep litter smelled healthy. She filled the other troughs, detached the long hose from the wall, opened the tap and poured the water into the drinking vessels. She straightened her back and watched, smiling at the feeding flock, their busy pecking a lullaby of contentment. She put some clean straw in the bottom of the bucket and began to collect the eggs.

Herself and Joe met at the tap on the wall outside. He hosed down his boots, thinking about something.

'Isn't it a beautiful day, Joe,' she said. 'You might get the last of the hay drawn in today.'

'I might,' he said, looking up at a small, dark cloud away on the horizon and checking the direction of the wind. 'If it holds. I think there's a change.'

'It'll hardly break before this evening,' she said.

'Maybe not.'

She wondered to herself why his sentences were always so short. Words spilled over in her own mind so much. She had to hold them back, conscious always of his brief replies and afraid she might become garrulous in her effort to fill the void. 'Communication,' she reminded herself sometimes, 'is not only made with speech.' And then she would fancy herself and Joe drawing pictures on the wall, painting excitedly and beaming in satisfaction when they understood each other. The idea so amused her once when she was washing the dishes that she smiled with pleasure. Joe caught the smile as he was passing the kitchen window and asked her about it later. She couldn't tell him. 'It was only a funny thought,' she said. 'You're a queer one,' he said, laughing at her as he went out the door. He wouldn't have laughed if she had told him. He hated to be analysed. Once she had told him crossly that he thought self-knowledge was masturbation, but he pretended he didn't know what she meant.

When he had gone to the creamery, rattling the churns on the trailer over the potholes on the avenue, she brought the eggs into the kitchen for cleaning. She took out the dish of cooked tripe and onions from the fridge and put it in the oven. He'd like that for breakfast. She liked the oniony sauce, but not the spongy feel of the tripe. She'd have an orange herself.

'Any post?' she asked him when he came back half an hour later.

'Not a thing,' he said.

'Any news at the creamery?'

'Not a word.'

It was almost a ritual. She clutched at the few sentences he let fall without prompting, and would sometimes go over them afterwards, savouring each preposition, each monosyllabic word. Once when she had the temerity to reproach him for not talking to her more often, he said she'd have something to grumble about if he was out every night in the local with the boys, or running after some flighty woman who wanted to be run after. She had to agree that it surely would be something to grumble about, but it wasn't a fair comparison. He was a just man, so he said, 'I've got a lot on my mind,' and went away before she could retaliate. She wanted to scream after him, 'I've got a lot on my mind, too, but I need to share it. If I don't share it with you it might be with one of your friends who holds my hand too long when saying goodbye, or squeezes me when we're dancing at the hunt ball.' It wouldn't do any good, of course. And she didn't want to start screaming. She calculated that one scream led to another, and she might end up screaming at herself.

'The tripe's good,' he said.

'You always like tripe,' she smiled at him. He had queer tastes.

'You like oranges.' His smile was a reading of her thought.

Eagerly she said, 'Are you sure there was no post?'

'Well, nothing much, only the notice about the TB test.'

'Oh. When is it?'

'On Wednesday. He's coming to me first. I'll have to get them in at half past nine.'

'You can keep them in the paddock after milking,' she said. 'I could hunt them into the yard myself while you're away at the creamery.'

'That would be handy,' he nodded his appreciation. 'We'd better move now. Have you the water boiling?'

'I have,' she said, and was glad to be ready for him.

The calves bawled hungrily when they heard them mixing the linseed and boiling water outside the house. She put two measures of the hot sticky mixture into each of six buckets. He lifted the churn of skim milk and filled the buckets almost to the brim. Inside the house the calves jostled for the best position. Two of them got their heads stuck between the bars of the wooden railing and had to have their noses whacked to make them pull back. They put the buckets up on the ledge in front of the bars and the first six fed eagerly. Five times they refilled the buckets, marking each calf as it finished with a splash of milk. They noticed the thrivers and looked for scour in the young calf whose coat had lost its bloom. They were pleased at the success of their rearing methods and discussed it together. When the thirty calves were satisfied, they let them out to graze. Martha scrubbed out the buckets and tankards while Joe finished cleaning the milking machine and hosed down the cement floors. It was eleven o'clock. She went back into the house to do the tidying and prepare their midday meal. She was tired. She sometimes wondered how her neighbours managed with young children to care for. Nappies to wash as well. No wonder they looked exhausted. But happy just the same. A child is a candle in the house, was the old saying. Her mind created an image of a great golden candle flame dispersing shadows of loneliness. The sigh that came from her startled her and made the long-held-back tears spring to her eyes. Stop it, she muttered to herself. Tears are for townie women with no guts. It was a habit she had got into, admonishing herself, reminding herself to count her blessings. And there were blessings to be counted. She thought back to the struggle they had in the early years. Even last year. The calves had got blackleg for the first time and four had died; they lost four from hoose pneumonia; two from a virus pneumonia, and one calf had been lain on by its mother. She had cried quietly over that one. The others she had nursed, bottle-fed and injected with antibiotics, and it was useless. 'That's farming,' her husband said. It could be worse, was her neighbour's comment, a kindly woman who had put twenty years of farming behind her and knew what she was talking about. There was no good making a litany of disasters, storm damage, pests, disease, accidents. They had known them all. This year they were over the top of the hill. Joe had built up a herd of cows, with his usual patience, culling the poor milkers ruthlessly, and now they had thirty good Friesian cows, milking well and all in calf for next February. Every penny they had went back into the farm, and neither of them grudged it. Nothing was gained without work, patience, skill. She felt happy again. She left the dinner cooking and ran down the fields to meet Joe as he brought up the first tram of hay from the meadow. He laughed at her sunny face and reached down to pull her up beside him on the tractor.

'Isn't it a lovely day, Joe?' she said, kissing his rough cheek.

'A beautiful day,' he said, kissing her back. He sang 'Oh Mary this London's a wonderful sight' with mock pathos, and she knew that he was happy too.

On Wednesday morning she got up earlier. The weather was holding. It was an Indian summer. There had been no rain for three months. Where the soil was thin over the limestone rocks the grass was singed. The early morning dews prevented a complete parching. Her wellingtons glistened as she walked. 'Hup there, hup there,' she called softly to the old cow who always hung back because her hoof nails were long, horny protuberances and because the young cows would bully her if she went too far ahead. Martha coaxed her along, then ran to head off a few straying heifers. To her right, Joe was bringing up the rest of the herd with the dog, Shep. The sweet tangy smell of early morning fields delighted her. The sun was just beginning its slow climb from the east. A thin finger of smoke pointed to the sky from Cahill's chimney. They were stirring too. Mrs Cahill would be hanging the heavy iron kettle on the crane in the open fire, raking the wood and turf ashes over the kindling until they blazed. She had to milk the cows by hand before she got the children off to school. Her husband's body was twisted with arthritis. Twenty years older than herself, he was an old, worn-out man at sixty-five. They had married late and now had a young family to provide for.

Martha hooshed the last of the cows up to the yard gate. Joe closed it behind them and shouted, 'Thanks a lot,' smiling and nodding at her. A brown curl, with a streak of grey, crisped under his hat. She wished he could have a long holiday so that the hollows and the grooves in his face would fill out. Maybe next year. Surely next year they could manage it. The thought lightened her step and she skipped like a young girl up the back field to start her chores with the hens.

That evening, as she sat rubbing the odd dirt spot off the eggs, preparing them for their journey on to the breakfast tables of the town hotel, Joe said, 'I noticed a few lumps already on the cattle.'

'Oh,' she said, 'that's very quick. We'll have a few down so.'

'It looks like it.'

'It won't matter if it's a few bullocks,' she said. 'We'll get a fair price from the Department for them.'

On Friday morning the vet came to check his testing. He worked quietly and without comment. She sensed the silence when she came out to them.

'How's it going?' she asked.

There was an unusual intensity in the faces of the men in the yard. Joe looked around at her and his eyes slipped from her stare.

'Not so good, Martha, not so good.'

'What do you mean?' Her voice rose a tone, but she didn't care.

Pat Meehan, the vet, used a deliberately conversational voice when he said, 'They're all down, Martha, every one of them. You've had a right flare-up.'

'You're pulling my leg,' she said.

'I'm not. I wouldn't joke about a thing like that.'

She turned quickly and went into the house. She could feel her jaw-bone contracting in the effort at self-control. She moved hurriedly, getting coffee ready for the men, as if by outpacing her thoughts she could keep that dark cloud of anxiety away. Anyway, there could be a mistake, she thought, and knew that there couldn't. The vet's car started up. They weren't coming in for coffee. She heard him bumping down the avenue. She ran out to help Joe hunt the cattle down to the river field. 'What'll we do?' she asked, childishly slipping her hand into his.

'I don't know in the hell,' he said grimly.

They watched the cattle move easily ahead of them through the open gate, their coats sleek after a good sum-mer's grazing, the cows' udders still showing a fullness of milk, although autumn days were upon them. She recog-nised the heifers she had bucket-fed from the time they were three days old, remembered how they had bawled helplessly for their mothers, how the cows roamed the fields outside for two days and a night, listening and answering plaintively.

'How could so many have gone down the same time?'

'I don't know,' said Joe. 'I just don't know.'

He drew the last of the hay in that week. As they built it up in the hay barn, limbs aching and eyes smarting from the seed dust, they knew there would be no gentle cows munch-ing contentedly at it in winter time. They couldn't bear to talk about it, yet each knew that the other thought about little else. Martha wanted to blame someone or something. Had the vet made a mistake the last time and passed a cow he shouldn't have passed who had infected the herd? Even so, five or six might have gone down, but not the whole herd. Was it the milking parlour? Was it the drinking trough? She knew Joe would be going over all the possibilities in his mind, too. When she questioned him about it he was morose and said his mind was buzzing from thinking about it.

'We'll have to wait and see how they kill out.'

'Will they really be slaughtered? All of them?' she asked unnecessarily.

'Of course,' he said, 'all of them.'

If she had found a nest of rotten eggs out in a field she might even have believed in the pishogue that someone had put a curse on the farm.

Sunny days following one another made a mockery of their misery. It was difficult to accept that the brilliance of blue skies could look down on anything other than lovers or holidaymakers, or contented old people drowsing in deck chairs. Nights were diamond bright. When the sun went down, still late and reluctantly, the stars sprinkled the deep blue canopy with luminous spots. Martha and Joe worked doggedly, but now without satisfaction. Aching limbs were witness only of the fickleness of a treacherous world. They wished the cows were gone. Perhaps some primitive instinct for survival made them want to remove all trace and reminder of doom so that they could start clean, from the depths of existence, all over again.

Martha did not cry until one morning when she watched the bully cow elbowing her way to the front of the queue waiting to be milked. She had always reminded Martha of bossy women at sales. In the past it had made her laugh. Now she cried. And for the next three days she cried unrelievedly from morning until night. She lamented not only the loss of the herd, but the wheat crop blown flat by storm, the hay barn they had watched collapse like a pack of cards under the hurricane, the sows that never farrowed, the hens slain by the fox, the blighted potatoes rotting in pits, the long-gone dead calves. She cried the way the keening women cried at wakes over the transience of life, the frailty of human effort, the weakness of the human spirit. She cried in despair, and she cried for envy of her town friends who worried about appearances, good manners in their children and which part of the Continent they would visit for their next holidays. Joe looked at her blotched face, but could say nothing that would comfort her.

Her tears were a sedative. The knot of grief loosened and she took on again her accustomed role of comforter or silent witness. She coaxed him to eat, but his taste for food had died. He grew thinner and quieter. The house held silence in every corner. She began to talk to herself. 'What really kills me is the injustice of it all. Of course, he wouldn't think of that. All he'd say is, "Those things happen." As if that explained it all. Or "That's life." It's as if his whole philosophy could be circumscribed by those two sentences. I don't accept it. Ten years I've been struggling, doing without things, never buying a stick of furniture for the house and doing with hand-me-down clothes from my sleek city sisters.' She indulged lavishly in alliteration during those monologues. 'It's not worth it. Life must be more than an upward climb, with the summit a hole in the ground, six foot long, and an epitaph, "Here Lies". Here lies all right. A pack of self-deluding lies. Well, God, if you are there at all, it looks as if the more patient and tolerant we are, the more knocks we get. The broader the back, the heavier the burden, or some such idiotic proverb.'

Her monologues were successful therapy. In the past, she had talked herself out of gloom, neurosis, over-confidence, inhibition. She could intone her predicament to the sink, word for word, until it hung there quivering under her accusing eye, and finally disintegrated with the bubbles in the dish water. Joe's healing process was slower and perhaps more painful because he was not able to articulate his despair. Their fathers would have said, 'God's holy will be done,' and slipped the problem easily on to divine shoulders. Such faith and such relief were not a part of their lives.

It was on a day in October the trucks came to collect the cows. They were up long before dawn. Martha was sick and couldn't eat breakfast. Joe swallowed two cups of tea. They hunted the cows up to the yard for the last time, through the drenched grass. The cows called to one another in excitement and played games, poking at the ground with their hooves, tossing their heads and frisking elephant-like with one another. Only the old cow, ambling along slowly, scorned such indecorous behaviour. Martha's mind recoiled from images of victims being led to execution, of sad trails of humanity walking innocently into gas chambers, of Abraham with the knife poised over his unsuspecting son, of the sacrificial lamb. She felt miserably that they were adding another flame to the great pyre of human misery which would one day consume the earth. 'They're only cows,' she repeated to herself. 'They don't understand.' And did not believe either supposition.

In the yard the lorries waited. Three men helped them load. As if sensing the anxiety in the air, the cows were uneasy and kept doubling back out of the truck, or dodging around the corner. The men waved their arms and sticks, shouting hoy there, hoy there, goback, goback, goback. The old cow was first to give up, and Martha shut her eyes tightly when she saw her take the first shambling run in. Through the clamour and the excitement there flashed, like a pain to her optic nerve, a recollected picture of pastures yellow with buttercups, of this, their first cow, nudging her newly born calf on to its legs. So strong was the image that it superimposed itself on the dull, cool morning, and she felt on her face, not the damp wind of an early autumn, but the warm sunshine of the long gone summer and smelled the grass at the full peak of its lushness before seeding. It was the smell of fear from the sweating herd which made her open her eyes and jump to intercept their last break for freedom. The ramp was lifted up and locked into place at the back of the truck. Joe turned his face away and she went back alone to the house.

When he didn't follow she went to look for him. She found him in the machine shed, sitting on an upturned cement block. He was nearly crying.

'If you cried,' she said, 'you might feel better.'

'What's the use of anything?' he replied. 'It's a bloody waste of time. And it's no life for a woman.' He looked at her with sudden perception. 'And I haven't even given you children.' Coming from him it was like an accolade.

'Well, it wasn't for want of trying,' she smiled, trying to tease him into good humour. 'And it wasn't your fault. Look at me. The original biblical barren woman. In some societies I might have a rock tied to my neck and be thrown into a bottomless well.'

'I'd say you'd put up a bit of a fight first,' he said. 'Let's go out and get drunk. What is there left but booze and sex?'

'There's fight,' she said. 'What's life if it's not a fight?'

'We've lost all the battles so far,' he sighed. 'I'll soon be too old to fight.'

She put her arms around him, cradling him until he

responded. 'We'll never be too old,' she whispered into his ear. 'And we'll never give up the fight until we're dead.'

It began to rain. 'God,' she said, 'you forgot to fix the leak in the roof and the rain will be coming in on my polished table.' They ran into the house, getting basins and buckets ready to catch the drips from the ceiling.

'What did Pat say in her letter this morning?' he asked her suddenly.

She looked at him solemnly. 'She said she had to sack her Ayah again, that the heat was withering her roses, and that the Mercedes is in being repaired so they'll have to manage with one for a few weeks.'

'One what?' he asked, astonished.

'One car, y'oul eejit. Very awkward for them.'

She began to laugh, and so did he. They sat on the floor watching the raindrops pelting in faster on the plastic buckets, hitting the sides and splashing out on the floor. They laughed at the enormous joke of life, at the huge, side-splitting, star-shattering, cosmic comedy of it all. Then Joe cried for his empty fields and for the poor victims of their last campaign.

The Vain Woman

Sitting beside the fire he annoyed her. His legs thrust out to their full length captured most of the heat. She got up from her chair and said 'Excuse me' as she bent to lift the lid of the coal box. He did not move. He grunted and craned his neck around her bent back to stare at the television even more fixedly. She placed two pieces of coal deliberately at the back of the fire, and looked full into his face as she turned around. His eyes flickered a little but did not change the direction of their gaze. She sighed and his mouth closed tight.

'That old telly,' she said. 'I'm sick of it. It ruins conversation. I'm sure all that shooting and killing is bad for the children.'

He looked at his watch. 'I'll have time for a quickie.'

When she heard the door bang she moved into his chair, stretched her legs out in front of the fire and stared at the distorted faces on the screen. 'Thank God it's not in colour,' she thought. 'All that blood.' She hoped her only daughter would be home soon. It would be dreadful if she had a boyfriend. It was the end of the world when you got tied up with a boy. The end of life. The end of dreams.

She was twenty when she married, twenty years ago. She had fifteen pregnancies, ten full-term births and six surviving children. They were familiar calculations. She subtracted and added the born and the unborn, the dead and the quick in a careful way. She was superstitious about remembering the miscarriages. Remembrance was their only immortality. She thought about her own age, carelessly added a year too many before arriving at the correct forty-one. What age did that make him? He must be coming up to fifty. His age and the contents of his pay packet were nobody's business but his own. She wondered would he have much to drink. Would he have time for much? How quick was a quickie? Funny how he used the same word for drink and sex. He might look for a quickie when he came up to bed. She could pretend to be asleep. Once a month at the safe time he came regularly to her and rubbed his hands and said, 'Is it time, little mother?' Other times after a drink he might look for 'a quickie'. A long time ago she had looked for it herself. What was it like then? Wanting it. They used to laugh a bit then. Not much, but a bit. Once he said tenderly that she was a terror, a divil. She clasped her hands violently together at the thought. She brought her fingers up to her face, gently smoothing the skin. It felt soft still. She ran her middle finger along the hollow under her eyes. It wasn't baggy. And what did it matter? It didn't matter, of course. Nothing mattered. There was no meaning to anything.

She didn't go to Mass any more. She expected him to say something about that but he didn't. They had never gone together anyway. He went up the men's side and she went up the women's. She used to envy the young couples who didn't care about small town traditions and braved critical stares by sitting together. She watched them holding hands coming down the church aisle, or whispering together during Mass and sitting close up to one another as if they could never get near enough. Then she stopped envying them and began to pity them.

The reason she didn't go to Mass any more was silly. On her last Sunday the priest was the new curate. He had a thin mouth and defensive eyes. His sermon was on the subject of vanity and he gave as an example the vanity of a middle-aged woman who tries to delude herself and others by painting her face. He went into some detail about the application of mascara while smilingly admitting that of course he knew very little about such matters. She noted his carefully smoothed hair, his clean-shaven face, his manicured nails, the several inches of lace on his surplice.

She pondered on the identity of the lace maker. It might have been the widow, Mrs Crilly. She belonged to the Ladies' Guild who also made the embroidered vestments. It was truly beautiful work and must have taken countless hours of labour. Then the curate left the dais and John Thompson stood in his place to read the lesson. He slurred the words thickly but read with a loud voice so that she could hear the noises and make out an occasional phrase.

Mrs Rogers, who sat beside her, said, 'I've left the chicken in a slow oven. I wish I had John Thompson in it too.'

She giggled and whispered back, 'He'd be a tough old cock for your chicken.'

She tried to remember the reason she had been given why women were not allowed to read the epistle. Something about them being a distraction to the men. She looked furtively at Mrs Rogers's fat face with the hair sprouting from the mole under her ear, and thought, I must remind her to cut it. When it gets too long, it shows. That's very distracting all right.

Then it happened. The revolutionary thought made her gasp. It was all a swindle. It was a man's church for a man's world. The clarity of the revelation was astounding. A terrible, oppressive sense of betrayal settled on her. She stared at the tabernacle, the flowers, the candles, at the priest in his lace and John Thompson in his best suit. And she knew that nothing mattered, nothing mattered. The words began to sing dizzily in her mind. It made her feel weak and a little faint.

'Are you all right?' Mrs Rogers whispered.

'Yes,' she mumbled back.

'You're not that way again?' Mrs Rogers said accusingly.

No. Not any more. Once a month, 'Is it time, little mother?'

She was sick so often for the first baby that she felt like a sewer inside. It was an indescribable feeling. The constant fainting and the terrible, slow recovery of consciousness. It was hard for a man to be patient, she supposed, although she had hardly expected such impatience so soon. Any cow in the field can have a calf, he said. It's natural. I'm not on four legs, she remonstrated once, reasonably. The whole business seemed to disgust him. Again she felt you could hardly blame him. Being a woman *was* a messy business. Monthly periods or babies. It was such a humiliation having to strip for a male doctor, especially in pregnancy. Pretending it was normal and you didn't mind. But she did mind. She minded very much. When the baby was born he suggested she go for the blessing. What blessing, she asked. He said his mother had done it after all the children. The Blessed Virgin did it. Did she not know about the Feast of the Purification? She remembered then that there was such a feast day but she had not understood its significance. She had simply thought it was another Jewish custom transferred into Christianity. Don't pull that education muck on me, he said. She protested that she did not need to be purified for having a baby. That was going too far. The baby was beautiful, a beautiful boy, just what he wanted. Did he think the baby was soiled too? He got angry and said she was always arguing and she was to do what she was told, or by God she'd hear about it from him, it was the custom and she wasn't going to make a holy show of him. So she went. Up after Mass to the altar in front of everyone to kneel down before the priest for a blessing and to be purified. Why don't men get purified, she wondered. It's their seed. And why doesn't a woman give me the blessing, she wondered, just for a change. Of course it is only a custom, she consoled herself. It's only a religious performance.

The next baby came too soon. When it was born she had two infants under a year, and she was too ill to go for the purification. Then she had her stillbirths. Then she had her only daughter. She cried with delight when she had a girl. Even he was pleased to see the dainty creature, since he had his full quota of sons. She went once more for the purification, thinking it would please him, but he didn't seem to notice. The house always smelled of nappies, he said. She agreed. She was tired of babies' bottoms. Her whole life seemed to be spent wiping them, washing them.

Her whole life seemed to be spent in a great orgy of pushing food in one end and cleaning the other end. Cleaning up and tidying up after people, that was her life.

'Why don't you pick up your clothes?' she said to him. 'Why do you always have to leave them on the floor? Haven't I enough to do?'

'Nag, nag, nag,' he said. 'Like an old hen. Cackle, cackle, cackle.'

He was right of course. She *was* like an old hen, shrill and cackling. 'We ought to talk more,' she suggested, after reading an article in a women's magazine. 'It's bad for us not to talk.'

'What is there to talk about?' he asked.

And there was nothing. The weather, his work, her work, the children, the price of things, that was nothing.

He burst out laughing when she said they ought to go to evening classes. 'Go if you like, and make a fool of yourself,' he said. She didn't go.

The terraced houses were in the old part of town. Once the genteel occupants had used them to entertain their country cousins at weekends. Solicitors and doctors and merchants lived there in those days. When they left, the houses lost slates and plaster and the arched doorways sagged and the new owners did not care too much about paint and repair. But he admired the proportions of the rooms and took delight in showing them off. He even helped her to paint and wallpaper. The house gave her a status and she repayed it by decorating it. The walls and roof did more than protect her from the elements. They shielded her from the prying looks of neighbours, from the buffetting of passersby. When the baby smell stage was finally over she planted geraniums in pots and left busy lizzies trailing around the bathroom. Noisy boots and the rough passage of boys had to be borne with, but by scolding and cajoling she kept their worst excesses at bay. The house protected her and she protected the house.

Since she no longer went to Mass and Teresa did most of her shopping there was rarely any need for her to go out. At the back of the house a long narrow strip of grass stretched to the canal and outside her back gate a little single plank bridge spanned the water to link up with the farmland. On summer days she sat in the open gateway, staring out at the stretching fields and murmuring to herself with pleasure. All the houses were walled in along the sides and backs. The luxury of this privacy was enhanced by the spaciousness of the view. If she heard any of her neighbours scurrying down their pathways to open their own gates, she would draw in her chair quickly and hide in the shadows of the garden until they had gone.

When he went to football matches or into the public houses she turned to the fields and to the house for companionship. At one time her children had compensated. But they were older now, with their own interests and their own friends. Her last four pregnancies had ended in miscarriage so her youngest was independent. When they were at school or at work she had conversations with the cat and the furniture and whatever she happened to be cleaning at the time. Her monologues had an Alice in Wonderland quality about them. 'Dear, dear, dear. Look at that. Dirty again. You look very nice today, taps. I've managed to get the scum off with this new cleaner. It's amazing the inventions there are nowadays. It's no bother at all keeping you shiny. Well, I won't say it's no bother. But it's not much, and it is certainly worth it. And a pleasure to do it for you. A real pleasure.' It seemed as if the house responded by warming and enfolding her and radiating the kind of happiness known only to those who feel loved and cherished. The cat arched and purred, following her from room to room or stretching in abandon in front of the range. When the seasons allowed, she put flowers in every room. When that was not possible she sprayed with perfumed aerosols. Each day she had a momentary feeling of resentment when the children came bounding in through the front door and took possession again. During the holidays she found it even more difficult and had to work hard at keeping her relationship with the house alive. Sometimes she got out of bed at night to steal around the rooms, touching and looking, or she peered out the windows at the garden and fields, shadowy and still.

In spring she caressed the sticky buds of the chestnut tree and watched them unfold. On those occasions she regretted her loss of faith. She longed to thank some supreme God for the chestnut tree. Once she thought wildly that she needed a father figure just as men needed a mother figure, and was filled with terror at the thought. Her hands trembled to think that her self-sufficiency was only a pose, her love for the house a substitute for something unobtainable. But then she recalled her own father and dismissed the idea as ludicrous. Her mouth wrinkled in contempt at the thought of the weak, vulgar men she had known. Out of her contempt was born a new pride, almost an arrogance, which she saw discomfited her husband.

Often she caught him stealing sly looks at her, looks of distrust and doubt. But his routine was unchanged. His conversation remained as dull as ever. A small tingle of malice at his look revitalised her and she talked animatedly to the children. They indulged her by feigning interest but were caught up in their own activities and escaped from her when they could. She did not resent their flight. She had often longed for release from them and it amused her to see them hacking their eager way through new jungles. Desert at the end for them, too, she thought mockingly, and drew in a sharp breath of anguish. When those warm maternal feelings flooded through her she was laid bare to pain again and she had to seal herself off by indifference or forced activity. There were always times when she was caught unawares and she accepted her weakness with resignation.

As she relaxed in the now empty room it was easy to concentrate on her book. He had stopped mocking her new interest in philosophy, psychology, sociology. 'All codology,' he said at first, but when he saw it had no effect he resorted to mute disapproval. She was thankful for that. There were times, after all, when his silence was a blessing. It was extraordinary how her brain seemed to expand in middle life while his stultified. She wondered did the beer have a pickling effect. She discovered resources of intelligence she had never known she possessed, and was occasionally filled with awe at her ability to understand even the most complex and abstract of ideas. After one blazing row with him when she discussed the splitting of the atom with her eldest son during supper, she was careful never to display her knowledge before him. It was easy to hide her books and she read only when he was not at home.

When the front door-knocker banged imperiously she sighed with irritation. He was home early and without his key. She opened the door and stood back to let him in.

An amused voice said, 'Madam, are you inviting me inside at this late hour? Your husband will not mind?' The man standing at the doorstep was short and had thin pale hair straggling across his pink scalp. His eyes twinkled through rimless glasses.

She laughed back at him confidently. 'Oh, so you've met the man of the house.'

'I had that pleasure just a few moments ago in the local hostelry and he directed me to you, because you have the key of number eight in your possession and I am interested in buying that delightful residence of character.'

'How nice,' she responded coquettishly, 'to have you for a neighbour.'

He raised a cautionary hand. 'Do not presume too much, madam. If the house does not meet my very particular requirements, you will be deprived forever of my neighbourliness. It is not advisable to indulge in false hopes.'

'It might need some decorating,' she said. 'The two old women who lived in it for years had no one to do anything for them. Poor things.'

'Poor things,' he echoed. 'What has become of the poor things?'

'Dead,' she answered.

'Dead,' he repeated hollowly, with a look of such lugubrious sympathy on his face that she laughed. He did not respond. 'I do not require decoration,' he said. 'All I need is a large north-facing room with good windows.'

'All these houses face north-east,' she said. 'The gardens at the back face south-west. They get all the sun.'

'Perfect,' he said. 'It sounds perfect. If I might have the key I will not detain you longer.'

'I'll open the door for you,' she said. 'Let me show you the house.'

'I don't know what to call you. What is your name?'

'Mary Murphy. And yours?'

'Patrick Murphy.'

'That's funny,' she said. 'We are two Murphys.'

'Not so strange,' he answered. 'Have you ever looked in a telephone directory for a Murphy? It's the commonest name in Ireland.'

'I could believe that,' she sighed. 'Of course, it is only my married name. I do have another. My real name. This one is only borrowed.'

'The borrowed one will do me,' he said. 'I find it hard enough to remember my own name, common and all as it is.'

'That's funny,' she said. 'I do that too. I forget what age I am as well. I often find it hard to remember *who* I am. Not just my name. But my self. I look in the mirror and I say, "Who are you?" And then I say, "Who am I? Who is me? What is me?" It's weird. I suppose I'm crazy,' she added smugly.

'Probably,' he agreed. 'It sounds rather like it.'

He had a cheek agreeing with her. 'I don't really think I am mad. I only pretend to think it. It's because I am too polite to let everyone else know how mad *they* all are. I can bear it. They might not be able to.'

'Very considerate of you,' he said. 'Could I have the key now, please? My feet will fall off on your doorstep.'

She was apologetic. She ran ahead of him along the pavement to the end house in the terrace. She rushed up the steps and, breathless, inserted the key. 'There,' she declared. 'There.'

He was a painter. He hauled his canvases, easel, his carrier bag with brushes, paints and palette.

'You're an artist,' she cried with delight and clapped her hands childishly. 'It will be marvellous to have an artist living near us.'

He frowned. 'I did not say I would stay. The house may not suit.'

'It will suit. It's the perfect house for you. I'll help you clean it.'

'Well, I may need a little assistance. I'd appreciate that kind of help,' underlining the word 'that'.

'Don't worry,' she cried. 'I won't interfere. I'm not one of those nosy neighbours. I keep myself to myself. You're the first person I have talked to, apart from my children, for ages. I don't know why I'm talking so much to you. It's funny.'

He sighed wearily. 'You keep saying everything is funny. It's not a very precise word for the meaning you have in mind.'

'You don't know what meaning I have in mind,' she said and ran back to her own house, laughing all the time. She felt exhilarated. Once inside the front door she danced along the hall, clutching herself as if hugging an exquisite secret. The television blared at the empty sitting room. Turning it off was an act of war and she did it with aplomb, raising a military hand as if signalling the firing of cannon before turning the knob. 'That will shake your man when he comes home. That will give him something to think about. If he's capable of thought.'

She was asleep when he came grumbling to bed, really asleep, not just pretending.

Her own house now took second place to the painter's. On number eight she poured new love, almost adoration, turning it into an altar with flowers and perfumes. Patrick worked from early morning in the north-east facing room and accepted her service without comment. She planned new colour schemes for the rooms and cajoled the money out of him for paints and paper. When he grumbled, she reminded him that it was an investment and that her labour was free. 'I'd really prefer it if you would cook me a meal,' he told her. She replied indignantly that she was not his servant and in a burst of revolutionary fervour, added, 'Cook your own bloody meals.' He laughed gently and made himself a sandwich.

Her children teased her. Her husband did not refer to her new interest. Communication between them was reduced to the most basic of signs and grunts. She savoured the conversations she held with the artist. Over the years she had become almost inarticulate and now found miraculous release for the ideas she conjured from her reading. Verbal skills were a delight and she practised them constantly. Each morning she hurried out of her house, and the neighbours listened for the sound of her skipping feet as she rushed back to prepare the family midday meal. 'You can tell the time by her,' they said. 'But it isn't right. Pity her poor husband.' When the house decoration was completed and the empty paint cans disappeared from the rubbish bin, her daily visits continued. 'What is she doing now?' they asked, leaning out of their front porches to whisper confidentially. 'An artist like that and a simple woman like her. Something will come of it and it won't be any good.'

'Where did you learn that?' the painter asked her one morning when she sketched his hand and arm holding the brush.

'I could always draw,' she shrugged. 'I went to art school for two years. Drawing was important then.'

'Why did you give it up?'

'I met him.'

'You didn't have to marry him.'

'He wouldn't leave me alone. I wasn't able for him. I was too quiet. I couldn't fight anyone in those days. Even in class I could never bear to be first so I just did as much work as would make me second or third. I could gauge it very accurately. I wanted to be ordinary. It's very lonely being different.'

At that he groaned in exasperation, and shouted at her, 'God blast it woman, have you no pride?'

'Pride? What's that?' she yelled back. 'What woman has pride? Vanity maybe, but not pride. That's your prerogative.'

'Are you a women's libber?' he challenged.

'You make it sound like a disease,' she said. 'I don't know what you mean. I told you before I don't know what I am. I only know I am. That's all. It's enough for me. It's enough for you.'

'Crummy philosophers I can do without,' he grumbled, and went on painting. But he lent her his paints and his canvases and he spent as much time watching over her as she did over him. She began to criticise his work, and once when he had spent all day painting and over painting until he was in despair, she said all it needed was a little more white. He covered his eyes with his hands and said, 'Will you go away, woman, and don't ever come back.'

'Kindly call me madam when you address me,' she said. It was five days before she came back and saw with satisfaction that he had painted nothing while she was away.

'Don't imagine,' he said, 'that I have been idle without reason. And *you* were not the reason.'

'What was?' she asked disbelievingly.

'I am simply refuelling. Every now and again I have to stop to recover and examine what I have done and decide where I am going.'

'Going?' she asked, her heart pounding.

'Not going away. My progress. Now I must paint from life. You are convenient, if you are willing to model.'

'I am convenient,' she repeated bitterly. 'Am I a private or public convenience?'

'Sarcasm does not become you. I am serious.'

'So am I.'

'Well, if it's too much for you, say so.'

She sat down, thinking fast.

'I have just one condition.'

He turned his back and, facing the window, said, 'And what is that?'

'You must model for me, as well. I need a convenience too.' He didn't move or speak for a few moments and she was afraid she had been too daring. Then he turned round and said, 'It's a deal.'

They took weekly turns at posing. For the first few days of her roster she was self-consciously naked and he cursed her for it. His abuse was so impersonal she could not be offended, and, besides, his turn was coming. She consoled herself with that thought until by the end of the week she did not need consoling. The weather was warm and it was a new and enormous pleasure to recline near the window with the green world of high summer reaching in to touch her. At the end of the week he allowed her a glimpse of his work. 'I suppose it's hideous,' she said, expecting some gross distortion of her body but resigning herself to the fact of his artistic integrity. If that was the way he saw her she would have to put up with it. 'Modern painters see a woman's body with a clerical eye,' she said, 'a kind of perversion.' He said nothing and waited for her comment.

It was 'Oh', an exclamation of pleasure and recognition. 'It's very good,' she said then, slowly, and he nodded his agreement. 'It's like seeing myself with a better pair of eyes,' she said. 'Thank you.'

'Thank you,' he acknowledged gravely. 'Of course it needs a little more work.'

'It's my turn next, don't forget.'

On Monday he was ready for her sitting in his dressing-gown at the window.

'I don't know if I want you there,' she said. 'I think I'll try it in deep shade.'

Her fingers tingled as she prepared her palette. It was an excitement she had forgotten existed. He moved to the position she wanted and sat stiffly, grimly determined to keep his bargain. She smiled a little to herself as she mixed paints. Already the completed picture was in her mind's eye. It did not occur to her that his twenty years of patient, painful practice might be an advantage. At the end of the first day she knew what she had lost.

'Don't worry if it's a failure,' he comforted her. 'You are a long time away from it.'

'It's in my head,' she cried then, frustrated and angry. 'It's in my heart. Locked inside and I can't get it out. The same as when I hear a tune clear and true in my head but it comes out different when I open my mouth.'

'As long as you have it inside, you aren't too bad,' he said. 'Worse to have skilled hands and no heart. Worse to have technique and no vision.'

'I don't know about that,' she said, 'but perhaps tomorrow will be better.'

By Thursday she was exhausted and begging him for a fresh canvas.

'Clean the other one again,' he said. 'It will be all right.'

'Just one new one,' she said. 'I feel I might be lucky with this.'

'Luck,' he scorned. 'No. Use the old one and don't talk about luck.'

'I've only two more days,' she groaned, 'and nothing to show for it.'

'You can try again after my week,' he said.

She took her discoloured canvas and glared at it. It had a warm beige tint after its constant wiping clean. She began to work on a new idea. She saw him in colours of sepia and beige, impersonal, distinct, even his kindness touched with cruel self-possession.

'You have never had children,' she said.

'I have never borne a child,' he said drily.

'Have you ever fathered one?' she persisted. 'Ever loved one?'

'To the first question – not to my knowledge; to the second – no.'

'Have you ever loved anyone?'

His look remained impassive. 'Love is a word I do not lightly use because I am not certain of its meaning. But I have been extremely fond of a number of persons. I am extremely fond of you, for instance.'

And that was how she painted him, extremely fond of you for instance.

On Friday evening she stood back to let him see it, in agony for his approval, steeling herself for his rejection. She watched his face and was intrigued to see him colour a little.

'Are you embarrassed?' she asked anxiously.

He shook his head. 'Of course not.' He put an arm around her and kissed her. 'You have given me too much tenderness. And too much cruelty. I am more mediocre than your idea of me. But it is a magnificent picture. They are both magnificent pictures. And we are magnificent people.'

They made love in his shadowy bedroom. They made love for the next three days. They became careless, forgetting the large north-east facing window and the long rows of gardens. On Monday night when she tried her front door it was locked against her. She knocked and rang and called through the letterbox. There was no answer. She spent the night uneasily in number eight and there was no love making. He caressed her and consoled her, but it was no use. When she said sadly, 'Ah, my children,' he left her alone.

It took the intervention of the parish priest, the pleas of her children, her own repeated avowals of repentance and promises of good behaviour before her husband would take her back. 'She can stay,' he said. 'But she's only a common prostitute and will be treated like one.'

'Christ forgave the woman taken in adultery,' the priest said softly. 'She seems to be truly sorry. Can you not be a little Christ-like in charity?'

'She has made a mock of me,' he said, 'and I'll never forgive that. She is a vain, lewd woman, but she has my name.'

'Are not all women vain?' said the priest. 'We have to be strong to make up for their weaknesses.'

Number eight was put up for sale immediately. No one saw the painter leave. One morning the house was empty and in the afternoon the 'For Sale' notice was on the gate. The neighbours were sympathetic to the children, indulging their Christian charity to excess, full of just pride in their tolerance. Only occasionally did a bitter comment break out to remind them that they also were human. A few were openly disgusted and thought the incident had lowered the tone of the avenue, which had been so laboriously pulling itself back to its earlier dignity. The men winked knowingly at each other near her house. The women shunned her. She had one communication from the painter. It was a picture postcard of Christ crucified and underneath it he had printed the words, 'Ah, my children.'

Pilgrim's Tale

The moment the train pulled out of the station the boys at the end of the carriage began to beat their tom-toms. Fingers and palms drumming furiously on the table, heads down attentively awaiting replies from distant jungles, they filled the carriage with their noisy presence. Every now and again they burst into raucous song.

'It's more like a football train than a pilgrimage,' a woman opposite Helen said wryly.

Helen shrugged. 'Boys,' she said expressively.

Across the corridor four shiny new girl communicants with an average age of six and a half years brandished their dreadful dresses. Helen shuddered and closed her eyes to exclude further conversation and the awe-inspiring vulgarity. With a feeling of doomed resignation she faced the long journey through Clare, Galway and Mayo, having shaken off the dirt-trailed hem of Limerick. Her niece, school uniformed and temporarily docile, took her bearings. A week ago Helen had promised the outing when tears and reproaches had failed to move the atheistic heart of the child's mother. A week ago it was just a gloriously unfulfilled promise.

'Never make a promise you can't keep,' her sister Margaret said, a week ago today. 'You know it was someone experimenting with a magic lantern. How can you encourage such superstitions?'

'Don't be so unimaginative, Margaret. You'll bruise the child's sensibilities. Anyway, that has all been disproved. Who would have such a thing in such an out-of-the-way place?'

'The local joker. The parish priest. Who cares? It just got out of hand. Things do. That's why we have a nuclear crisis. We don't know how to stop. It's the human predicament.'

With the death of Sartre, Margaret had revived her student interest in existentialism and quoted chunks of Nietzsche at breakfast. His nihilistic obsession with abysses suited her current mood. Her husband dived for the antacids. Helen prescribed a dose of hormone treatment for her sister and a total censorship of European philosophical thought.

'Unless you go back to Duns Scotus,' she said. 'A practical religious.'

Privately Margaret thought that her sister was becoming more like the caricature of the nursing sister ex-missionary nun every year. It was all that physical business of dealing with death, laying out bodies, closing dead eyes, removing dead tissue. As if that was all there was to life. But then, of course, poor Helen had never had children. She gave practical assistance at deliveries and she was no doubt very sympathetic, but the experience, the actual experience she would never understand. And had she ever been in love? Another experience she had missed. Was she not a teeny weeny bit in love with her own Tom? But that sister-in-lawish feeling could hardly be compared with the real thing. She advised him on his ulcer, suggested diets for him that she, Margaret, would have to prepare. Quite simple, she said. It was very easy when you were on the outside. Very easy to give advice. Very easy to take other people's children on a day's pilgrimage when you could go home to your own flat and not have to face the day's ironing before you fell into bed.

'Why do you iron the sheets?' Helen asked in amazement.

'Tom likes his bed linen crisp,' Margaret said with proprietary martyrdom.

'But you always say you have so much to do. Can't you cut it down? What about those American non-iron sheets? Percale or something.'

'Ugh,' Margaret said. 'Tom wouldn't like those flowery things. Sprigs of blossom and nursery colours. They're fine for you, Helen. But they hardly suit the dark passions of the marital bed.'

Helen blinked twice, knowing it was meant to shock her single prudery. Married women were quite childishly knowing about the plain facts of life. It hardly required much imagination to know what went on between husbands and wives or their unmarried peers. Dark passions indeed. Comical convulsions. If one wanted to, one could easily let one's mind wander into other people's boudoirs, and find nothing at all surprising there. Not even black satin sheets. Middle-class daring. Margaret would have been surprised to have found such ideas lurking in her sister's ascetic soul. Margaret had been cross at the reference to hormones. 'If I hear one more programme,' she said, 'or read one more stupid article about the menopause, I'll –' her imagination failed.

'Kill yourself?' her daughter suggested helpfully.

'Throw yourself in the Shannon,' her son said longingly.

'Oh yes. You'd like to be rid of me. That would suit you fine. Free houses and all-night parties. You'll be sorry, though, wait and see.'

A million years of male seventeen-year-old frustrations echoed in his sigh, re-echoed through the slammed door, the scraped boots dragging their way across the parquet flooring. Anguished, Margaret looked after him, tears showing.

'Lucky he can't see that,' her daughter said philosophically. 'He'd really make a laugh of you.'

Helen often wondered why she punished herself by spending weekends with her sister and her family, husband, two girls and three boys, two pre-puberty, one on the doorstep, another sunk in the abyss, and the last with a lingering spot where he hadn't yet had to shave. When she was young, Helen thought, no one had puberty. No one had a 'teen' age, at least no one but the Americans who had other marvels like electric kitchens, instant food, instant education and instant unnoticed death. And here they were thirty years later with all the disadvantages and none of the advantages of the American dream. Even their own private Vietnam on their own bloody doorstep.

In some ways the pilgrimage was a relief. Apart from her acknowledged need for spiritual refreshment and the deeper need to face a new and gnawing fear about her health it had been good to escape from the breakfast atmosphere, the silent crumbling of marmalade and toast, the Saturday morning resentment towards Saturday morning chores, the rival switching from one radio wavelength to the other, the expressive glowers and sighs. Even the cherubic youngest was contaminated and complained that someone had used her mug.

'I gave it to your Auntie Helen,' Margaret said firmly. Helen started guiltily to expiate and the eldest grinned knowingly.

'Little twit,' the resident of the abyss said. 'Who cares about your stupid mug?'

'It's not stupid, it's the Pope's mug.'

Helen looked aghast.

'Don't mind her,' the pilgrimage niece said. 'We only found it at the Pope's picnic. Everyone left everything behind them. Daddy just picked it up.'

'Mammy wouldn't go,' the youngest said pathetically. 'Mammy has lost her faith.'

'Heavens! Who told you that?' Margaret said, half laughing, half guilty.

'I wish you were like Auntie Helen and said the rosary every night. Sister Teresa is always asking us at school who says the rosary every night. We have to put our hands up.'

'Tell her to mind her own business,' the eldest said cheerfully. 'Tell her your mother is an atheistic, humanistic feminist.'

'I will not,' the little girl cried. 'Tell her yourself.'

Helen fled to the back kitchen to pack sandwiches and flask.

'Don't forget your staff and shell,' Tom said, coming through from the garage. He used heavy humour with her to clarify their relationship for himself. It didn't need any clarifying for her. Still, it was useful to know that she wasn't entirely sexless, even if it was a bit late for all that. Dreadful if she became one of those maiden aunts who appeared at their nieces' weddings begging guests to sign anti-contraceptive or anti-abortion appeals. Not that she was in favour of the second, whatever about the first. But it was, after all, the business of the pregnant and the pregnable.

'My God,' Tom exclaimed in wonder when he saw the sandwiches and lemonade and fruit and crisps and the flask of coffee. 'Are you sure it isn't a bacchanalian orgy you're off to?'

'Take a whiskey for the coffee,' Margaret said, 'and you won't feel the journey. It's four hours by train and bus.'

'I'm not walking. I'll be sitting down the whole way,' Helen said patiently.

'Wait till you do Lough Derg or Croagh Patrick. Then you'll know about pilgrimages.' Tom did both every year to pray for his wife's conversion, he said, half joking, whole in earnest.

'We were never a pilgrimage family,' Margaret said with unnecessary pride. 'I wonder why? Never did Lourdes or Holy Wells.'

'The pride of intellect,' Tom said, shaking his head.

'We did Faughart for St Brigid's day,' Helen pointed out. 'Don't you remember walking out to her well?'

'That was a pagan well.' Margaret lifted her chin as she spoke to indicate her moral and intellectual superiority. 'Mother went and so did we, because she said Brigid was one of the few genuine Irish saints. Patrick was only a "runner" and the others were part politicians or petty chieftains or male chauvinists trying to get away from their women.'

'I wish you wouldn't libel poor Chauvin in that way. He was never sexist. And I never heard your mother use the word in her life. I don't believe anyone used it when you were a child,' Tom remarked reasonably.

'Well,' Margaret said in that quick impatient way she had, when someone disagreed with her and she wasn't sure enough of her facts to be able to counter-argue. 'Whatever she said, that's what she meant. I can't remember her exact words.'

'We went to Ladywell on the first of May,' Helen reminded her. 'I brought Danny and it cured his warts.'

'Psychosomatic,' Margaret said. 'Another pagan feast. And by a funny coincidence – did you notice what day today is?' She sang a jingle:

> The seventeenth of May
> The big fair day
> We all got a holiday
> And we all ran away.

'Leave Helen alone,' Tom said, putting his arm around her shoulder. She steeled herself against sinking into its magic masculine circle. 'It's you should be bringing Miriam, Margaret. It shouldn't be left to Helen. It's very good of you, pet, and we're grateful. Say a prayer for all the old heathens here.' He kissed her on the ear like a boy at his first mixed party.

'Well excuse me,' Margaret said and then began to laugh. 'You should see your face, you goose. Don't let him have that effect on you. You can have him, you know. Any time. On loan of course. You're welcome to him for practice.'

She wasn't even worthy of jealousy. But perhaps that wasn't fair. Margaret wasn't the jealous type. She probably would be glad to share Tom with her, just as she was glad to share her children and never minded when they went through passions of devotion to her. Was that because she knew they always came back to her in the end, with their secrets and their complaints?

The train was full. Her niece, Miriam, sat demurely, ankles crossed, flashing amused, inquisitive glances around. She was very like her mother.

They passed over an unexpectedly magnificent stretch of the Shannon as it curved around to enclose a portion of the town. By the back doors of the newest corporation houses, by the town dump spewing litter on to the pavement, the train bore its pilgrims. They peered into ramshackle junk yards at the rusting carcasses of civilisation until, within minutes, they were up into the lush woods of Cratloe, festooned with hawthorn blossoms and the flowers of the mountain ash. Gallows Hill, where the sheep stealers had dangled, looked down on them and on the sprawling estuary below.

'Don't forget to look out for Sixmilebridge station,' Margaret said, before they left. 'When Johnny was a baby we brought Mother to catch the train to Athenry and they had to open the station for us. All the passengers hung out the windows and laughed because there were no tickets in the ticket office. I think we were the last to use it before it was closed. A day like today. A lovely, rich, green-field, blue-skied, golden, whitethorn-blossomy day. Oh what a day. I wish I was going now.'

'You can't,' Miriam said importantly. 'You haven't got a ticket. You book in advance for pilgrimages.'

'Oh boo,' Margaret said and blew kisses of derision at her. Helen envied those kisses and the laughing scorn of the child rejecting them.

Sixmilebridge was a painted name that vanished before they had time to note its peeling letters. Behind it, the rose-entwined cottage, which used to lift its golden thatch to the sun, was a sheet of concrete with a stark new bungalow.

Margaret's eldest, Johnny, had sipped porter from a mug almost as big as himself by the fire in the old thatched house. They were all innocent then, Margaret newly into marriage and motherhood, Helen off on her first mission to Africa a few weeks later, Johnny newly into life. The old couple who watched with glee his first tentative sips relinquished life without complaint a few years afterwards. They seemed to fade into death. Margaret's letter, bearing the news to Helen, had been full of sadness.

'All things pass,' she wrote, 'even the good and wise.' Helen, labouring in tropical heat to save the lives of children, wrote back to say how fortunate people were to live to old age. 'If I reach fifty,' she wrote, 'I will consider myself lucky.'

How pompous and smug she had been, she thought, noting her reflection in the carriage window. At fifty, life was even sweeter. So many things to do. So much undone.

The little abandoned railway stations flashed by like beads on a rosary. Near Athenry apple blossoms tumbled against the sky. And then suddenly there were rocky fields and stone walls, stretches of bog and the familiar landscape of the west on its permanent pilgrimage into the past. The carriages snaked around bends and were waved at by families busy cutting turf. The end carriages swivelled as the train slowed to take the curves. The sun, scorching through windows, lit up the pre-exam pallor of the youths. Helen softened towards them, thinking of their gruff, bristling, anxiety-ridden lives and the unadventurous world ahead of them – office boxes, assembly lines, production machines. A pilgrimage without faith.

Across the passageway a fat girl could not resist her lunchbox. She smacked her lips over an orange and afterwards licked her fingers with the delicacy of new love's kisses. Miriam felt hungry by association and attacked her sandwiches. Helen restrained herself from admonishing her to keep some for later. Mothers could say those things, not aunts.

The boys at the end of the carriage grew restless and sang bawdy songs, one about St Peter shovelling coal.

'Anal humour,' the woman opposite proffered. Helen nodded and shrugged again. The woman looked curiously at her shoulders as if expecting an exclamation mark for added emphasis. Helen did the next best thing by raising her eyebrows and smiling ruefully. The woman closed her eyes.

The heat burned her face and prodded her body, a relentless reminder of her flesh and its frailty. As if in response a pain twisted through to her spine. She jolted forward. To hide the reason for the sudden movement she crossed to the other side and sat opposite the fat girl who looked at her as if she was about to be dispossessed. Her foot, resting on the seat beside Helen, lingered for a moment and then relented, surrendered, withdrew. Helen mentioned the heat apologetically and patted her skin in excuse. The fat girl looked with disinterest, almost contempt, at the flush. Helen closed her eyes. She wished she could have walked. She wished she could have worn pilgrimage sandals and carried a staff and begging bowl. Today was the perfect day for abandoning routine. Today could have been the beginning of a journey into the soul, into the world of myth and magic and great unselfconscious belief.

At Claremorris they changed to waiting buses, lined up ready for the moment of release. When each had its complement they charged off, along the dusty road, by the new bungalows and the unvarying bog. Half an hour later they were disgorged into a bus park near the shrine. Miriam had found some friends and they raced to the souvenir stalls.

Helen gazed around her. Here had stood the Polish Pope on that rainy day in autumn. Here people saw a vision of the supernatural, a maiden mother with attendant, a lamb to symbolise sacrifice. Here she might find healing, if not of the flesh, then of the spirit. She clasped her hands like a young novice venturing into meditation and closed her eyes to pray.

'Is chughatsa a tháinig ag gearán mo scéal leat, is ag iarraidh mé a leigheas, ar son Dé ort.'

The air was bountiful, honeyed by heather and bog. In such an atmosphere, scented with the accumulation of ages, she might pull from the imagination the hosts of the dead, those who had peopled other pilgrimages and filled the nights and days with their hymns of praise and their penitential psalms. Between them all they would make powerful persuasion. And those other women, clamorous and pagan, keening their dead, exhorting their menfolk to battle, beseiging the gods, would align themselves with her and would accept no denial.

'Is chughatsa a tháinig ag gearán mo scéal leat, is ag iarraidh mé a leigheas, ar son Dé ort.'

She opened her eyes and saw the stalls, the shops, the slate roofs, a great glass dome at the end of the old church enclosing a great white representation of the vision. And erupting – it seemed – like a volcanic mountain from banked-down pagan fires, a new basilica, shining and challenging, bristling with steel and glass.

She was stunned by this new evidence of man's vigour and enterprise. While she stared, a voice of welcome emerged from a hailer. Detached from corporeal source it welcomed them boomingly. It filled the air around her as she twisted, eager to locate its source. A thousand or so people, about three quarters of the number women, moved around in quiet order. Were they all in need of healing? She closed her eyes again, this time to remove the persistent image of diseased female organs. Had the Pope pleaded for mercy for all those abused, diseased female organs? She could not remember. Had the Virgin Mother died of cancer of the uterus or ovaries? And why did the thought seem blasphemous? Atheistic Margaret would have been shocked. Tom would have been saddened and disillusioned. For him she represented the spiritual. It was not easy to be spiritual when one knew intimately the secret workings of the body and the crazy chaos of its disorder.

Two young men, with peaked caps set at rakish angles over their foreheads, pushed wheelchairs with occupants towards the special WC marked 'Wheelchairs only'. A procession of elderly women, sprinkled with a few elderly men, walked around the old church, reciting the rosary. Miriam came to show her purchases – a clockwork spider, a holy picture set in a shiny frame, a plastic bottle with 'Knock, Holy Water' written on it.

'Why aren't you going around with them?' she pointed to the procession.

'They look a bit old for me,' Helen said.

'Oh. Are they?' Miriam looked at her and at them, puzzled.

'For goodness sake, Miriam,' Helen said crossly, 'can you imagine your mother going around with them?'

'That's different,' Miriam said.

'I'm only a year older than your mother, you know.'

'There's somebody young,' Miriam pointed to a frail woman being helped by her tired old parents. 'It's nothing to do with age, you know. We aren't here because of that.'

'Why are we here?' Helen asked cruelly.

'To pray to the Virgin Mary of course.'

'You're only buying things.'

'That's just for now,' the child said with a look of disbelief at such stupidity. 'We'll be going in with the nuns to the basilica. You can stay at the back if you like. I know Mammy would. Then you can leave if it gets too much for you.'

The perception of nine-year-olds was alarming.

They had their picnic, gorging themselves like everyone else on sandwiches and fruit and flasks of tea and coffee. A quiet, self-satisfied munching pervaded the allotted territory near the bus park. Loaves and fishes, Helen thought. Manna from heaven.

Afterwards she sat with a thousand others in the basilica and watched the concelebrated Mass. Five white priests and two black priests officiated. Earlier one nun, white, female, had prepared the altar, shaking and unfolding cloths, adjusting candlesticks and flowers, like a busy housewife. Why Helen noticed such insignificant trivia she could not tell, but they lodged in her mind, like a cerebral toothache, nagging her to a new discomfort. She escaped outside to the sunny benches.

A youth passed, sticking labels on everyone with panache and authority, while his transistor radio played the latest pop record. Helen recognised him. On the outward journey he had sprawled across four seats as the train filled up with shuffling petitioners looking for places to rest their bones. Through each carriageway they moved, to be met by his mates, brothers, peers, each covering four seats. No one complained. The women dragged their eager children and laden baskets through the carriages while the prime of Irish young manhood held fast to their territory. And here he was, lord of the realm, pinning on labels. He flashed her his well-rehearsed smile. She removed her label instantly and read it before crumpling it into the waste bin. 'Catholic Family Pilgrimage,' it said.

'Don't look so glum,' the young man said. 'It might never happen.'

'It has,' she said loudly, to his surprise and her own. 'You've happened.'

'Lady,' he said, and the inflexion on the word was tinged with violence, 'don't worry. I haven't raped you yet.'

If she had been a man, she thought sadly, she could have punched him on the nose.

She wandered into a missionary exhibition where a priest modelled native African apparel. A public relations exercise. She wandered out again. The black Swazilanders emerged wearing white surplices trimmed with a foot of lace. One bore a simple cross. Behind them four stocky men with earthy features carried a platform on which stood a plaster replica of Christ's mother.

The large congregation, mainly women and girls, followed obediently, reciting a litany. The montonous, mechanical tone of the response contrasted oddly with the poetry of the symbols. Tower of Ivory, House of Gold, Ark of the Covenant, Mother of Divine Grace, Mother most pure, Mother most chaste, Mother inviolate. The little girls, newly communioned, tripped their tongues over the phrases and beamed while they sang of freedom from sexual sin. Blessed be the fruit of thy womb, they chanted artlessly. Immaculate virgin. Conceived without stain of sin.

Helen retired to the old church and sat in the last seat, luxuriating in its darkness and quiet. The pain had come back, clawlike this time. Outside a confession box a large crowd of women queued. The confessor's door opened and he came out and waved his arms in a gesture which had as much of despair in it as of dismissal. No more, no more, he seemed to say. Disappointed whispers spread the bad news among those who had so patiently waited to be shriven. They moved apart, he exhausted, overburdened, they still replete with undisgorged gossips and scruples. How he must long for a good male sinner with lusty malevolences, or a beautiful Magdalene abandoning her wayward flesh at his word, washing his feet with her tears, wiping them with her magnificent hair. Rapunzel, Rapunzel, let down your golden hair, Helen thought. Arise my love, my dove, my beautiful one.

My soul exalts the Lord, my spirit rejoices in God, my
Saviour,

For He that is mighty hath wrought great things in me,
And holy is His name.

Outside in the sunshine the voices hymned in chorus:

> Sweet heart of Jesus,
> Fount of love and mercy,
> Today we come
> Thy blessing to implore
> Oh touch our hearts
> So cold and so ungrateful
> And make them Lord,
> Thine own for evermore.

Helen buried her face in her hands.

A pair of agitated sisters, so alike they must have been twins, rushed past her, whispering, 'We'll be late for the Stations. We'll be late for the Stations.' She followed, expecting a pair of white gloves, rabbit whiskers and a knee-high table with a bottle labelled 'Drink Me' or a cake begging 'Eat Me'. This is my Body. Who eats of this has life in me. Confused images and memories jostled for room and were cast out by the strength of the present, then brought blurringly into half focus by the recurring pain. Again from the hailer came the voice.

'Jesus falls the first time,' it said. The procession, winding from cross to cross, responded with prayers. She sat on a bench and tried to join in. An old couple beside her shared with enjoyment their flask of tea and ham sandwiches. They gossiped, darting bright looks about them, their lives welded together by time.

'Jesus meets His afflicted mother,' the voice said.

A woman leaning heavily on two crutches stood up and tried to genuflect. She tottered and regained her balance as Helen jumped futilely to save her. The old couple finished their sandwiches. The procession wound its way around her, locking her in its serpent-like curve. She gasped for air, caught in a boa constrictor of grief, remembering and lamenting the death of the son of God. The statue of the Virgin lifted a face of pudding-like serenity. Helen stared at it, reflecting on its prototype, the white goddess, the all-wise, all-seeing, merciful Mother of God, the ambitious Jewish girl who dreamed of a new world and saw her dream transformed and taken out of her hands. Somewhere, perhaps in exile, perhaps with a community of women who still shared her vision, she died, alienated and disillusioned. Did someone diagnose her condition, prescribe sedatives for her despair? Did some expert explain away her grief?

'It's not usual in a virgin,' the gynaecologist had said to Helen. 'Cancer of that sort is more common in married women. But it does happen. And we can treat it. I think we have got it in time.'

She was assaulted, vanquished by terror. Her hands shook as she sipped the water he gave her to drink. It tasted bitter. Vinegar and gall, she said, and he looked uncomprehending. He was cheerful and practical, reminding her that each day of life was valuable, that she could be killed crossing the road, that she mustn't think in terms of time left. Each day is a new day, he said. She agreed.

She had anticipated the pain but not the despair.

It was no longer possible to pray. An unrecognised ember of rebellion suddenly took fire within her and she felt, for the first time, real kinship with her sister and their dead freethinking mother.

A woman rushed past on high-heeled shoes, saying to a friend, 'I'm delighted we came, aren't you?'

So commonplace a remark should hardly make a sane woman wish to scream. Helen's mouth yearned to stretch and open wide to release newly discovered rage. She placed a hand to her lips in horror and was relieved to find them closed tight. The youth, his gluteal muscles rippling through his jeans, came by, still sticking on labels. The women allowed themselves to be selected without demur.

'I'll put you first on the list,' her gynaecologist had said. 'And quite soon. By the twenty-fifth. We'll have a look inside.'

Her face closed like a nut on its kernel, private, secret, protective. In other processions of desolation the Virgin's cousins were numbered and labelled for convenient destruction. What would she have said to that, Christ's mother, long ago, when she was a teenager, unmarried, pregnant? Did she dream of the cruelty and prejudice that would simply continue in another name, in her name, in her son's name? That effigy, that plaster-pudding-mock-up had nothing to do with her.

Helen looked around for a stone. The tarmacadam was smooth. She took off her shoe and threw it. It missed the statue by several feet and fell harmlessly to ground. No one noticed. Her body shook with relief and then laughter.

When Miriam found her she was still laughing sporadically to herself.

'You look like Mammy when you laugh. I never noticed that before,' Miriam said, crunching potato crisps.

Helen was grateful, remembering her sister's screwy, puckish face and the demonic giggles she indulged in to relieve what she called life's tawdry untruths. She could be told. She would help.

The statue was reversed back into its sanctum with little ceremony and forgotten. The bearers dispersed for refreshment. The day died.

On the train the boys resumed their ribald songs. Miriam chewed and blew bubble gum. Helen took two painkillers and dozed peacefully.

The Fortress

The castle is still there at the end of the road. It was a watchtower for the monks who could see over the harbour. When the enemy boats were spotted they ran down the secret tunnel which connected the church with the tower and had time to hide their precious treasures and manuscripts. They weren't always in time of course, nor were they even always alert. But at least the old church still stands, its copper spire a monument to their industry, and the castle tower is a reminder of their good intentions.

For the little girl who was ill in the upstairs bedroom across the road it was a magic finger pointing to the lazy, hanging moon. It was a fortress silhouetted against ragged clouds, withstanding all storm, all threat of disaster. Although she did not know it at the time, its outline was to be forever etched into her memory, to be recalled as a sort of talisman and used in moments of stress, especially in moments of despair. At night time when she couldn't sleep, and out of a mature pity didn't want to waken her mother, she found comfort just in looking at it. The castle hadn't known darkness since the first streetlamp was erected alongside it. On blue winter nights the frosty moon illumined it, making the streetlamp's glow pallid by comparison. But on rainy November evenings or slate grey February nights the little girl smiled to see the ruggedness made soft by artificial light. She had learned from experience that the pain behind her ribs grew worse when she thought about it, and lying on her good side didn't always help her distressed breathing. So she stared at the castle, examining every pock mark and cleavage in its structure until her eyes were sore and they closed and she fell asleep.

There were nights when she was afraid to sleep because of her dreams. Her terror at times drove her to waken her mother, who would patiently soothe her and tell her it was the fever that made her dream so terrible. Once she dreamed that the side where the pain was had burst open and was pouring blood, and when she opened her eyes her hand was clutching her flesh and it was wet and sticky. She waited for death to come, in whatever form it might take, so sure of its coming that she did not say as she did at other times, Oh God oh God, let me live until tomorrow and I'll be good. I'll be a nun, I'll sing hymns all day. I'll say a hundred aspirations for the holy souls, I'll make sacrifices. It must have been five minutes before she realised the wet stickiness was only perspiration. A little sheepishly, the following morning, she said a few aspirations, did without sugar in her tea, and put the nun business on the long finger. The hymns were not a sacrifice at all for she loved singing, but she was afraid some of the neighbours might hear her and call her a little angel and other nauseating things which would make her brothers and sisters tease her, and her mother might look at her fearfully as she had done once, when the missioner had called her that. It was unfair to have had the sort of ill health which gave her waxen skin and blue-veined hands to match pale hair, like the holy pictures they got at school on the first Friday of each month. It was cruel to have a raging temper and a fierce independence shackled to such frailty of flesh. So she did all she could to disabuse her family and friends of their ideas by joining in the rough and tumble of family life. The greatest compliment of her life had come from her father who one day affectionately ruffled her hair and called her his little tomboy. But that was months ago and she might never again earn such praise.

The thought was painful and had to be quickly pushed back where it didn't obtrude. She listened instead for the sound of her mother working in the kitchen. Sometimes the door was closed – she knew by the softening of familiar noises, the lid of the range being lifted, the coal bucket rattling as it was put down, saucepans being moved around. It made her feel lonely and isolated, all the more so since she was afraid to call in case she became breathless. She hoarded oxygen without being aware of it, knowing only the panic brought on by a suddenly depleted supply.

There was no timepiece in the room so she marked the passing of the hours by the routine of the street. The factory workers wheeled by at ten minutes to eight every morning.

On wet mornings the swish of their bicycles was like an ebbing tide. Their thin faces so grey in the winter light were a reproach to her comfort. Whenever she grew pettish at her confinement, her mother would remind her of the poor who had to work in spite of their own ill health, of the children who had no mothers to nurse them, of the people who were being bombed out of their homes in England that very day. Such tragedies were no longer remote accidents in an adult world. Her own pain and weakness made her part of them. When her brothers and sisters came bursting in the front door from school, coats, football boots, camogie sticks clattering into the cloakroom under the stairs, she felt so far removed from them that she had scarcely a twinge of envy. And though at times she longed for their company, their energy so exhausted her that she was glad when they were bored and left her after a few minutes.

Downstairs behind the closed kitchen door her mother winced at the clatter of the coal bucket as it slipped to the floor. She reached to the mantelpiece for her cigarettes, then sat smoking peacefully, thankfully relaxing with each inhalation. She looked at her legs now, propped up before her on a kitchen chair. As if they belonged to someone else. It made her smile to think it. The way they ached was her proof of ownership. It was good to sit down. She looked at the door, then up at the ceiling, visualising the anxiety of the child upstairs, yet for both their sakes needing this respite.

It would be heaven to have a week of sitting up in bed.

Her varicose veins might finally stop hurting. I must get a new elastic stocking. But they're so expensive. I really can't afford it. It will just have to wait. She had ten minutes before peeling the potatoes and slicing the onions. Her husband didn't like onions. They gave him wind. Peas gave him wind too. They made him fart, he said. She thought the word fart deliberately, daring her mind to recoil from it. He used it sometimes to tease her, because he knew it offended her. Ooooh. You're very refined, he'd mock, irritated, but proud because it was true. She smiled tenderly, thinking of him, his warmth, his zest, his jokes, his affection. His eyes filled with tears sometimes when he looked at their pale little daughter upstairs. Are you sure she'll be all right? Did you see her hands? Her legs? Sure there's nothing in her at all. Is that fella doing his job properly? Is he a quack or what? Anxiety made him unreasonable, so that she had to be twice as calm, twice as tolerant. She'll be all right, you'll see. It will take time, but she'll come. Her words were sparse, each one expressing its precise meaning, whereas he used words with lush extravagance, rolling them off his tongue, relishing the embroidery they added to his thought. She envied him his verbosity sometimes, because she felt traitorously that if she had such words within her control she would make better use of them.

Voices in the hall startled her. There were sounds of reassurance mingled with the hollow tones of someone in distress. She heard her husband groan her name and sat staring at the door, unable to bear the thought of a new crisis while her cigarette burned its way into the table. When the door opened and her husband, grey-faced and sweating, collapsed from the arms of his companion into a chair, her first reaction was not of pity but of anger. Then there were things to do. It was time for action, not for feeling. The onions were unsliced, the potatoes unpeeled, but he was in bed, the doctor was there, and he had double pneumonia and it was better to call the priest and have him anointed. Of course, she said bitterly to herself, he had to go laying wreaths on Republican graves in the pouring rain, and he with a cold on him. Much good it did him or me. Self-pity welled within her, smothering her anger. And finally pity for him came to her and she stood looking at him, sadly shaking her head all the time, listening to the respiratory grunt as his lungs laboured for life. She put her hand absently on the head of the little girl huddled in the bed at the window and said, 'Say a prayer for him darling' – and on her way down the stairs to meet the first of the children home from school, 'and pray for me too, God help us.' The last words were a sigh trailing over the banisters, but caught and worried over by the child.

It had all happened so quickly. The excitement, the tension, had filled the room with terror. And there he was, her father, dying there over near the door. She pulled the sheet over her head to keep out the noise of his breathing. It was the end of the world. There will be weeping and gnashing of teeth. Fire and brimstone. Terror and despair. Grief for his suffering, loneliness at the thought of the world without him made her cry for a few minutes. It was sunny outside. The castle reflected its captured warmth. There were no clouds looming, no distant crackles of thunder, no crumbling of the castle's foundations. Children called to one another in the street below. She decided to pray. Oh God, let him get well, don't let him die. Make him better. And then the ultimate sacrificial offering – I'll be a nun if you really want me to. The escape clause was an involuntary protection; even in this moment of crisis it was better not to commit oneself utterly. She was beginning to understand the ifs and buts that went with survival. Good health and happiness were purchased at a price, and the price was compromise. It was better always to hold an if in reserve or a maybe or a perhaps. But still it was a poor sacrifice that made reservations. She stared at her father's agonised face and cried, Oh God, I will be a nun, truly I will. Swallowing the if nearly choked her. She waited for miraculous relief. Miracles, she finally thought, don't happen. Surely the time had been ripe for a miracle just then. Never in her thirteen years had so much drama been packed into such a small space of time. Her own periods of near death had held no drama for her. They were just hazy occasions of whispering and subdued lighting and hovering laces. It was different now. Drama, she discovered, lay only with the audience, never with the players.

Her father groaned her mother's name. Oh Kate. His voice paralysed her so that the tears dried up. It was better to lie absolutely still. If she didn't move a muscle it might all go away and everything would be just the same as it had been. Why had she never appreciated the peace and happiness of her life before? It was nothing to be sick yourself. Lying there like a lazy lump, just feeling a bit sick, or a bit breathless, or a bit sore. With a mother to nurse you, and a father to tell you stories and make you laugh, what greater happiness was there than this? Oh, but you're a selfish thing, she abused herself. Serve you right if you're left without a father for evermore. At this she sobbed so bitterly under the blankets that she fell asleep, mercifully oblivious of the waning afternoon.

It was a strange, dreaming feeling to be awake at last in a muted world. The terror of the morning had faded with the light. She lay partially anaesthetised, aware that full consciousness could bring some pain or fear. She smelled the burning wax of the candles before she saw the flicker of shadows on the wall. Her heart thumped a little, but there was neither fear nor pain. A soft voice was murmuring a Latin prayer. Her father mumbled some responses. A young man was calling him 'My son'. It seemed ridiculous yet it was comforting. Dusk was creeping over the fields from the quayside. Like a mist it swathed the little houses and the stone walls and finally the lamp posts, until click, the lights were on again, almost ahead of schedule, a little too officious perhaps. She felt slightly cheated. After so much change in one day, a little lengthening of the no man's land of twilight would have been welcome. They hadn't put on the landing light yet. Downstairs there was tea. The smell of frying bacon reached up to her. She visualised her brothers and sisters eating with their usual lusty appetites, each in his or her proper place at the table. Her eldest sister would have buttered all the bread first and left it on the plate in the centre. It wasn't really butter. Her mother mixed half margarine and half butter to make the ration go further. So she mused, her lifeline the activity of the kitchen below, impending annihilation in the room beside her. When her mother's footsteps came briskly up the stairs her pulse quickened in happy anticipation. Perhaps there might be time for a few words of conversation.

Her mother's thoughts were racing ahead. She'd have to move the child out of the room. In with the girls of course. They wouldn't like it. They'd have to put up with it. One good thing, the doctor said she could skip the 2 AM medicine from now on. She was improving after all. And now this other upset. Why did he have to do it? Obstinate, of course. Knew the risks he took with his bad lungs, and yet he took them. And then she had to carry the burden. He was like a naughty child beyond the reach of chastisement. She felt fury and frustration mingle with exhaustion. She willed herself to unclench her teeth, to soften the hard set of her mouth. The smile she gave the priest was polite habit.

'Don't worry,' he said. 'I'm sure he'll be all right. God is good.'

'Ah sure, I suppose you're right,' she said, a slight tinge of cynicism betraying itself. Instantly she regretted the doubting phrase. She should have said, as her neighbours would have done. 'Of course you're right, Father. I know that. God is good and His holy will be done.' He was only trying to help her and comfort her, and there was no help in the world for her. It wasn't his fault. Poor young man. She chatted politely to him, escorting him to the front door, to make up for her lapse. It was necessary to steel herself to mount the stairs again. She recalled with envy the one-storey thatched house in Co. Clare, where she had been born. Remembering the great widening out of the Shannon Estuary, where river and ocean became one, made her eyes mist over with loneliness. She wished as she reached the top step that she had never married, had never borne children. She wished that she was a little girl again, rounding up the shorthorn cows with her mother on a summer's evening, sitting on the stool and milking them in the paddock next the house, intoxicated with the scent of honeysuckle and elder flower.

The room smelled of brandy and disinfectant. The little girl watched her mother move to her father's bed. It pleased her to see the tender confidence with which she felt the sick man's forehead, and then his wrist where the pulse could be counted. Her mother knew everything. She was better than any doctor or priest. She could cure him if anyone could. The girl remembered with pain all the times she had disobeyed or ignored the wishes of her mother. She promised, this time without reservation, that never again would she be so ungrateful. She moved uncomplainingly into her sisters' room and paid no heed to their grumbles.

Yet theirs was not the only home to know sickness. It frightened her when she understood that in other innocent-looking houses there was also enacted the same sort of drama. Behind subdued doors and immaculate curtains the struggle to survive went on. Even in their own street the tentacles of disease had reached out to another and clasped in their suffocating embrace an only daughter. This pale girl, now nineteen years old, had to bear the added affliction of an hysterical mother. To that woman sickness was an abomination, a revenge by God on the wickedness of the world, a visitation on the innocent for the wrong-doings of others. Not only did she bewail the humiliation which such corruption had brought to her home, but she acclaimed her lack of responsibility for such suffering to all who called on her. For the poor, dying girl there was constant exhortation to get well, to walk, to exercise her limbs and thereby exorcise the demon disease. She did not know the kindness of gentle hands, of soothing words, of coaxing and reassurance – did not know it, that is, until the little girl's mother and two sisters called to see her and were aghast at what they found.

Late in the night the child listened as the two girls relived for one another the evening's visit. A new uneasiness crept into her. The unshakable strength of motherhood was not universal. If not universal, then could not her own mother be fallible? She did a quick mental resume of the various crises in her family life and was reassured when she could find not one instance of a failure to cope. Yet how could it be her good luck to have been born to her parents and Pauline's bad luck to have been the daughter of such an irrational mother and timid, fearful father? Was it chance or providence or divine intervention? Or was the seed of strength sown in everyone and nurtured only by some? Was there a moment in everyone's life when the seed was neglected and began imperceptibly to perish? All during the next few weeks she puzzled and pondered without being able to put her thoughts into words. Instead, she watched with a blazing intensity every action of her mother's and listened avidly to every word. Sometimes in despair, she fancied there was an imminent break-down in the sigh 'God help us' which her mother let fall now and again. Yet the proof was there. Her father grew better and stronger and there came a day in summer when she herself was able to totter out of bed on her two sticks of legs and laugh at the comical sight she made in the long mirror. It was the turning point. From then on, her progress had to be upward. A few steps around the room at first and some day she would be up for tea.

Her mother noted abstractedly the returning energy to the wasted muscles. Her husband had bounced back to full vigour, hardly even chastened by his experience. The routine of the house was almost back to normal. The end-of-term exams would soon be over, and then there would be holidays. The long, long winter was over, the cold wet spring had faded. There was no need to light the fire every day. The summer sun penetrated even the damp old walls of the kitchen and left its warmth behind. Her antirrhinums and sweet williams were blooming. She would pick a few and bring them to Pauline tonight. She felt cold at the thought of the visit. She hated the sickly odour in the girl's room and recoiled from the touch of those clammy white hands. And no doubt Mrs Carter would be weeping as usual. But it had to be done. Somebody had to ease out the last days of that girl. It exasperated her when Mrs Carter justified her own inefficiency by saying mournfully, 'Of course, you country women are stronger than we are. You were reared tougher.' Her husband snorted disparagingly when she reported this to him. 'Don't mind that old besom,' he said. 'Reared in the back streets of town. *She* should know about toughness. Marrying a bank clerk gave her fancy ideas and addled her brains a little more. Why do you have to go there at all? You're only upsetting yourself.' 'I've got to do it,' she said. 'The creature. If you but saw her. You'd pity her too. Maybe it's my thanks to God that our own are all right.'

And maybe it was. Whatever the reason, plain pity or her practical nature seeing something to be done and doing it without fuss, every evening she spent a couple of hours with Pauline. She would dab Cologne water on her forehead and press a little sweet tea between her lips. Mrs Carter would come in, sighing heavily, to throw holy water in great splashes on the bed, and then she sat in the kitchen, rocking to and fro, mumbling aspirations all the time. Her daughter showed no interest whatever in her presence, sensing perhaps that there was no help to be got in that quarter. Instead she followed with her two brown eyes, made luminous now by her disease, the slightest movement of her visitor.

When she died, the last bubble of oxygen squeezed through her raddled lungs, that practical efficient woman wept on her husband's shoulder out of pity, out of exhaustion, and out of relief.

He used the traditional clichés to comfort her. 'She's better off now. It was a happy release.'

'I wonder,' she said.

The day of the funeral was hot. An expensive mahogany coffin had been brought from Magees. In it lay Pauline, more cossetted in death than she had ever been in life, resting in white padded silk, dressed in her blue Child of Mary gown, and her long black hair, dull as old bog soil, was brushed carefully down each side of her expressionless lace. Her bony fingers were clasped in artificial embrace of the crucifix. People came all morning to kneel and look and pray and whisper 'Doesn't she look beautiful? Ah sure, God help us.' 'And God help the poor mother.' And they moved out again quickly into the sweet, open air. The hay was being saved in McDonald's field behind the castle. Its perfume, drifting across the street, was inhaled thankfully by the mourners. The little girl in the upstairs window opposite smiled to herself as she watched Jimmy McDonald and his son tramming the hay deftly. She'd miss the rides in the hay slides this year, but next year, oh next year, she'd make up for it all. She noticed young Jamesy topping off the last wynd with his feet and holding the twine between the two prongs of the fork while his father below tied the ends to a tuft of hay and pushed them well in underneath the wynd. They were rushing to the funeral too.

Her younger brother had to stay at home to keep her company. Their mother didn't approve of children at funerals. Soon enough they would be harrowed, she said. She didn't much like the custom the school children kept of calling in to the 'dead' houses on their way home from school, to pay their respects. And giggle and whisper excitedly too. However, she accepted it as a tradition of the place and was too well mannered to voice her objection.

The little boy came grumbling up the stairs as the front door shut with a click. He loved the horses kept by Magees for funerals, and was sometimes allowed to exercise them. 'I'm going to miss them bowing their heads passing the cathedral. And it's all your fault. You're an old baba. Why couldn't you mind yourself? You're older than I am,' he was raging.

She couldn't blame him. She wouldn't blame herself either. 'It's not my fault I'm sick.'

'Ah shut up, you,' he scowled. 'And you can tell Mammy I said shut up, I don't care. I'm sick of you, old pet. Always spoiling everything.'

She was delighted. It was great to be abused again. She was better. 'You can catch them at the shop,' she said. 'I won't let on. Mammy won't know which or whether.'

He was mollified, but just said, 'I'll see. I mightn't bother.'

They leaned out the window. The blinds were drawn in the houses. Some of the old cottages had black blinds especially for funerals. The horses were standing quietly waiting. The first four pulled the hearse. 'Jet and Midnight. Ebony and Satin,' her brother breathed their names ecstatically. 'I helped groom them this morning. Oh boy, look at the shine on them. And they're wearing the plumes too.' They were beautiful all right. Black as ebony, sleek as satin, shifting only a little in the heat. Pat Hayes was coachman. His yellow, wrinkled face took on dignity under his black, tall hat, his hands on the reins telling the horses he was boss and to behave themselves. There were two coaches behind for relatives and close friends, pulled by two slightly substandard blacks also bedecked with plumes. No doubt about it, her father always said, but Magees had the best funeral turnout in town.

A shifting movement cut across their admiration. The mahogany coffin was carried out of the house on the shoulders of Pauline's four brothers. It slid into the glass-sided hearse quickly. Then the wreaths and bouquets of flowers were placed on top of the coffin so that only the brass handles at the side and the panels below were visible under their gay colours. The door was closed, the four brothers lined up behind, the men friends of the family moved into position behind them, each one impressed by the solemnity of the occasion. At an old person's funeral people could talk or even smile, recounting maybe some amusing incident which had involved the newly departed. It would not have been proper or decent this time when someone cut off in the full bloom of youth was being buried. The relations piled into the coaches, among them the sad weeping father, too overcome to walk. Mrs Carter wasn't going. Everyone agreed it was best for her not to go. Pat Hayes whistled his whip lightly behind Jet and Midnight and the four moved into a steady trot, legs working miraculously in unison, heads held precisely at the same elegant angle. The coach had almost reached their window, Pat's tall hat just level with the sill, when they were stunned to hear an anguished scream echo round the silent street. Mrs Carter ran after the hearse, tearing at her hair and wailing, 'My daughter, oh my darling, little girl. Don't take her away from me. Bring her back to me. O great God, have pity on me.' Her grief was terrible to behold, her inability to restrain it an awful sight. The two children saw their mother run to comfort her and finally lead her back to her empty house. As the funeral moved towards the end of the street, the little boy burst into tears, overcome by the whole terrible enactment. But the girl herself, tight-mouthed, bright-eyed, stared woodenly ahead, without a word. 'Oh but you're very hard,' he burst out at her and sobbed afresh.

She could not explain to him, then or ever, for she was too ashamed, the hatred and disdain that burned away her pity at that moment. If she had words for it, she might have said why had the wretched woman not used the energy she now expended on grief when it would have been of some help to her daughter. It was too late now. It was too terribly late. She closed the window and said, 'I'm going back to bed.' He was enraged by such callousness. He could hardly believe it. He stared at her, mouth open, eyes still wet. She refused to look at him. He started to cry, 'You – you're –' when she sat bolt upright and said bitterly, 'Go away.' And he went.

Next afternoon as she sat gazing unseeingly at the castle, her mother came to do some mending by her bed. 'You've grown a couple of inches since you were laid up. I'll have to let down your clothes or you won't be decent.'

The child examined the face intent on sewing. Signs of crumbling courage ought to show. But there were none. Her serenity was still unravaged. She was like the castle, indestructible. Maybe her hair was a little paler. Perhaps her eyes were a small bit less blue – as if they were fading. The way the blue forget-me-not faded in strong sun. It was hard to understand such strength. The girl was filled with pride and love and relief.

Her mother said absently, 'You're staring again.'

'Am I?' she said. 'I was only looking at you.'

Her mother lifted her head, caught by some change of tone in her voice. And then, 'And sure you're entitled to do that, you poor creature you,' she laughed, hugging her daughter impulsively.

They looked out the window together. The street was hot and quiet. The fields beyond the wall were deepening to late summer green, except in McDonald's field where the aftergrass would soon be making a bright carpet for the old gold of the haycocks. The Greenore train rattled across the metal bridge. They'd all be home from Gyles Quay soon, sunburned, togs and towels stiff with salt. 'You'll be able to go next year, my love,' said her mother. 'And there's salad for tea. You and I will have ours together before the others come home.'

A Life of Her Own

Aunt Brigid died many years
ago and it is painful now
to admit that I can scarcely
recall her face. It is painful,
because for a while I loved
her with the kind of abandonment given only to the
very young or the very foolish.
There was nothing of heroine
worship in my feeling. Being
in her company simply meant
being contented, happy and
safe. All year round I looked
forward to the letter which
would come in mid-June inviting me to spend the summer
holidays with her. When the

letter did arrive, it precipitated an excitement of buying and packing new clothes, which, coupled with the long journey by bus and train and bus again, was a foretaste of the joys ahead. Coming from my father's town, where even in summer the east wind was sharply penetrating, the soft moist air of Mother's home was a beauty treatment for both soul and complexion. In my home town, a nod of recognition was sufficient acknowledgement that one's father's family had for generations tilled the little fields surrounding the town. Anything more would have been flattery, false and fulsome, a sin of unforgivable deviousness. Since they prided themselves on plain speaking and truth at all times, there was no room for the small graces my mother would have deemed natural. And since I was tainted with my mother's blood, there was a constant war between the weak longings of my soul and the forged honesty of my mind.

What a relief it was to be embraced in Mother's country with joyful cries and greetings which gave recognition not only to my own stature, but to hers and the generations who had gone before her. The fact that I had travelled such a journey alone gave me added importance, and evoked the kind of admiration only the childlike could share or appreciate. Their exaggerated response was taken by me as it was meant, not a practice of deceit, but an expression of their love, and it showed their anxiety to put me at my ease, back at home, their warmth would linger with me for a few months, and I would, puppy-like, tail wagging, greet friend and stranger without discrimination, until the continued warnings that I was being effusive or insincere finally wore me down, and I became like my peers, wary, suspicious and honest. But oh, those easygoing, lackadaisical few months, like paradise now in memory – were they so wonderful, I ask myself, or has memory again betrayed me? I do not think so.

Aunt Brigid and Uncle Jack were both older than my mother and Aunt Brigid was a year or two older than Uncle Jack. Like many other brothers and sisters of their time they lived their bachelor lives in apparent contentment. Indeed, Uncle Jack had occasionally given me the impression that he disapproved of the whole idea of marriage and considered my mother had made a foolish mistake. When he asked subtle questions about my father's work, or his prospects of promotion, I had the faint notion that both my parents were being censured. He appeared to regard their departure from the land as some kind of betrayal and he expected nothing of excellence to come from their lives. He was tolerant of their mediocrity and a little contemptuous, but never openly critical. Marriage is all right in its way, he implied, just as towns were all right for people who had failed the harsh test of country living. It was not too much of a surprise, therefore, when one evening in the summer of my thirteenth birthday, as we were sitting at table finishing supper, Uncle Jack said suddenly, 'A late marriage is like an autumn of the passions.' But the tone of his voice was a shock and I knew instantly that there was something wrong.

Aunt Brigid said, 'Autumn is my favourite season.' She said it quietly but with the firmness so characteristic of her.

'It's a queer thing,' Uncle Jack commented, 'for a woman of your age to be setting up home with a stranger. Aren't you better off here with me? Have you ever wanted for anything? Haven't I always been good to you?'

'We have known Anthony all our lives,' Aunt Brigid said. 'I believe I shall be happy with him. The child is listening.'

'Let her listen,' said Uncle Jack, scowling at me. 'She might as well learn now as later what a fool you are making of yourself. She can be witness that I warned you, when you come running back to me for comfort in six months' time.'

'I will not do that, Jack,' Aunt Brigid said. 'I will not look for comfort from you. And the child is young.'

'Not too young to learn the ways of the world,' Uncle Jack answered. 'I suppose you'll say now that you had no comfort with me.'

'I am not looking for comfort,' Aunt Brigid said. 'I have never lacked it, but it's a thing I can do without.'

'Don't tell me it's love you're after, or some such nonsense. I thought you had more sense.'

'Then you thought wrong,' Aunt Brigid said, and took my hand and guided me to the door. 'Go and see if you can find where that old hen is laying out. I'll follow you in a minute.'

She did not follow me for a long time, but I knew better than to go looking for her. I was missing all the delight of their conversation, exhilarating words and ideas I would never hear at home, but Uncle Jack's face was redder than usual and I was a little afraid that Aunt Brigid's calmness might not withstand his new anger. It was bad enough having to watch his expression change so horrifyingly. It would have been worse to be in at the death of their once thought indestructible love. Part of the pleasure of holidaying with them had been the sureness and security of their lives, the smoothness of their companionship, the predictability of their conversation. Listening to them just now had given me a peculiar pain in my stomach, yet what strange and terrible things I might have discovered if I could have been a fly on the wall. I waited, sitting on the flat stone beside the lake, reaching out with a stick for a water lily, knowing that it would wither almost instantly if I cut the long rubbery stalk, and thinking that I might just take the chance.

When Aunt Brigid found me I managed to let her know, by being very polite, that I felt aggrieved and neglected, she laughed and said, 'Well then I apologise. But there were things to be sorted out and better for you not to be there.' I longed to ask her why she wished to marry Anthony, who although pleasant and good humoured did not seem to have any of Uncle Jack's good qualities. He never, for instance, told jokes, carried glasses of water on his head, rode facing tailwards on the donkey or laughed with the great roistering, stomach-aching merriment of Uncle Jack. And if it was romance she was after, she might have picked someone really dashing, like the new sergeant, or even the new Protestant minister, who wore his pallor as if it were the result of excess spirituality and not the product of Mrs Anderson's dyspeptic cooking.

'You must understand,' Aunt Brigid said, 'that I have no life of my own with your uncle. The farm is his, the house is his. If he should marry, what would become of me? Can you imagine me a governess in Spain for instance, or house-keeper to a parish priest?' Such confidences were entrancing and I tried to look wise and reflective. 'You must promise me,' Aunt Brigid went on, 'that you will work hard at school and get yourself a profession. Don't let them give all the edu-cation to your brothers.' The conversation was gaining all the hallmarks of adult talk, boringly interspersed with good advice, and I stretched my arms restlessly, showing my dis-interest. She caught me roughly and said, 'Promise me you will do what I say.' I promised. I hadn't much choice, held in her angry grip, transfixed by desperate and pleading eyes. It was a relief when we went into the house and a greater relief when we never again touched on the subject.

I was back at school when the wedding took place. The photographs were good. Aunt Brigid looked beautiful and Anthony looked dignified and assured. Gazing at her image with an arm coyly tucked into his, I felt a sense of loss, espe-cially when I saw, to one side of the picture, Uncle Jack's face, forlorn and resigned. A shadow of disenchantment touched my thoughts but I dismissed it quickly. It was too soon to destroy that dream.

Next summer, my brother Tommy was included in the invitation. He was to go to Uncle Jack's house where a paid housekeeper had replaced Aunt Brigid. I was to stay in Aunt Brigid's new home. There was no point in protesting. The situation had obviously changed. Tommy spoiled the train journey with his kicking feet and uncouth behaviour. I spent the time feeling embarrassed and apologising for him. He aroused in me a passion of resentment I had never before experienced. He was ten and I almost fourteen but an aeon of civilisation separated us. The bus journey was no improvement. He was a bad traveller and was sick most of the time, spewing out of the window with an abandonment totally in character. I ministered to him from a safe distance but could not avoid some pollution. 'Poor little lad,' a passenger said. 'But aren't you the lucky fellow to have such a good woman to look after you.' Instinctively I resisted the role being thrust upon me. At his age, I reflected, I travelled by myself. I would not allow myself to be his mother figure or wife figure or whatever a 'good woman' should be. But the pain of mustering a polite smile to cover my spleen was almost unbearable. To have to carry the wretched boy into my territory was one thing, to watch him infect the beautiful landscape with the outpourings of his greedy, chocolate-filled stomach was another, but to have to grin at the banalities of his sympathisers was the ultimate in suffering.

Each year Uncle Jack used to wait for the bus at Poll Gorm, the lake which bordered the road before it twisted into town. We could then take the back road behind the mountain and every step of the half mile was a delight to be cherished for months afterwards. The recognition of familiar beloved objects was a pleasure bordering on ecstasy.

The Angel's Foot was an imprint on rock, a producer of miracles like a square of chocolate, an apple, a gelatine doll, and later a book or a box of paints. The game had ended by the time I was ten but it was still wonderful to recall it. Then there was the Mass Rock where the priests of old had held their services, and the Lookout Rock where the watcher guarded against the priest hunters. In the dim light I would look for the fern-covered stones which were monuments to the famine dead and I would stare at the little wood, shrouded in dusk, which hid the ruined houses of a small community obliterated by the famine as cruelly as the old towns of Europe were destroyed by earthquake or volcanic eruption. I would gaze at the hills, navy blue in the evening light, and run to greet Aunt Brigid, standing at the gate waiting. I can remember it now, the tangy smell of heather, the faint aroma of herbs and wild flowers mixed with the smell of peat and the smoke from the chimney. Always at that first greeting I would feel part of the past, part of the very earth, sharing the first ecstatic moment of creation when each living thing, plant or animal, had knowledge of its own existence.

Now all was changed. Even while I pressed my nose against the steamed-up window, I knew there would be no figure standing, pipe in mouth, Rex the sheepdog at his heels. There would be no joyful recognition, no exchange of news with the driver and conductor. Yet the disappointment when I was proved right was greater than I could bear and the tears began to pour down my cheeks. By the time the bus reached town I was sobbing openly. At the hotel, the bus stopped and Tommy, who was frightened and beginning to whimper, helped me off. Aunt Brigid was there, warm, comforting and loving, and when she wrapped her arms around me I cried louder and more despairingly than ever. 'The poor child,' she said, 'she's exhausted. What kind of fellow are you, Tommy, to let your sister get into such a state?' Poor Tommy could only mutter in his defence that he had been very sick, but Aunt Brigid pushed him aside. 'My pet. My poor little lamb. You're all right now. Tommy can stay with us for the night and your Uncle Anthony will bring him out to Uncle Jack first thing in the morning.'

It was stupid to have cried. I wiped my eyes and looked at her. She was vaguely different, I could not tell how exactly, and I did not care to analyse anything at that moment. I was, after all, exhausted. It was a relief to climb into the trap and be driven along the twilight roads to Anthony's place. The rhododendrons marched up the avenue ahead of us and exotic evergreen trees loomed darkly behind them. Their beauty was extraordinary but I could only dream of rolling heathery hills and bog lakes. I sat in their kitchen, drinking hot chocolate and swallowing my pain. Anthony was kind and concerned. Aunt Brigid tucked me into bed with a hot water bottle, kissing me as if I were an infant, and when she left the room I cried again until the pillow was saturated and I fell asleep.

The first days were spent exploring. Aunt Brigid showed pride in her new home, which it certainly merited. No one could deny the graciousness of the house or ignore the care and thought that had gone into the planting of the gardens. But it might have been any place in Ireland or indeed in the world, and that was its flaw. There were no plaintive memories, no famine ghosts to tap their fingers on the window panes at night. There were gun dogs and hunting trophies and all the paraphernalia of a man for whom farming was only a part-time occupation, and who could happily leave that to his workmen. Aunt Brigid had insisted on keeping control of the poultry. Collecting the eggs with her in the morning I hoped that perhaps all was not lost, and she seemed eager to continue the deception. She went out of her way to show me nooks and corners, places where Anthony had played as a boy. But there were too many alien touches for my liking, little tombstones for favourite dogs or cats, an elaborate monument to a dead hunter with an appropriate epitaph. The herb gardens were planted in patterns and were separated from their common cousins, the vegetables. Protestant order, I thought bitterly and Anglo-Saxon sentiment, for I was at the age for prejudice and I longed for the sight of a tall cabbage head, elegantly gone to seed, or a row of last year's turnips left in some neglected corner, their pitted skulls evoking memories and prompting strange thoughts of death and immortality.

Alter a few days when all possibility of excitement or adventure had faded I decided to visit Tommy. I cycled the five miles. Even now I can recall the twinge in my stomach when I approached the house and saw Tommy sitting, idly dangling his feet off the verandah. He looked miserable.

'There's nothing to do here,' he complained. 'I wish I was at home. Uncle Jack never talks to me, he never eats properly and the food is horrible.'

'You're too greedy,' I said. 'It won't hurt you to starve a bit.' But I did feel sorry for him and a little anxious. Perhaps he was not being fed.

I found Uncle Jack in the tool shed. I said, 'Hello, Uncle Jack,' forcing a cheerful lightness into my voice.

'Hello yourself,' he replied, without turning around. 'You're getting very high and mighty in yourself. I suppose staying in their fancy house is giving you notions.' It was too silly an accusation to answer. 'Your brother's not much company,' he said, 'always snivelling about something.'

I examined him. His bent head was greyer. He looked up at me, the slashers he had been sharpening still in his hand.

He was thin and lined and his skin was blotchy and his eyes looked sore. 'Are you managing all right?' I asked.

'You young hussy,' he snarled. 'Managing? What the hell do you think I am?'

I almost said I think you're a cranky old man.

'When is that baby due?' he asked. What baby? What did he mean? He stared scornfully at me. 'Don't you know she's pregnant? Anyone with half an eye could see that. Living in towns you learn nothing. You know nothing about anything and you think you know everything.' I began to understand the vague difference in Aunt Brigid. His stare became malicious. 'Remember, since you will soon be a woman, that in men desire begets love, in women love begets desire.'

I was afraid of him then and I stood looking at my feet, waiting for him to destroy me utterly. When he said nothing more I wanted to comfort him, I don't know why. Pity perhaps, or gratitude for withholding his dreadful adult knowledge. 'If you like I'll stay with you and let Tommy go to Aunt Brigid.'

He was indifferent. 'Please yourself.'

I was not deterred. I was filled with missionary zeal. My presence would renew the old life, I would be a miracle worker, touching the dead memories and resurrecting them. Everything would be restored to former glory.

If Aunt Brigid felt surprise she did not show it. 'Whatever you like dear,' she said, which was something better than 'Please yourself.' After her first demonstration of affection she had gradually slipped back into her routine of caring for Anthony. It seemed to me that she was unnecessarily attentive, even – although I hardly dared think it – a little maudlin. And Anthony was ridiculously complacent. I had a mixture of regret and guilt leaving her, regret because of my own involvement in betrayal, guilt because although I knew it was wrong of me I could not bear to look at her. Irresistibly my eyes were drawn to the bump of her pregnancy and I heard again Uncle Jack's sour tainted words. His use of the word 'desire' had a suggestion of sinfulness about it, an aura of distasteful secretiveness, associated with the dark whispers of the confessional. Somewhere there was an enemy to be faced, but not just yet.

I moved back into my own room with pleasure. I awoke the first morning, happy. There were no sounds in the house. Outside, the calves bawled to be fed. I dressed and went to the kitchen. The range was blackly unlit. One empty mug with the dregs of cold tea stood on the table beside the bread board which had a portion of stale loaf on it. There was a taint of sour milk and damp. When I opened the kitchen cupboard it exuded a smell of musty flour and the rancid odour of resident mice. Annie would come later on her swollen legs, to light the fire and prepare the midday meal, but that was obviously the extent of her duties. I wandered through the other rooms. The breakfast room had the ashes of last night's fire and the dust lay thick on mantelpiece and table. Uncle Jack used it as a sitting room.

The table was littered with books. He was reading *Gulliver's Travels*, I saw with surprise. Book IV, which I had never known existed, lay open. I read a passage about female Yahoos. I was revolted by their beastliness and flung the book on the floor and ran out. All through the day the memory of the paragraph stayed with me and I could no more look at Uncle Jack than I could look at Aunt Brigid. At lunchtime he picked at the food which Annie had thrown on the table. I was appalled by her slovenly habits and could hardly eat the meal myself, but I was too young to interfere and not confident enough to remonstrate with her. I might be called a young hussy again. But I *had* to make a start on my miracle working. At four o'clock I brought him a flask of tea and some scones I had baked. 'You're very kind,' he said distantly.

It was one of those chilly, misty days, neither summer not winter, neither spring nor autumn, but a hotch-potch of the worst of all seasons, not quite cold enough for the self-indulgence of an afternoon by the fire and not quite wet enough for waterproof and boots. One spent the whole day waiting for it to make up its mind and one went in bed frustrated at the wastage. I had not then the determination to live through all weathers, ignoring their uncertainties, and I felt miserable.

'I wish I were dead,' I said, perhaps out of bravado, perhaps because for a brief moment I did wish it.

'That's a good wish,' Uncle Jack said. 'There is reason to that wish. I'll quote something to you now if you have patience enough to listen.' He measured out the words slowly to me so that the weight of each one might not be diminished by a fraction. He quoted as if he saw the punctuation marks in his mind's eye, the position of each word on the page where he had read them, or as if he had written them himself.

'"Although reason were intended by Providence to govern our passions, yet it seems that by two points of the greatest moment to the being and continuance of the world, God hath intended our passions to prevail over our reason. The first is the propagation of the species, since no wise man ever married from the dictates of reason. The other is the love of life, which from dictates of reason, every man would despise, and wish at an end or that it never had a beginning."' Years later I recognised the passage in the works of Jonathan Swift, but on that day I saw no connection between Uncle Jack and the melancholy Dean. All I knew was the futility of reforming zeal, the hypocrisy of miracles. If a man wished to destroy himself, no one could stop him. My pity was replaced by anger and impatience. His anger, I thought, was not honest wrath. It was despair and self-pity. Aunt Brigid had left him. So what? He didn't own her. I had no time for adult folly.

For the following ten days I stayed obstinately with him. We were like two boxers, lurking in our corners, coming out now and again, he to jab, I to retreat. He despised everything, food, life and all humanity. I kept saying to myself, 'Let him, it's his own fault,' and I began to build a steel wall of indifference for myself. Sometimes at night when I heard him groan from his room, it was harder to be indifferent, but I managed.

'Oh, you're like her,' he said to me one day. 'That cold look.'

Another day he said, 'The young are cruel. I hope you will be old some day.'

'If I am,' I boasted, 'I will not be sour and cranky. I'll kill myself first.'

'It's not so easy to die,' he said. I felt cruel then. If you want to die, I thought, get on with it. Go and find yourself a corner, like the old donkeys, where you won't bother anyone. But it was agony to be cruel, more pain than I could bear, and I ran away from him finally, from the house, the hills, the past, the brightness of childhood. Tommy stayed on with Aunt Brigid and Uncle Anthony because he was having a wonderful time with them and I went home.

Aunt Brigid died in childbirth. She was not young and the risks were greater in those days. Two months later Uncle Jack died. Mother said he died from malnutrition. Anthony remarried eventually and had a second family. I have met Aunt Brigid's daughter several times but I have never been back to either place. The old farm was sold and is now a health resort, which is strangely comical when you think of the hungry dead around it.

Lovers

A heavy, late-hanging chestnut, still inside its armoured car, hit Tom Conway on the nose when he lifted his head to stare at the threadbare branches above him. He rubbed his nose tenderly. Violence everywhere, he said to himself, lurking in men's hearts and even on treetops. 'There's no end to it,' he said aloud. His wife heard him, coming from the pig pen, clanking buckets.

'You're a lovely sight,' he said bitterly.

'If it's beauty you're after,'

she replied, 'you'll have to be content with yourself and the mirror.'

He watched her defiant back and nodded approvingly. 'Spunk is better than beauty,' he called after her. Her shoulders shrugged in mock contempt. She hadn't thought of a reply. He had her there. A late marriage was like a late autumn, full of the knowledge of recent summer and coming winter. Their words had to have fire in them to fend off old age, to substitute for youth's passion.

'Are you feeling all right?' he asked her when he followed her to the kitchen. 'Any tea in the pot?'

'Yes,' she said. 'No.'

'Are you making any?'

'For you I'll make it.'

There's beauty, he thought. 'Have some yourself,' he said.

'I haven't time to be sitting down gossiping.' Her voice was tart.

He pondered over it for a moment. 'Are you sure you are feeling all right?'

'I said yes.'

'Yes isn't enough.'

'It will do for now. There's cow dung on your nose.'

'That was a chestnut.'

'That's new,' she said mockingly, 'chestnuts wearing cow dung.'

'I don't know about it being new,' he said. 'Everyone wears cow dung nowadays. Didn't you know? The most plentiful product in Ireland. During the last war they made cigarettes out of it, so who knows? Perhaps it will be reconstituted meat soon.'

'What in God's name is that?' she asked and didn't wait for an answer. 'You're in a very talkative mood today. Did you get another bill?'

He was furious. 'You're a suspicious old hen,' he said and was satisfied to see her look guilty.

'I'll get you the tea,' she said placatingly. 'And you might like some apple cake.'

Chalk one up to me, he thought. But it didn't do to overplay his hand. Self-righteousness was all right once in a while. Twice it was teetering on precipices. Three times it was a long drop into the valley of her contempt. 'Thank you,' he said graciously, and winced from her side-long look. But she swallowed it. She knew when to swallow.

'It's November,' he said.

'Well?'

'Doesn't it make you feel lonely?' He took her silence to be agreement. 'Sunshine gone,' he continued, 'and –'

'What sunshine?' she interrupted harshly.

He took a moment to recover. 'It's the idea of sunshine then,' he attempted, feebly.

'That's good,' she said. 'I like that. An idea. That's all it ever is.'

She slopped his tea carelessly into the cup.

'You're a terrible woman,' he said sadly, not caring. 'You've no nature in you. You've no heart.'

'You knew that when you married me.'

'I did not.'

'"Annie will make a great wife",' she quoted with unexpected bitterness. '"She's no beauty, not much nature, but a great worker."'

'Who said that?' he asked indignantly.

'The parish pulpit kisser, Donnelly.'

He relaxed. 'Who'd take notice of him?'

'You said it too.'

'You know I didn't mean it.'

'Once it isn't meant, twice it's established.'

'I didn't say it twice.'

'It doesn't matter who said it, as long as it's said.'

'It matters.'

'Look,' she said fiercely. 'Once, it's a prig's opinion, twice it's godalmighty dogma.'

'You're an awful woman,' he said bewildered. 'I don't know what to do with you.'

She smiled at him.

'Finish your tea,' she said.

It was lovely to sit in the kitchen, listening to the pots simmering and sighing. It was lovely to waken on a November morning and watch the mist strangle the rising sun and the sun tear the mist into shreds. It was lovely to see her in the bed beside him. It was comforting and exciting at the same time.

'You were carrying buckets this morning,' he accused. 'You know you're not supposed to carry weights.'

'Old wives' tales,' she said scornfully.

'You've lost three already,' he said angrily.

'I can count,' she said and the words dropped like stones into the spreading silence they created. I can count. One baby, two babies, three babies. All lost around the fatal three months. And last month was a near thing. 'I cannot stay still,' she said, as near to apology as he had ever known. 'I like to be doing things. I don't take chances. I just can't coddle myself.'

'It isn't just yourself,' he reproached her.

'I know,' she sighed. 'I suppose I'm too old. We're both too old. Nature's telling me I shouldn't be having children. I'll be over sixty by the time it's reared.'

She was right. There was no answer to that. The November day began to weigh more heavily on him. 'I'll get at the potatoes or the frost will get them for me.'

'I'll help you in a minute,' she shouted after him.

'You will not,' he said. 'You'll stay there.' He almost said in the kitchen where you belong, but saved himself in time. Doing a woman's work like other women, rearing babies, tidying up, preparing his meals, being around when he wanted her. But no, out she'd be in five minutes, cap pulled down over her ears, windcheater hiding the bump of her four months' pregnancy, wellingtons covering the first varicose veins. 'Watch the chestnut tree,' she shouted after him. 'There might be another one waiting for you.'

If women were trees, she said to herself when he had gone, how handy that would be, dropping your fruit so casually. But does the earth groan and heave when it is thrusting up a young tree? That chestnut tree was a miracle growing where it did in the corner of the stony old yard. Maybe I'll have a miracle too.

The wind lifted Tom's hair as he passed the stables. The sky had cleared suddenly, swept clean of scudding clouds. He wondered briefly where they had gone, if they huddled together in some stormy corner, building up moisture, threatening already flooded fields. A stable door banged suddenly and the wind died and even more suddenly a great silence covered the farm. Beside him, the sheepdog cringed, tucking its tail between its legs. Looking back at the chestnut tree he saw that the last precarious leaves hung motionless and he had an eerie feeling of impending danger. 'Get up you fool dog,' he snarled, angry at his own weakness, and the dog whimpered and ran into a stable. At the cowhouse Tom paused, listening to the faint rustle that seemed to be giving birth to heavier soughs. A great sigh of wind came through the chinks of the stone walls and a slate rattled down from the roof over him. 'A storm,' he said, enlightened. 'A storm.'

It hit him while he latched and bolted the half-door

beside him, tearing at his coat, searing his cheeks to redness. It bludgeoned him while he staggered, gasping at its ferocity, dodging the next slate which missed decapitating him by inches. 'Christ,' he said, 'that's all I need. Slates for enemies.' The thought of battle was strangely exhilarating. He tried to yell defiantly, but his voice was sucked back into his throat, almost choking him. He turned his back and his trousers stung his legs, whipping into them like thongs. He stretched his arms out and leaning backwards yelled, 'Come on, big wind, come on, big wind. I can take you.' Vengefully the wind lashed his ears and he turned, facing into it again, arrowing his body forward to give less resistance. 'Brain against brawn,' he gasped. 'It's got to win or we might as well all lie down and give up.' His words hiccoughed back and he gasped and struggled for breath. 'Bastard wind,' he tried again. 'Bastard, no good, base born out of some rotten hole in the universe.'

Annie laughed when she saw him weaving towards the kitchen window, his eyes screwed up against the airborne debris of the yard, his fists jabbing forward against some imagined punchbag. The hosts of the air might be arrayed against him but he would take them all on. She ran to open the door and he fell in, sprawling helplessly at her feet, while she slammed the door, locking it quickly. 'It's breezy out,' she said, looking down at him. 'You were always prone to exaggeration,' he said when he had caught his breath. She helped him pull off his boots. They moved to the window and stared out at the slates hurtling from the roof and splitting and scattering across the yard.

They thought of the cattle out in the fields but knew they would find shelter in the craggy places where the hawthorn trees sprouted and linked branches, forming tunnels where the animals could lie in wild weather. Tom worried about the heifer who was due to calve and Annie voiced his thoughts.

'We should bring up the heifer. She's due soon.'

'You're right,' he said. 'She'll be safer inside.'

'I'll go with you.' She rushed to get cap and windcheater and he did not protest. He took the rope looped on the hook of the back door and slung it over his left shoulder.

They linked arms at first and then held hands as they forced themselves over the fields, leaning against the wind.

Their ears were battered by the whine and screeching around them. From the yard came the crashing of milk churns and cans sent flying from their habitual places and rolled backwards and forwards, banging against the stone walls. Annie had a strange sense of joy in their linked hands. They were two puny objects of no account to anyone, to be missed by no one if these delinquent air currents should lift them up and throw them into the estuary. The cows would be milked by their part-time helper and someone else would walk their fields and don a new armour of hope. It was a strange and fearful thing to be able to walk almost upright against this challenge. She thought how fear imprisoned hearts while courage liberated them.

Tom pointed towards the river and they watched in wonder the great heaving mass cast itself helplessly in white foam against the banks. Below it their last field of hay, saved by inches, it had seemed, during the late days of the wet summer, was now irretrievable. The hay trams, left hopefully until the field might dry out, now tumbled into the pools around them. It was painful to have to accept again that one hour could so ravage the careful toil of many days. Whatever poet talked of the slow unfolding of seasons had been no farmer, Tom thought. But then, what poet could be a farmer? They hadn't the stomach for it. Spinning words and ideas was a queer way to spend a life, and he shut off with scorn the faintly remembered poetic dreams of his youth. It was difficult to think of anything with the distraction of a hurricane tugging at his sleeves. Better perhaps to surrender, to forgo the pleasure and effort of intellect, to unload from strained muscles the burden of labour, to lean on this mad dog of a wind and let it take over. What bruises could it give him if it whirled him into its vortex and sucked him into the silence of death?

Beside him, Annie pulled restlessly. 'Hurry, hurry. I don't see her with the others.' They searched along the hedges and by the sally trees, until they found her lying in a corner of the field, neck thrust up, legs splayed out, and heard her groan loudly.

'She's started,' Annie said. 'We'll never get her up to the house.'

'She might be better here,' Tom said. 'Healthier and cleaner.'

'But it's so cold,' Annie protested. 'And what if she takes too long?'

'We'll leave her alone for a while,' Tom said. 'Let her get on with it.'

Annie suddenly put her two arms protectingly across her stomach. 'I'll go up to the house,' she said.

Her unexpected meekness alarmed him and yet he could not bring himself to ask her was she all right or offer to accompany her, but he could not resist whispering, 'Be careful,' when she left him. He shouted it aloud then when it was too late for her to hear and the shrieking wind tore his words in tatters. He watched her all the way up the sloping field, lost her when she dipped into a hollow, followed her again with his streaming eyes as she neared the farm gate. Flying slates made the yard more dangerous than the open spaces, but she was out of sight then, and he could only hope that she was safely in the house.

He crouched under the hedge away from the heifer and tucked his head into his knees. He hated wind. Its irrationality depressed him. Like a mob or a cowardly bully one never knew what to expect from it. The human skull was frail after all when it could be crushed by a casually falling tree or split by a slate. Perhaps open desert was the safest place. But they had sandstorms, clogging your nose, suffocating, burning eyes. And the sea was worse again, hands clawing for substance, an unnatural element. He smiled to himself and touched lovingly the earth at his feet. Worst of all was the rational violence of men, weapons discharged with accuracy, words and bombs and bullets all aimed to destroy and kill. For a moment he felt affection for the chaos around him, because it was irrational and without malice. He heard the heifer's bellow and lunged forward as if catapulted by the frantic appeal. She had probably been labouring for hours and was exhausted. The calf's forelegs were showing. 'Christ,' he said prayerfully as he tied the rope and began to pull.

Even in the cold the sweat oozed from his pores, trickling under his armpits, lodging freezing inside his shirt. The heifer's groans mingled with his own and with the wind so that he lived through an eternity of anguished noise, each second of effort a condensation of the labour of his whole life. Surrounded by primitive forces he was possessed of superstitious fear. If he failed in this, he failed in everything. If calf or mother died, what of his own child and its mother? 'Christ,' he said again, summoning the forces of good to his aid.

When the calf flopped on to the ground he fell beside it, panting and gulping. Then he began to clean the mucus from its mouth and nostrils, stretched its neck, forced open in mouth, pressed on its side to encourage oxygen to take root in its lungs. The air whistled around him and he cursed it and implored it to penetrate the limp animal under his hands. When it gave a little kick with its hind legs he worked harder, praying and cursing at the same time. The heifer stood up and came over to them, lowing softly. He stood back and watched while the calf moved more strongly in response to its mother's tongue. Around them the creaking hedges sieved air, loud, drunken, raucous and uncaring. He took off his coat, wrapped it around the calf and hoisted it on to his shoulders

Annie saw them as they came over the rise of the land, man, calf and cow riding the wind.

Anglo-Irish Relations

Perhaps it is envy, perhaps it is genuine sadness that makes me think of the days of my youth with a pang. *Salad Days* is how I remember them. That was the time of the musical by Julian Slade. Somewhere among my old records the bright voices are still captured – 'The Things that were Done by a Don' and 'We Said we Wouldn't Look Back'. And in the background the piano tinkling with all the fresh, green enthusiasm of youth.

All summer we played it, until it was ousted by The Goons and 'I'm Walking Backwards to to Christmas' clonk, clonk. There were parties and outings and picnics. There were occasional gala events where we dressed up and thought we were beautiful and perhaps we were. One of my friends borrowed my only evening dress to go boating on the Isis with some tipsy, newly fledged graduate from Magdalen College. She was reputed to be the daughter of a Polish count – there were hundreds of them in England after the war – but since I had actually known a genuine Polish countess whose frozen gentility was a far cry from Marietta's gay insouciance, her disguise wore thin very quickly. Not that I minded. But I did mind the loss of the only evening dress which never recovered from its adventures in the muddy depths of Oxford's most famous tributary.

There were other evenings which required no fancy dress, merely an acceptance of the enchantments of Oxford: *Twelfth Night* performed in New College Cloisters, a trip to the Bodleian with an aged uncle who had translated Pliny's letters fifty years before and always checked that his copy was catalogued, a visit to Christ Church where the same aged uncle scowled and complained if a chair had been moved or a pew damaged. He was then almost eighty years old and he endeared himself to all of us, who were only his nieces by marriage, because he was the most blatant lover of Ireland we had ever met. He used to declare that had he been an Irishman he would have been a Fenian, and he loved my grandmother when he went to visit her in Connemara because she confessed that she had been of that very persuasion in her youth. He knew G.K. Chesterton, who was at the time a passion of mine (and for that matter still is), and said he was the sloppiest eater he had ever known. Since he himself was a fastidious old man, elegantly handsome, his curl of contempt at the memory of food-slopped waistcoats was without equal. He had been at college with F.E.

Smith, later Lord Birkenhead, and told me that he was the wickedest man he had ever met. He himself was a socialist, the first socialist mayor in the Borough of Willesden, and perhaps that had something to do with it. He was Mayor at the time of the Coronation of George VI, and his account of the paper bags with sandwiches tucked under the regal robes of titular bishops and lords of the realm was hilarious. Pomp and circumstance were treated with mockery, and the lack of toilet facilities for all those aged bladders made him by turns angry and amused when he recounted the other splendours of that day. Every now and again, when I met up with prejudice because I was Irish, I was consoled to think that the most English of Englishmen loved his wife because she was Irish and shared that affection with me. If all this seems irrelevant I can shortly make clear that it is not.

And before I go further I must also make clear that I was not one of Oxford's embryo scholars. One of my great weaknesses throughout my training as a student nurse was that the smell of the theatre made me ill and when I qualified after four years, my knowledge of surgical techniques was so poor I could not assist at a simple appendectomy. The hospital in Oxford offered a year's training for nurses who wanted to specialise in surgery. I didn't want to specialise. I didn't want to spend the rest of my life behind hospital walls. But I had utopian visions of changing the whole system and to do that I had to learn as much as I could. The academic and cultural delights of Oxford were fringe benefits, about the only fringe benefits available. But they were enough for me. I was lucky, I suppose, because a young man with a motorbike who had got a second in history (considered barely acceptable by the aged uncle who had a formidable intelligence) happened to fall in love with me, or so he said. Although I treated such declarations with a healthy scepticism, I enjoyed his company and we soared across the Cotswolds on his machine, investigating Laurie Lee country and Roman remains and Norman arched churches with equal enthusiasm.

Those excursions were magnificent relief from a life which I began to think was hardly worth living. I still felt ill in the theatre, sometimes hardly able to breathe, and the instruments which everyone else took for granted had for me the appearance of medieval tools of torture. Part of my training involved learning their names and their uses so that I could reel them off with the speed, accuracy and soullessness of an abacus. Then each surgeon had his own particular likes and dislikes. The instrument had to be slapped into his hand with just the right degree of pressure so that no irritation could interfere with the great man's concentration. The fact that I was constantly irritated by the piques and foibles of great men was of no account to anyone, and after a while I began to see myself as a kind of robot, computerised to give satisfaction at all times. But my programming was faulty. The body on the table remained a real live human being, and not, as I tried to convince myself, an anonymous mound of green cloth with an aperture of flesh in the centre. And the deified person beside me was a kind of glorified plumber, a graduate of barber-school days. He could be admired for the risks he took with other people's lives, and therefore for the responsibility he had thrust upon him, but had to be judged as well by the consideration, or lack of it, which he showed to his menials, among them – and way down at the bottom of the list – myself. Once I forgot a particular Allis forceps when I was setting the trolleys for major surgery and the fuss created was almost as bad as when I dropped the radioactive gold on the floor and the theatre had to be vacated for two days. For weeks afterwards the Geiger counters were croaking in odd corners. I was quite sure I would die of leukaemia at an early age since I had got the full blast of the thing.

I certainly felt tired. The boyfriend began to complain.

'I thought you Irish girls were full of the joys of spring.'

'What do you mean, "you Irish girls"? I thought you English boys had impeccable manners,' I countered.

He laughed. 'I told you I was only a scholarship boy.'

That was the first time he had brought up the racial difference. It was almost as if he had said 'you peculiar aliens'. When I mocked him with, 'Take me to your leader,' he didn't think it funny.

'I don't think of you as foreign,' he said. 'But you are different. You don't giggle like the girls I know. And you look at me when I talk to you.'

'I think you are well worth looking at,' I teased and he actually blushed.

'Now look what you've done,' he said. 'Nobody makes me blush but you.' Our little darts of racialist repartee stayed at that level.

But then the letter bombs started, or took up where they had left off. Now and again and without warning, people's hands were blown off because they opened a package. Sometimes they were British hands, sometimes West Indian hands, sometimes even Irish hands, but they were always Irish bombs.

'Your lot are at it again,' he said once, angrily. The aged uncle never said things like that. He merely sighed and looked grim.

'I am not up for bid at auction, lot twenty-two, one average-sized Irish colleen full of queer tricks and trades with thirty bombs up her knickers,' I jeered.

'How crude,' he said reproachfully in his flattened Reading accent.

'That's the kind of response prejudice brings. One can only be crude,' I answered.

'I don't blame you,' he cried. 'You know how I feel about you. You are the first girl I ever loved.'

'What a pity I happened to be an Irish bog-trotter,' I sneered.

'What does that mean? Your background is probably much better than mine,' he said magnanimously. 'I don't feel any social difference.'

'*Oh.*' I seized on the slip. 'Being Irish pulls me down sufficiently to reach your scholarship boy level.'

'Did anyone ever tell you what a damned pompous racist you are?'

Talk about the kettle calling the pot black. I fumed for days. When the chef in the hospital pretended not to understand what he chose to call my brogue I bit his nose off.

'Brogue?' I said. 'What do you mean? Brogue means shoe. Every ignoramus, even those unversed in the subtleties of the Irish language, which is the oldest of the Indo-Europeans, knows a brogue is a shoe.'

'Oi. You speak Erse then?'

Erse my arse I said under my breath. I didn't want to go too far.

'Want some more booter then love, yerrah begorrah,' he called out.

'Not booter. Butter. B-U-T-T-E-R.'

'Oi. She means botter.'

'I don't want botter. I want butter. The stuff they make out of milk.'

'That's cream, you know, love. Don't your Irish cows make cream, then?'

How could one compete against such ignorance?

Then there was the boyfriend's special subject: history. The aged uncle asked him had he got a first and the boyfriend looked suitably scathing at so outmoded a value. When pressed he admitted he hadn't.

'I suppose a second for history is acceptable,' the aged uncle said with a pointed charity.

'From what dusty archives did you drag him?' the boyfriend asked me later. 'Methusaleh in person.'

'He is very fit. And intelligent,' I said loyally.

'When was he at Oxford?'

'In the 1890s I think. He was the same year as F.E. Smith.'

The boyfriend looked stunned.

'You look as if you didn't know whether you were shot or poisoned,' I said. 'You could learn a lot from him.'

'I learn more from you,' he said, winking lasciviously.

The aged uncle referred to him as a blurb. 'The fellow's a blurb,' he said confidentially. 'Don't know what you see in him.'

His knowledge of Irish history was certainly limited. When I sneered at the gaps, he explained that he had specialised in European history. That was before the EEC and we were a mini-continent all on our owney-oh out in the Atlantic. And of course our greatest mistake in Ireland was to have left the Empire. He waxed lyrical on the topic.

'What resources do you have? No coal, no minerals to speak of. Thousands of acres of bog. You're mad.'

'Any minerals we had you stole. You ruined our trade to protect your own. Destroyed our forests to save your own. Savaged our religious beliefs to entrench your own. Rapacious plunderers. And left a bastard culture behind you.'

'Some convent you went to. Always wondered what those nuns got up to.'

He enjoyed himself hugely during these encounters. The angrier and more vicious I got, the more he loved it and the more he swore he loved me. He had the intellectual arrogance of the newly conferred with just enough confidence to water it down to acceptable limits. Even so, he had to admit that we came out about even, mainly – though he would never admit it – because his ignorance of Irish affairs was truly abysmal. My own knowledge of European and British history was diffuse, scattered through the centuries in dilettante fashion, but I had enough ingenuity and common sense to keep myself afloat when he tried to drown me in a deluge of facts and dates. Since my education had a much broader base than his, he might confound me with detail but I confused him with generalisations thrown in with abandon. However, on my own ground of things Irish or even medical, I won hands down. He tried to isolate and condemn. I related everything to everything else.

'Facts are facts,' he would say.

'Truth is relative,' I would respond to his despair.

'You are a mere empiricist,' he would yell.

'What's a historian for God's sake? I suppose you call yourself a scientist.'

'It is a science. A most exact and precise science.'

'Second-hand news and biased reporting. That's all history can ever be.'

'What do you know about it? What have you read?'

That's when the going got tough. But I was not to be done down by lists of reading and I capped his personal bibliography with fictitious titles and authors and magnificently imaginative quotations. I quite impressed myself. I began to plan a career as a popular historian. At times I went too far. He collapsed into laughter when I used the lost vernacular.

'Say that again,' he said in mock wonder one pleasant sunny evening in the park. 'It sounds as if you're trying to spit and can't quite manage it.'

'You English are so prejudiced, so how could you possibly escape?'

'I'm British,' he corrected me. 'My mother was Welsh.'

'Being born in a stable doesn't make you a horse,' I threw back.

'Oho. Fee fie fo fum. An expert on Wellington.'

'It's useless talking to you. *Briseann an nádúr trí shúile an chait.*'

He fell on the hallowed grass in the hallowed Oxford park and had hysterics. There were some sheep droppings near by and I picked up a small handful and dropped them into his wide open mouth. People have been hanged for less. It took him two weeks to forgive me and he came ostentatiously to one of our awful hospital hops with Marietta.

'Dahling,' she said, 'he's a perfect poppet. How can you throw him over! I love him. I could eat him for dinner. He's simply adorable. And so bwilliant.'

'Does he call you Your Countessness?' I said cattily.

'Weally dahling. There's no need for that. I gave up all claims to title. You know what I suffered. Those dweadful Germans drove all that nonsense out of my head. And you know how poor I am.'

Of course I was filled with remorse and said she could have him for breakfast as well as dinner, if she liked.

'Gluttony, my dear, is a cardinal sin. We Catholics know that.'

She went to the Black Friars for Mass because it was the snob thing to do. I went blatantly to Cowley where they had bingo. If I must play the part, I should play it to the death. I repaid him by going to the Spider's Web, a dreadful dank dungeon where everyone leaped around doing Bill Haley's rock, with a classical scholar who was as bored by me as I was by him. The boyfriend glared from a corner. Marietta had found a Polish count and they were exchanging reminiscences. I smiled radiantly at the classical horror before

me as we bounded past the corner, just to prove what a marvellous time I was having. Marietta whizzed off with the
definitely suspect count and the body in the corner wilted.
My partner thought I was ready for higher things and made
noisy advances. I kneed him where it hurt and ran for the
bus stop, clutching my handbag and my virtue with equal
determination. It began to rain. Miraculously the boyfriend
appeared, complete with umbrella which he silently raised
over the two of us.

'When all fruit fails, welcome haw,' I said, and he smiled
gratefully. Marietta passed with the classical scholar, both of
them beaming. I said, 'Let them off, fine weather after them
and snow to their heels.'

He collapsed, leaning on the bus stop and laughing so
much that the tears trickled out of the corners of his eyes.
'I've missed you.'

Actually I had missed him too, and I felt it only fair to
tell him.

'Perhaps we should get married,' he said, but I knew he
was only joking and ignored it.

Our reconciliation made life bearable again. I was having
a rough time. Our theatre sister had been in the army and
brought army discipline to our overloaded routine. She even
examined our nails at morning parade. One of her boasts,
and also ours, was that there was never a case of cross-infec-
tion in our theatre. No porter was allowed inside the swing
doors, which meant we had to do the heavy lifting as well as
the skilled work. Every eight days one of us was on call for
emergencies. There was no such thing as an eight-hour shift.
On a busy day you just stayed on. It was bad luck if you got
a call at midnight after being on duty until 10PM, and I was
as susceptible to bad luck as anyone else.

I found the theatre stuffy and blamed the lack of air

for my shortness of breath. One night I had a call as I was climbing into bed. The French girl whose turn it was gave some garbled explanation about an abortion and her conscience. 'You should refuse too,' she said, 'but there's no one else around, and I always get the feeling that your religion doesn't mean as much to you as it does to me.'

'You've a bloody cheek,' I said. 'What the hell do you know about it?'

'See what I mean,' she said. 'The language you use,' and she stalked off.

There were new degrees of exhaustion, I decided, never before experienced by man. The boyfriend was off in Norway. He sent a card or letter every day with declarations of love on each one. The next time he made a proposal of marriage I would take him seriously and further the cause of Anglo-Irish relations. I'd even become a British citizen and abandon faith and motherland if I could escape from this dedicated drudgery. Fair exchange was no robbery. Not even for Kathleen Movourneen and all that would I swap life and good health. I was not the stuff of which martyrs were made. Even at twelve years old I had discovered as much about myself. Having seen a gory religious film called *The Twenty-Seven Martyrs of Japan*, amongst other equally gory films which were regularly shown to convent schoolgirls to improve our moral fibre, I decided I would be a permanent coward. If I am ever tied to a stake, I said, or thrown to the lions, I'll have to turn Protestant or Buddhist or heathen or whatever is required at the time. It was a decision I stuck to firmly, and having made up my mind to be a coward, my nightmares of being buried alive in a coffin or being kicked out of heaven because I got there too late, wearing only my vest and bedroom slippers, miraculously ceased. Cowardice has its advantages. My mother almost ruined it by saying she was sure I would get whatever strength was needed in my moment of trial. I didn't want to be strong. I wanted to be a weak, snivelling renegade living a life of ease and comfort. I assured her earnestly there was no hope for me and she gave one of her wondering sighs and said, 'The things you think of.' How could one *not* think of them with the twenty-seven martyrs of Japan groaning behind every bush. And here I was lurching into dedicated uniform after a mere two hours' rest. The time for cowardice and high treason was nigh.

The poor young woman on the trolley in the anaesthetic room was not there for an abortion but because she had had a back-street job done. The smell of infection and her cries of pain were suffocating. She was a beautiful, olive-skinned Italian girl with no English and she cried constantly *O mama mia, O mama mia, O mama mia,* before the anaesthetic delivered her. If I needed any convincing of my cowardice and gutlessness I was confirmed in it when I bawled after it was all over while I scrubbed out the theatre for two hours until even our martinet would have been satisfied. I had four hours' restless sleep before facing the day. Before breakfast I went to see how our patient was faring. She had died just half an hour earlier. I couldn't eat and went straight to theatre. It was my turn in the sterilising room and I carried the first tray of boiled instruments to the surgeon who had already started. Again there was that feeling of suffocation and I had a terrible need to cough. Out on to the newly sterilised instruments came half a pint of my own frothy bright red blood.

Even in my last extremity, as I believed it to be, the look on the surgeon's face gave me enormous satisfaction. As I fell clattering to the floor, still holding on to the tray of instruments, I prayed that some magician with a camera would appear, capture his expression for posterity and have it pasted on the theatre wall to remind him and his successors that nurses bleed too and when they do it's the same colour as anyone else's. I think I must have been hung up on prejudices – class, social, race and all the others. I retired in ignominy having messed up the antiseptic conditions for another while. It had to be someone Irish – I could imagine everyone saying – who would infect the place with the tubercle bacillus.

I prepared to meet my Maker, reminding her/him that all my intentions had been honourable and imploring him/her to make due and merciful allowances. I was put into a glass-walled room with a spyhole into the office from which I could be observed, while I cried with apparently suicidal intent for three days. They thought I was wallowing in self-pity and that it might be good therapy, but I cried for *Mama mia* and another foreigner who had died in a strange and hostile world, and who had to have a room scrubbed out after her visitation. In the end I was told I would have another haemorrhage if I didn't stop and what a lot of nonsense it was and Streptomycin, Para amino salicylic acid and I.n.a.h. would soon see me as bright as a new penny. As it turned out it wasn't quite as simple as that.

Meanwhile, back at the ranch, the boyfriend's letters and cards piled up. What with bouncing around on his motorbike through the hills and dales of merry old England I hadn't much time to get very friendly with the other nurses, though there were a few, apart from Marietta, with whom I exchanged groans over conditions of work and the sexual frustrations of nursing sisters. Eventually, after some weeks, Marietta arrived with a new young worshipper in tow, shielded her nostrils against my contamination, and deposited the parcel of mail before fleeing as if from the plague. I shouted after her, 'I'll need my evening dress any day now,' and heard her wistful 'O dahling, don't, you'll make me cwy. It's all so sad. And you're so bwave,' from the safety of the hallway. 'Your lisp is slipping,' I said bitterly. I never saw her again, or only faintly in the distance. And I'm sorry about that too. She was quite a character.

I went through the mail. There were six communications from the boyfriend in Norway and I read them in chronological order as I made out the dates on the postmarks.

The first was full of the usual chirpy nonsense about the scenery and the weather and the people. The second was more interesting. He certainly missed me. I had dug deep into him and he couldn't get me out. He would be at the enclosed address and would I please write and tell him that yes, he and I should be wed forthwith and spend our lives in bliss for evermore together. And just to prove how much he loved me he enclosed a rude doggerel of Ogden Nash's about hips being fleeting or something. The next one was slightly reproachful. He was a master of the reproachful reminder. Perhaps my reply was on the way. Had I not noticed his telephone number? Was I so impoverished I could not spend a few quid on a call about such a momentous matter? But he was certain my letter would arrive, or better still, a telegram, or better still, the phone would ring any moment now.

The fourth had a dash of malice to it. Apparently the Irish government was making perfidious statements which would encourage terrorism in England. He must have had the *Daily Telegraph* posted to him. The fifth was an angry and bitter series of accusations about treachery and disloyalty and betrayal and countries who weren't grateful when other more enlightened countries tried to do them favours, about political traditions, and historical firsts, and Magna Cartas. The aged uncle was right. The fellow was a blurb.

The last letter was a sad acceptance of the inevitable

without any reference to history or national pride. He had been a fool. He had been conned. He would know better the next time. He thanked me for giving him such a hard lesson because he was sure it would be of great benefit to him in the difficult years ahead as he made his millions because after all what was there left but money and he was ambitious and he didn't need to be saddled with encumbrances however sexy and attractive and foreign.

He little knew what an encumbrance he had just missed, I thought. Bad enough to be female, but Irish, a nurse, woweewowee, and now tubercular. All that was left was to be black. I peered hopefully into the mirror but the pink and white gleamed back at me. If I had even turned pale and interesting it would have been something. The classic tubercular complexion, one of the medics said, after tapping me all over. The haemorrhage had given me a rather neat shade of green, I thought, but it had soon passed.

I turned my face to the wall and contemplated its blankness. Every now and again a cheerful nurse would dash in, puncture my tail-end with a needleful of raw acid, ram dozens of tablets the size of half crowns down my throat plus hundreds of mini varieties and make me drink another bucketful of milk. The glass doors were left wide open to freeze out the b-b-bacillus since that was the fashion in those days. My pink and white turned to deep violet which was very apt. One of the medics remarked on my name outside my closed door in one of those clear penetrating English voices which can laser beam their way through ten-inch steel. Is it Mauve? What an odd name. Is it Oirish har har? Oh victimised nation! The butt of every joker through the uncountable class structures of English society. Some weeks later when I realised death was not as imminent as I had first imagined and I would therefore not be depending on aliens to get my foreign corpse back to the green isle of my birth, I told him, 'Maeve was a famous queen, a fact which is no mere legend, but is well authenticated historically. I am not deaf. I am not retarded. All that is wrong with me is that the muggy mists of this damp town and the insanitary conditions of your hospitals have aggravated an infection which was at one time so common in this country you managed to spread it all over the world, both to Ireland and the plains Indians and the Eskimos.' I was breathless for two days after that speech but it was worth it.

He said, 'Dear me. She not only bleeds. She talks too.'

I resigned myself to a slow and patient recovery. After the initial shock it was quite pleasant. At least one could look on the bright side of it. Perhaps it is an exaggeration to say it was pleasant, but the days of servitude were temporarily over. Perhaps permanently over. Someone else would have to take up the torch for Florrie and put up with insults and abuse in order to be of service to the sick. History offered possibilities. All one needed was nerve, imagination and plenty of bias. I didn't think about the boyfriend. My lungs felt as if they were filled with lead and when I thought of him the lead shifted over to my heart. I put him out of my mind.

The aged uncle occasionally visited me but his attitude had changed. He seemed to be saying, without putting it into words, that anyone who could allow themselves to be in such a predicament was guilty of gross negligence, not to say Catholic fecklessness. At eighty his pink and white complexion was unscarred and his round of golf every morning with occasional triumphant birdies added zest to his disturbingly springing step. Born more than half a century after him I ebbed and waned and wilted while he waxed and flowed and thrived disgustingly. Look at me, his lustrous white hair declaimed. Behold the wholesome, hard-working English gentleman, behind him centuries of order and good clean living, and fine traditions and noble, victorious wars and independent thinking and sharp, decisive intellect and glorious monarchy and the British Way of Life. Wake up and get on with it. None of this nonsense about being ill. I was never a day ill in my life.

My mother was never a day ill in her life and she lived to be ninety-nine and three hundred and sixty days. His father died at thirty but that never merited a mention. The child has no *joie de vivre,* he said to the aunt standing bewilderedly beside him. Thank you for coming, I said. But I'm sure it's too tiring for you. Please don't bother any more. Tut tut. You're not taking offence at anything I say. You know I'm just a silly old man. Take no notice, take no notice. It was good advice to someone with two lungs full of lead. I took him at his word and he went off in a huff. The British, I decided, with pleasant prejudice, are a very huffy nation. Shortly after that visit I opened the door to totter down to the bathroom and bumped into the boyfriend who was standing outside, a look of stark terror on his face and a potted plant of freesia in his hand.

'What,' I asked furiously and rhetorically, 'are you doing here? And who told you where I was?'

'Marietta.'

'Marietta,' I mimicked. 'La contessa blabbermouth. Trust her. I'm not allowed visitors. Go away immediately. I'm highly contagious. You should be wearing a mask even now.'

'The nurse said it was all right.'

'The nurse! The nurse! You know what nurses are. Would you take the word of a nurse? Menials. Peasants. Is she English or Irish?'

'Spanish, I think. Knows very little English.'

'Another of the underprivileged.' I coughed deliberately into my handkerchief and he didn't even flinch.

'I was only joking,' I said, when safely back in bed. 'I'm not infectious at all. They've tested my sputum, and I don't even have a cough.'

'I don't care if you are infectious,' he lied nobly. 'And you are more beautiful than ever. And I have been a perfect beast to you. Those terrible letters I wrote and the terrible things I said. And here you were being ill and I didn't know. Why didn't you tell me?'

'It all happened so quickly. And it's not the sort of thing one likes to boast about,' I said. 'And I feel such a failure.'

'You can't help being ill. It's nobody's fault.'

Some kind soul had given me Thomas Mann's *Magic Mountain* to read so I had other ideas.

'I think it is a wilful act of self-destruction.'

'What rubbish,' he said. 'It's just like getting a cold.'

'It's all in the mind,' I said. 'But what's the use of sulking? Here I am. I'm stuck with it. I'll just have to get on with it.'

To be fair to the boyfriend, he tried. Anyone less noble would have fled. Marietta, for instance. I could see he was a little anxious and I didn't blame him. I was a little anxious myself. Was I contaminating the air every time I exhaled? I wouldn't borrow books in case I infected the paper. I carried out as many of the aseptic practices I had learned as was humanly possible. If I had known about Howard Hughes I would have had sympathy for his fetishes. Only in this case I myself was the malignant source. Another Typhoid Mary. Thank God no one gave me Kafka's *Metamorphosis* or I would have been properly depressed. It was a new experience in alienation.

The boyfriend tried to resume where he had left off, but it was useless. I had been all alone in the bottom of a sewer and nothing could change that. Besides, he had gone a bit far in his letters. Words like 'perfidy' could not be bandied around so casually. I forgave him, of course. There was no question of holding it against him, but I began to see him in twenty years' time re-enacting British victories on the dining room table, with war maps instead of Van Gogh prints, Union Jack table mats and dinner service, and myself desperately and secretly wearing the crude tricolour knickers. I began to dream of the green fields of home.

We both knew it was all over when one day I said nostalgically, '*Níl aon tinteán mar do thinteán féin*' and he didn't laugh. He asked me to translate it. How could you turn firesides and storytelling and warmth and acceptance and common origins and shared disasters into that transfer embroidered 'There's no place like home'? I swore I would join the Gaelic League the minute I got back and I would never utter a word of English again, since it was so ineffectual an instrument for expressing the finer subtleties of the Gael. And I thought of G.K.C. and his sloppy waistcoat with even greater affection. 'The great Gaels of Ireland whom all the gods made mad, for all their wars are merry and all their songs are sad.' I wallowed in euphoric fantasies. One evening on one of the permitted trips out of the san, I called at the Irish Catholic Gaelic League Bingo Hall to watch the merrymaking. I sagged in a corner and a gay, red-haired, blue-eyed Irishman asked me would I bate the floor with him. When I apologised because I just wasn't able he said, 'Well, you poor creature you,' with the proper mixture of sympathy and unconcern. It put everything in perspective. I knew I was lost to the Empire and the boyfriend for ever. It had to be back to the bogs.

We parted good friends. I kept his letters with others in a trunk in an outhouse, always meaning to burn them. When

I finally got round to it I discovered generations of mice had used them as nesting material. It seemed a very inappropriate end to Anglo-Irish relations, or Hiberno-English relations – depending on your point of view.

The False God

His sisters met Tom at the airport. At first sight he did not appear to have altered. They rushed to greet him, arms outstretched, eyes glistening. Only when he was near enough to be kissed and cried over did they see that the eighteen-year-old youth had gone and that his thirty-three years were printed indelibly on his weary face. He looked at them in mock wonder and said, 'It's not fair. You haven't changed a bit.' They crowed with delight, each of them clutching at a hand or a sleeve, hustling him away from the crowds, ushering him into the Austin parked outside. 'I don't believe it,' he said. 'It's not the same old Jenny.'

'It is, it is, it is,' they shouted with glee. 'Goes like a bomb, like a bomb.'

He closed his eyes thankfully when he sat into the front seat. 'Poor old Tom,' they sympathised. 'You must be jaded after your long journey. We won't bother you with our chatter.' But they did. How could they help it? He'd been away so long.

As soon as there was a pause he said what he had been rehearsing all the way over in the plane, in fact from the moment he had decided to return home. 'I'm sorry I didn't get home before Mother died. I never expected her to go so suddenly.'

For a few seconds their silence seemed of such intensity he feared they would show him no mercy, perhaps ignore his remark, condemn him to frigid boycott of his mother's name, perhaps reproach him with his callousness, his indifference. He was about to burst out that he needed their forgiveness, their old smothering cossetting love, when Brigid, who was driving, remarked gently that they understood perfectly. 'Mother never blamed you, Tom. You had your life to live. It's only natural. Every bird must leave the nest.'

'Except for female birdies, of course,' said Jane. Tom chuckled, but stopped when he realised his laughter was not echoed. They drove through a fragment of time, icicled over by something so cold and forbidding he could not touch it with understanding. And then it was gone. Warmth and laughter and storytelling cushioned him all the way home.

The house was as he had left it. The arched doorway set in the cut-stone walls had been repainted in his honour, but in the same shade of wine red. The rock garden at the side was covered with alpine plants, some of them blooming now in competition with primulas and narcissi. The pond was fringed with daffodils which had ousted the narcissi from self-admiration. Even the bird house had been carefully patched up so that it looked just as it had done on the day of his departure fifteen years before. Yet the closed door gave him a feeling of loss. Foolishly, he expected it to be open, framing his mother in its elegant curve.

'Where's Maggie?' he asked, while Millicent poked in her bag for the door keys.

Again there was that icy silence. And again it was Brigid who spoke gently. 'Ah, poor Maggie is gone. Dead and buried.'

Remorse gnawed painfully at him. 'You never mentioned it in your letters.'

'You never answered our letters,' said Alice calmly, 'so it hardly seemed worth mentioning.'

Oh, Maggie, he thought. Fat, jolly, inefficient Maggie. The trial of his mother's life. Maggie, who poured whiskey over the rice pudding in grand abandon, and set the visitors arguing. Maggie, who sang so beautifully, but who was carried away by her own magnificent voice, so that she crashed the fragile best tea-service off the sink.

Millicent opened the door and led him beamingly inside. Jane drove the car around to the back garage. Alice rushed to open the kitchen door for her. Brigid lifted the bolster from the Aga and pushed the kettle on to the hot plate. 'You must be famished,' she said. 'Sit up there beside the fire. Supper'll be ready in no time at all. 'Tisn't worth setting it in the dining room. It's warmer in here.' He wanted to explore. He wanted to walk around touching the photographs and ornaments. But nobody suggested it to him. So he sat obediently on the chair near the fire, watching them set to work to prepare the meal.

Alice cut the bread. Jane brought out the rashers and sausages, eggs and black pudding from the fridge.

'You've got a fridge,' he cried, delighted. 'That's new.' They laughed. 'Ah, you think we're behind the times. And we're not at all. You'll see.'

Millicent set the table, mumbling to herself as she placed the knives and forks in position. 'That's Brigid, that's Alice, that's me, that's Jane, and' – she gave a little sigh of loving pleasure – 'here's Tom.' It seemed perfectly natural that she should have set their places in the old order of procedure. He, being the youngest, was at the bottom of the table. Brigid replaced their mother at the head. She hummed while she placed the rashers and sausages carefully on the pan. Jane, who had never been plain, and wasn't now, even in her forties, was putting the plates in the slow oven. He stretched himself and looked out the window. The hills were lilac-coloured in the distance. The fields were emerald pools under the evening sun. It was good to be home again.

That first meal set the pattern for the ordered days that followed. It soon became clear to him that his sisters carried out the business of house and farm with dedicated efficiency. Every morning and evening, Jane machine-milked the cows in the long dairy while an anonymous farm boy lifted the tankards of milk on the car trailer. He mucked out the yard and house while Alice cleaned and disinfected the milking machine with its great glass jars. Brigid cooked the meals. Millicent made beds and tidied up. In the afternoons they worked busily at the garden and greenhouse, each one again with their separate and never changing chores. His labour was superfluous. Fifteen years ago they had learned how to do without his young strength. Now they allowed him to help them in small ways, acting like indulgent parents, encouraging him and praising him for his most trivial of tasks. When he hung around the milking yard, waiting for a chance to be useful, he was told, 'Don't kill yourself, Tom. Take it easy, now, can't you.' The farm boy grinned at him but was not permitted to accept help. Several times Tom had tried to relieve Millicent of her bale of straw as she staggered to the stable with it, but he was firmly rejected, the last time with something like venom. Little by little, he was given the message. He was welcome as a guest. He was loved. But he had lost his right to share the sisters' burdens.

He took to wandering around the fields during the daytime, and sometimes plucked up enough courage to ask could he borrow the car at night. It was given ungrudgingly, by Brigid, but without enthusiasm. He used the opportunity to visit the local public houses and sucked peppermints on the way back in a hopeless attempt to deceive them. They never asked him where he went. Merely if he'd had a pleasant evening, was he hungry, was he cold. Their solicitude was unfaltering. When he returned later than usual one night, and sang his way up the stairs to bed, they rushed from their rooms to get him a hot drink, to reheat his hot water bottle, to plug in the electric fire. As to his whereabouts, what he had seen and done, whom he had met, they were totally without curiosity.

About a month after his arrival, as they sat one Sunday evening around the drawing-room fire, he was jolted out of his dozy relaxation when Brigid said, 'You'll be thinking of going back any day now, Tom.'

Back? Back? He was horrified. He was at home in his own house, and she was asking him such a tactless question. 'I hadn't thought about it,' he answered.

'Isn't it time you did?' asked Alice. Millicent said, 'It's amazing how time flies.' Jane poked at the fire.

'Are you getting tired of me?' He resolved to use a mock

serious tone, so that the conversation should not go too far.

'Not in the least,' said Brigid. 'But you must consider yourself. After all, it's not good for a young man to be tied up with four middle-aged spinster sisters.' Jane lifted her head and Tom scented danger.

'I don't know about that,' he said. 'Four good-looking women like yourselves could not be called middle-aged spinsters.'

'I'm fifty-two and unmarried,' remarked Brigid with pointed accuracy.

'I'm fifty-one and unmarried,' said Alice.

'And I'm fifty and a blissful spinster,' giggled Millicent.

He looked at Jane, waiting for her contribution.

'I'm a bloody virgin too,' she said viciously. 'And I'm ten years older than you. And that makes me forty-three. With all my chances gone. And you took them all, boy, the day you walked out that door, fifteen years ago, on the 23rd of May at half past two on a sunny afternoon.' The epithet seemed to shudder off the inlaid chairs, the French gilt mirrors and the silver-framed photographs, but she might as well have sung 'Bless This House' for all the impression it made on Alice, Millicent or Brigid. On Tom the effect was obvious. He felt personally affronted. It was quite out of keeping to use such an expression in this house. It reminded him of the sleazy steak houses he had worked in, back in the States – and to which he hoped he might never have to return. Her accusing words bewildered him. What did she mean? Jumping on him like that! It was uncalled-for. He bristled a little and stuck out his chin as far as it would go.

'I don't know what you're talking about.'

'And sure how could you, Tom,' said Brigid. 'You've been away so long.'

'And you never answered our letters,' put in Millicent gently.

'What difference did that make?' he cried exasperatedly. 'You kept writing anyway.'

'All the difference in the world,' said Brigid. 'It made a difference to Mother, you see. And that made a difference to us.'

'You're talking in riddles,' said Tom.

'I love riddles,' sighed Alice. 'They're such fun.'

'Stop.' It was Jane who spoke so commandingly. 'He deserves an explanation.'

Brigid assessed him thoughtfully and then agreed. 'Of course, Tom dear, we really must fill you in on our lives here. You see, Tom,' – she put her knitting down and looked through the great many-paned window as if she were reliving the memories she was recalling – 'when you were born, I was just about to start at medical school. I'd got a place. Father had agreed to pay. All my life I'd wanted to be a doctor. Maybe go on the mission fields and work for God as well as for the afflicted. I was idealistic when I was young.' She looked deprecatingly around at them, and her three sisters nodded their heads reassuringly at her. 'But then, you came … And Mother was very ill. She was forty-seven, you see, and you were rather a surprise. To all of us. But you were a boy. And Father had wanted a boy so much. He'd given up in fact, and had got more or less used to us. Well, I was the eldest, so Father said I should stay at home for a while and help. Mother couldn't bear any strangers near her, and poor old Maggie, well – you know what Maggie was like. I didn't mind. It just meant postponing everything. I cried at first, I remember. But Father said I wasn't to be selfish. Nothing he hated more, he said, than self-centred women. "Take an example from your mother," he said. "She never thinks of herself." And then of course he was so delighted to have a son he started drinking again. And he couldn't seem able to stop. And he wasn't able to look after the farm, and the farm hands began to play up on him. So Alice had to help.'

'I didn't mind, really,' said Alice. 'Mother promised me I should do domestic science when I finished school. At that time I was very keen. And quite good, I think, really. But you were a year old by then, and I said I could stay home for a little while. Besides, you were such a dotey little fellow. We all loved you a lot, Tom. We wanted everything to be perfect for you. And you were to have the farm. And we didn't want it to get run down because of our selfishness. Selfish people are so horrid.' Alice smiled dreamily over at the wedding picture of their parents. 'So – where was I – oh, yes. I learned how to milk. Jack Hanly taught me. Do you remember Jack? No. How could you. You were only an infant. I liked Jack – and he, he liked me.'

'He wasn't suitable,' said Brigid firmly.

'He was very nice,' said Alice. 'And I liked him. I liked him a lot.' Her words came a little faster. 'He was much cleverer than you gave him credit for. And he was very decent. And nice. And he liked me.'

'Yes, dear,' sighed Brigid. 'And he married little Annie Shaw from the cottages.'

'They have five children,' said Alice. 'Live in a lovely bungalow outside town. When Father sacked him he got a job in a machine shop and learned a trade. He has his own workshop. They're very well off, I think.'

'Father shouldn't have sacked him,' said Millicent. 'He was the best of the lot. But Father was crotchety then. After the stroke his speech got so slurred and he was hardly able to walk. So of course I had to help Alice. The other farm hands left. I learned how to drive the tractor, and I used to do the vegetable garden until it got beyond me a few years ago. Remember how I used to take you for rides on the tractor, Tom? You'd wait on the back step for me every morning with your little boots on. And then of course Father died. You probably don't remember.'

But Tom did remember. He remembered loud sobbing, black-draped windows, people with gloomy faces filling the house, black coaches, black horses, the box bearing his father edging over the curve on the first landing banisters on the way downstairs. He remembered being hugged by Maggie and wishing that she would stop slobbering all over him. And being glad that the old drooling, cranky man, his father, was safely out of the way.

I remember, he thought. A house full of hysterical women. And then a quiet house. No more whisperings on the landing in the middle of the night. No more pounding on the kitchen ceiling which was underneath his father's room. No more being dragged unwillingly into that room reeking of whiskey, to have his fat hand gripped and caressed by the one useful and horribly bony hand of his father's. And the relief of never having to kiss the slavering mouth in the stubby face.

'I remember it very well,' he said.

'You were five,' said Jane. 'And I was fifteen. Did you know, Tom, that I was clever? I was away at school. Mother Mechtilde said I was a genius. She exaggerated, of course. But for my age I had a good brain, I suppose. It's still good, of course. Better than yours could ever be, Tom, if you'll forgive me saying so. But Father left debts. And they had to be paid. Mother wanted to take out probate. The farm had been left to her until you were ready to take over. And there were death duties. So I was called home. Mother said, "You don't need all that education with your looks." I hated you, Tom. I begged and begged and begged to be let stay on. I said I'd earn my own living. I'd do anything if only I could finish. But Mother said no. We must not be selfish. We had to think of Tom. I got sick of Tom, Tom, Tom. Do you know that I once thought of drowning you in the rain barrel?'

Tom was aghast and looked at the other three for support in his feeling of outrage. They were quite unmoved.

'She felt very strongly,' said Brigid calmly.

'I didn't do it, of course,' said Jane. 'Or you wouldn't be sitting here. So there's no need to look so martyred. Anyhow I got fond of you.' She laughed. 'You were a funny little fellow. Always up to mischief. And on for a joke. Nobody could help loving you, Tom. But we were all acolytes at your altar.'

'And then when you were eighteen and we were all thinking we could relax, because you were going to do agricultural science and be the best farmer with the best farm in the whole country, you left.' Brigid's tone was harsh. They are judge and jury, he thought, and I am about to be sentenced. He had no defence. He was guilty because he had been born a male.

Then Alice broke the silence. 'It wouldn't have been so bad if you'd answered our letters. If we'd known something about what you were doing, or why you left. And there were so many things to do. And poor Mother killing Maggie like that. It was an accident, of course. But she got so nervy after you left, and kept blaming herself.'

'Mother killed Maggie!' Tom began to think he was going mad. Or they were all mad. The conversation was getting crazier all the time. It was too much to bear. He couldn't listen to any more. He started to lift himself off the chair. 'Sit down,' said Brigid. 'It was an accident. Mother was weeping one day in the kitchen – you were gone a few years at the time. And Maggie said it was time she gave over lamenting, that you were always spoilt and selfish. Mother got furious, and pushed Maggie. You know how fat Maggie was. She fell very heavily, and hit her head off the stove. She died a few days later. Cerebral haemorrhage they said it was. She was getting on of course and it might have happened anyway.'

'But you see,' said Millicent, 'Mother blamed herself for that too. So she went very queer. One of us had to stay with her all the time.'

'Couldn't you have had her put into a psychiatric hospital?' he asked.

'You mean a madhouse,' said Jane. They looked at him, four pairs of eyes sadly judging him.

'We couldn't have done that to Mother,' said Brigid. 'It wasn't her fault. Her only crime was that she was so unselfish, she expected us to be the same. Jane was engaged to be married to Mark Purcell from Burdoyne. But she told him about Mother and we think he got cold feet. Perhaps he thought it was hereditary. In any case he emigrated to Australia.'

'*He* never wrote either,' said Alice.

'Men haven't much moral courage,' said Millicent contemplatively.

The silence that followed seemed to encompass their whole lives, past, present and future. There was no more to be said. They had been the sacrificial offerings to his godhead and he had been a false god. Their lives were to have been his sanctuary and he had allowed them to be looted and despoiled. There was no place more fitting for a false god than the brassy temples of American eating houses. He would go back where he belonged.

The Tattooed

The sunlight on the end of
the bed was anaemic, its life
and warmth almost overcome
by the frosty air. Her breath
puffed into clouds when she
blew vainly on to her cupped,
chilblained hands. The glass
door, which was the fourth
wall of her tiny, box-like room,
was wide open. Beyond it, on
the veranda, the patients who
were allowed up in the afternoons stamped their feet and
slapped their hands off their
thighs. Graded exercise it was
called, the peak of progress
being reached when they were

allowed up for meals in the day room. An incongruous collection of people whose common denominator was the limiting factor of their disease. She had shuffled past some of the women as she made her way in her slippers to the bathroom at the end of the corridor, and had heard male voices beyond the kitchen and staff room. The segregation of the sexes was achieved with an air of nonchalance, and indeed it wasn't easy to imagine any fusion of the two in such an atmosphere. Which of us, she thought, half in amusement and half in despair, could fall in love with another victim of the bug. Now and again she would practise saying to herself, 'I have an infection of tuberculosis in the apices of both lungs. It is a curable disease. I am lucky to have survived to an age when there is an effective cure for it. Amen.' Sometimes she cried at night because she felt desecrated, contaminated. She imagined her visitors stood unnecessarily at the open glass doors, as if death by pneumonia were preferable to possible pollution by her breath. She was shocked by her own occasional overwhelming self-pity and resentment, and in an effort to fight it she agreed to do the prescribed amount of basketwork every day. Today it was impossible. It was too cold even to turn the pages of her book. Observation of the human species may have a therapeutic effect, she muttered into her blanket. Outside, the afternoon procession had dwindled to a solitary walker. Mr Matthews, shoulders thrust forward in an effort to protect his frail lungs from the bitter air, moved aimlessly in and out of her vision. She began to count the seconds between each appearance and had a compulsive desire to shout at him if he went over the limit of fifty. The gardener had been digging new flower beds, adding fresh soil and compost by the wheelbarrowful, and she wondered if Mr Matthews was stopping to talk to him now and again. Once, when he passed her window, she thought he looked a little less hunched as if the exercise was beginning to straighten him up. The sun dropped discourteously without warning behind the black limbs of the trees. The wheelbarrow creaked away to the potting shed, and Mr Matthews reappeared no more.

A nurse came in to close the glass doors. Through the naked glass darkness crept catlike, enveloping the corners of her room, draping itself over the foot of the bed so that she lay in a little island of light cast by the lamp behind her bed. A reawakening of interest in the outside world filled her with a tingling pleasure. Today she had wondered, however briefly, about someone else. Today, Mr Matthews was not just a name cheerily called by one of the staff. He was a pair of lungs cringing against the cold. He was a grey face under a felt hat. She reached for her book and began to read. In a few moments the tea trolley would rattle to her door, her evening medication would follow and the day would be over. Only the long, tedious, dark hours had to be lived through. She would read a little, listen to the wireless a little, or she might visit the room next to hers where there was a Scots girl who could play chess. What can't be cured must be endured. The old saying slipped into her mind. Yet stoic endurance was the last thing she had ever expected of herself. Was it a foretaste of middle age? At twenty-five middle age might only be around the corner. A surge of panic assailed her and she groped for her pocket mirror in the locker and peered in at her reflection. She looked like a droopy spaniel, so comically like one, in fact, that she stuck out her tongue, blew out her cheeks, and panted derisively. That made her feel better. At least there was no sign of the set face, the hallmark of so many women who had endured more than they could cope with. Not yet. She shivered at the thought and concentrated on her reading.

The gardener was a woman. This revelation threw an interesting light on Mr Matthews's new-found pleasure in herbaceous borders and rose beds. It might also, perhaps, have accounted for the slight straightening of his shoulders and the resolute way of his walking. They were working in front of her room now. The sunlight was warmer, the days a little longer. Somebody said the daffodils were thrusting their way up. Soon their golden heads would burst to glory. She imagined masses of yellow worshipping the budding trees above. New exciting smells filtered through the clinical atmosphere of her room, fresh-turned earth, the growthy smell of spring grass. At home they would be saying there's a bit of growth there today. Spring and a hope of better things to come made her feel relaxed and happy.

The gardener's hair, cropped like a man's, was burnished by the sun. Pepper and salt hair, sandy hair growing grey. Brown slacks tucked into Wellington boots and the heavy windcheater above them were part of her disguise. Her hands were big and strong and efficient. When she smiled, as she did now at something Mr Matthews said, it was obvious she was a woman. Otherwise it was anybody's guess. But what did it matter! Black or white, male or female, atheist or believer, to be healthy and able to work and earn one's keep was the only important thing.

Her relaxed feeling vanished when she heard the injection trolley stop at her door. She made bad jokes sometimes to stop the tightening of her muscles. 'My bottom's like a Picasso palette. All blues.' She flinched from the needle in spite of herself. 'Be sure it's the upper outer quarter,' she mumbled into her pillow. 'Mind my sciatic nerve.' And then it was over until tomorrow. Today she was told she might dress herself and sit up for half an hour.

She shuffled down to the bathroom. It took her a quarter

of an hour to dress. She felt civilised, renewed, reborn. The long Viyella nightdress and the bedjacket were like her corpse thrown across the chair. She flapped her arms and cast her eyes heavenwards as if she were leaving her mortality behind her. She practised long slow deep breaths. Her feet made a different noise in high-heeled shoes. Pitter pat pit pit pit they went on the tiled floor. Along the corridor and back to her room her footsteps were accompanying music, sharp, clear, decisive, fresh, ready for action. Shuffling was a thing of the past. Yet she was happy to sit down at the open door when she found herself panting a little. Mr Matthews came to congratulate her. 'You're up,' he said and smiled. She smiled back. He looks badly, poor man, she thought to herself. 'You have to take it easy at first,' he said. After a while he told her that he had been a miner in Lancashire, and that he had silicosis as well as TB. He had gone to live with an uncle when he was fourteen and had gone down the mines for the money. 'And what good is money now? Even if I had it.' There was no answer fit for such a question. No observation born of polite tradition could fill the silence that followed.

'I have a little money,' he said, then, apologetically. 'I'm entitled, they tell me, to workman's compensation. I'll go back to my own people in Clare. I'll buy a boat and I'll cruise along the Shannon and I'll visit all the islands from Kilrush to Limerick and on to Killaloe and up to Athlone. The good air will surely clear me.'

He looked wistfully, only half believing it, and she was reduced to saying falsely, 'Of course it will. The fresh air is great.' They sat in companionable silence listening to the muted sounds of hospital activity behind them and watching the gardener's efforts with the rake.

There was something different about the gardener today. What was it? Mr Matthews was walking over now and taking the rake into his thin hands with the clubbed fingernails. The gardener was smiling at him. She was wearing lipstick. Under the dark windcheater a glimmer of a brightly coloured blouse showed. Her strong teeth flashed white as she laughed at his poor work. He began to cough and splutter, shook his head despairingly and came back to the seat in the veranda to rest. There had been something pitiful in the contrast between the two pairs of hands on the rake, something infinitely moving in the difference between the woman's brawny width and the man's unnatural thinness. At the same time there was a flash of understanding between them as the hands had crossed each other without touching. He was silent now except for the rasping of his breath. As she sat beside him she was prompted to read aloud the English translation of an Hungarian poem:

Though the soul ache in such keen radiance,
Its diamond core grows harder, more intense,
Brother and little sister, we talk it over. I'm ready.
I sleep badly. No matter. See, I am calm and steady.
All the ways I have wandered to be sorted, at last
surveyed.
The word is what we need, more desperately now than
bread.
Blaze up, blessed hope, rekindle our souls – as you
sought it first in the alleys and every by-way and port,
mate.
You who bear the tattoo on your indelible heart.

'I only half understand it,' he said, 'but it's a fine poem. And who is it by?'

She was embarrassed after reading it. Somehow it seemed depressing and she had meant it to be hopeful. 'Lajos Tamási' wrote it, the time of the rising in 1956.'

'Ah yes, I used to love the poetry when I was a boy at school. And the hymns at the mission. I could have been a line singer. Fai-th of our fa-a-th-ers Holy Faith. We will be true to thee till death.'

She was terrified lest he should begin coughing, so she said quickly, 'That's lovely.'

'Things are different now,' he said. 'The reverence has gone.'

'Maybe it was only superstition.'

'There's a big difference between the two,' he said. 'I think we knew one from the other.'

She felt her immaturity wilt in the face of his confidence, and was silent.

Her last X-ray showed a big improvement. By June she should be home. She relapsed into a state of non-growth. Everything was suspended. It was as if for the next few months she was caught in a bubble of time while the world outside bustled about with important things to do. Even Mr Matthews did something positive. He and the gardener had established a relationship with each other which the rest of the inmates watched with dispassionate interest. There was a brightness about them when they were together as if the one halo enclosed them. It was pleasant to sit in the shade of the veranda and look at them. The daffodils faded.

She went for short walks in the afternoon and took an occasional bus trip into town. She felt shy and insecure when she was away from the hospital. People looked at her pallor and looked away again quickly. Her voice seemed tremulous to her when she asked for things in shops. The huskiness made her even more nervous so that she coughed unnecessarily and wondered guiltily if she was spreading germs. The sanitorium became a refuge from which to draw strength for her next sallying forth. As she grew stronger and more confident Mr Matthews slid inevitably towards his end. He no longer walked along the front or stood smiling and talking with the gardener. Propped up in his bed, he watched her vibrant energy hopelessly. Yet he did not seem unhappy. When the gardener came to sit with him for a few minutes at a time his breathing became easier. Their love was something to marvel at, like love in a prison or a concentration camp. There was no sentimentality between them, for there was no time for such mawkishness.

They had no need of the words and signs of more normal courtship. It was impossible to fancy either one of them indulging in flattery or persuasion. Each had endowed the other with a part of themselves, so that they seemed to look around them with one pair of eyes.

And yet it was a relief sometimes not to see them or think about them. The stronger and more confident she became the more it hurt her to look at them. Her instinct for service to others fostered by her upbringing was at war with her need to survive. She had to advance out of these shadows, yet she was pulled back into them by a terrible compassion and sense of comradeship. As the day of her discharge approached she saw less and less of them. She knew that the gardener spent every available moment with Mr Matthews so there seemed little need for anyone else to intrude.

On the twentieth day of June she packed her case and said her goodbyes to the staff and patients. The garden was at its best, the roses vying with one another in their thoughtfully planned colour schemes, the herbaceous hinder a blaze of different hues. Excitement and happiness mingled to make the whole world seem a sort of paradise. She didn't go in to Mr Matthews's room. She told herself he would be resting, that she might make him feel lonely if she said goodbye to him. It was a *lovely* day.

She didn't look back as the taxi drove her through the old wooden gates. She didn't see the blinds pulled down in Mr Matthews's room, or notice the chaplain hurrying through the veranda door. She didn't see the gardener, hair cropped like a man's, dark shirt tucked into dark slacks, moving slowly towards the potting shed.

Queen

Everyone said of Edna that her table manners were the expression of her perfect self-control. Even as a child, when others of her age were slumping and grabbing, she had remembered never to slouch over a meal and she seemed to have a natural flair for the niceties of table etiquette. The gross appetites of others, who could slurp the soup or reach rashly for the condiments or, worse, gnaw the asparagus down to its butt, shrivelled in her presence; the hungriest epicure repressed his desires in front of her restraint. When she grew up all her friends said that they loved her for her self-sacrificing nature, and at table, somehow, this martyrdom seemed to shine even more whitely. As was natural for a hostess, she was always last to be served yet, as she took the smallest portion of food on offer, there was invariably someone on hand who would beg her to treat herself better. Acolytes were never in short supply. She was the epitome of gentility, having qualities of graciousness which a country hurtling into the modern world with suicidal speed seemed to have forgotten. And everyone said, oh Edna is so refined and so gentle. You never hear Edna say a bad word about anyone. You never hear Edna swear or raise her voice. It's an archaic word to use but I suppose one had to say that Edna was always the perfect lady.

It was an experience later recounted with awe to have been offered afternoon tea in her drawing-room from an Irish Georgian silver tea service, and to forget that electroplating had ever been invented or that stainless steel or plastic could possibly exist. If there was a trace of patronage in the eyes glancing amusedly over the teacups it was not considered out of place in a woman of such fine quality. She was rather like an old master painting, in the artistry with which each layer of paint, symbolically speaking, had been applied, so that the original blank canvas was forgotten. The finished product was certainly a masterpiece, impervious to the wear and tear, the rough and tumble of the ordinary, workaday world.

Her husband had been the single great embarrassment of Edna's life. He had been a social disaster but she had borne his disgrace with a charitableness which, her friends said, gave her a claim to canonisation. The fact that she was a woman was a disadvantage. Edna's friends were not into feminist theology, so they lived in hope. Perhaps, they reasoned, by the time she reached that melancholy state of eligibility the Pope might have become emancipated. Edna modestly disclaimed any such ambition. She never grumbled about her husband and she never reproached him. At his drunken worst he had been maudlin, drooling over her perfection and weeping for his sins. On his few sober days he detached himself from his surroundings and from her. He died without knowing that it was not his alcoholism so much as his withdrawal from her influence that made her hate him.

The foolhardy few who disagreed with Edna were either never allowed to be in her company again or were made to feel the error of their ways and agreed slavishly with her opinions thereafter. These were held with great firmness. She had strong views on 'society'. The working classes, she said, were lazy and lacked intelligence. The middle classes were bourgeois and *nouveau riche*. The aristocracy (the few titled men and women whom she had known slightly in her fox-hunting youth) were decadent but had the advantage of 'knowing how to behave'. Her friends dared not ask her to which class she herself belonged. They would have got little satisfaction because in her own opinion she was classless in the way that people of culture ought to be and she would have dismissed the question as impertinent. One of her great achievements was this ability to dismiss with arrogance and destructive certitude the unwelcome questions of others. The airy wave of the hand which accompanied the words 'We won't bother with that now' was enough to demoralise the toughest opponent.

At Frank's death she had more of a sense of relief than any real grief. He had been a heavy burden. One never knew where his need for drink might lead him. Although she had willing assistants who rescued him, for her sake, from his worst orgies, there were occasions when she was forced to be involved. Then, it was humiliating to have to face the beery pub faces whose grossness her husband preferred to her delicate features. Those were rare occasions however, and happened only in the early years of their marriage when she had probably loved him and certainly worried over him. Perhaps the cold dominance she acquired later was an escape from an unrequited love. But if she had any regrets for the loss of something tender and wonderful, she did not reveal them. But then she never revealed herself. It was part of her attraction, a strange, impersonal, diamond-bright quality which made her strong and unassailable. Her friends gushed over these qualities. Her neighbours feared her dignity so much that they did not even permit themselves a sly smile. As for her enemies, if vulgar they were routed without knowing why; if not vulgar they had the good sense to keep their opinions to themselves.

It was strange that Edna should develop such a passion for a game. She gardened enthusiastically, but after all that was to be expected. Great gardens and great ladies went together. Twice-weekly a man came to do the rough digging and to mow the lawns. 'My garden is my life,' she would say. 'I am a poor cook,' (a lie, or at least modest disavowal of her talent), 'I detest sewing,' (the truth), 'but without my garden I would die, simply die.'

With or without the prospect of canonisation on the horizon, her friends rushed to encourage her to keep her interest at all cost. 'What would we do without you,' they cried. 'You keep us all going.'

She smiled deprecatingly, knowing their words to be true. Her garden flourished.

The game, incredibly, was chess. Bridge would have been understandable. In Edna's circle and in Edna's town a woman was not considered educated until she could play bridge, and she was a fair if unenthusiastic player. But chess, a game mistakenly believed to be played well only by men or boy prodigies, was not quite respectable. For one thing it had a nasty touch of cleverness about it. It was, moreover, a loner's game. Whoever heard of chess parties? Still, it was a proof of her intellect. And after all, she must have been clever to have rescued her business from the abyss into which 'that man' had allowed it to sink. 'That man' had inherited a chain of drapery stores throughout the country and had managed to dispose of all but two by the time he died. These two Edna brought back to life. They gave her a good living without too much distasteful dealing or wrangling. 'They are enough for me,' she said. 'I am a lot better off now than I ever was. Money is sordid but necessary. I keep an eye on things but I don't have to get too involved. Fortunately my managers are reliable. It leaves me time for more important things.'

Her interest in chess began by accident. At an auction she had bought an antique sewing table. Inside it lay a wooden Staunton set. She had often admired the beautiful ivory chess pieces, delicately carved by oriental craftsmen, which one or two of her friends arranged on tables for show, but since they were neither strictly functional nor purely ornamental her aesthetic sense drew her from them. The Staunton, with its severe lack of pretension, appealed to her. On a night when her husband was later and drunker than usual, she took out the pieces and handled them aimlessly. Next day she bought a book for beginners.

It became an obsession. She lay in bed at night watching the pieces manoeuvre across the ceiling. The bishop's diagonal, the knight's quick side-step, the pawn's even patrol, were fascinating. 'Wham' and 'wham' she breathed delightedly as she brought her rooks together for a final clincher.

She found little use for the queen. Such power was too much. It created an imbalance, she thought. There was no fun in winning with a queen. She longed for an opponent on whom to try out her skill. But there was no one. Her friends had their bridge, her husband was hardly more than a vegetable and shortly afterwards became even less than that when he drove into the river and drowned.

After thirty years of marriage she was free. At fifty she was a widow, not young, but not old, attractive and although not rich, quite comfortably off. She was not lonely because she had long ago learned to live with that little difficulty. But there was a vacuum. While he lived Frank had created a void. When he died he seemed to have sucked into himself the last reason for her existence. There was nothing to worry over and there was nothing to be pitied for. Her friends could hardly sympathise with her in her bereavement since the man had been such a torment to her – well such a nuisance, really.

She began to spend more time with her chess. She studied the openings, the end games, the great games of the masters, the problems and hypothetical situations, in newspaper columns and chess magazines. And one night she plucked up enough courage to join a chess club.

For her first game she had the luck to draw the club champion. She demolished him in nine moves. The members laughed and called it beginner's luck. He was not so sure and asked for a return game. He resigned after fourteen moves when he lost his queen and was in an impossible position. Afterwards she drove home, singing in celebration. The house was joyously empty. She locked the garage, the garden gate, the front door, with the pride that full ownership brings. 'This is all mine,' she said. 'The world is mine.'

Her friends said that after all she must have loved Frank. Only grief could have driven her to such mania, to such neglect of her garden and house. The afternoon tea parties were abandoned. She counted the days, the hours between club meetings. It wasn't a case of her always winning. She had her failures, but even those games were lost with a panache, a brilliance not usual in provincial clubs. The members began to boast of her prowess. A game between herself and the champion drew enthusiasts from all the neighbouring counties. She had no match nerves. Her cool, detached appraisal of each game was unrivalled. Her inventiveness and daring, the risks she took, the sacrifices she made to improve her position won the admiration of all. Her old friends faded into the dim, unhappy past. Her new friends brought her with them into the exciting world of youth, vigour, adventure. And the champion was handsome, civilised and a moderate drinker.

The oldest member watched her advance like an old parliamentarian observing a new, up-and-coming, potential head of government. 'Do you notice,' he asked the club champion one evening, 'how she always profers her queen before she mates? I don't believe I have ever seen her checkmate with a queen.'

'Are you hinting at something Freudian?' his friend laughed.

'I'll tell you one thing, Bob,' the oldest member said. 'You ignore her queen and you'll do better. Every player has his weakness. I'm nearly certain that's hers. Watch her. You'll see. For some reason the queen is an embarrassment to her. She has to get rid of it.'

It was the end of the season and the champion was ruefully counting his losses. 'There's no doubt,' he said, 'she's a brilliant player. I think she's a natural. I can't see myself getting the better of her. I hate to admit it. I always thought women were bad players, something to do with their emotionalism. Or perhaps they're too practical to be bothered with such futile occupations. And then, women aren't good at dealing with abstract ideas. Are they?'

'Rubbish,' said the oldest member. 'Train a monkey to play the piano and you'll get another Beethoven. Find her weakness and you'll beat her.'

'Well, we'll see,' Bob said. 'It doesn't seem fair. She's a widow and a good bit older than I am. It seems a little underhand to be looking for weaknesses.'

'It's the name of the game. One-upmanship, gamesmanship is the essence of chess. Try sucking your teeth like old Brennan. He caught you a few times. It might shake her.'

'You're a blackguard, Charlie,' said Bob. 'I won't play by those rules.'

'Then you're a loser. Do you want to lose to a woman who has more money than is good for her, who drove her husband to a lifelong binge? I knew him, you know. A decent fellow. A good sort. Until he met her. You disappoint me.'

Bob turned away from him. 'You play your way,' he said. 'I'll play mine.'

Edna was unlocking her car when he came down the clubhouse steps. He hesitated for a moment and then hailed her. She looked up at him enquiringly.

'I wondered if you would care for a drink,' he said. Her refusal was polite but instant. 'What about coffee then?'

Her eyebrows rose and he felt young and insecure.

For a moment her look softened and she appeared not quite so ageless, not quite so confident.

'Please,' he insisted. 'Please do.'

'All right,' she agreed brightly. 'I think it would be nice. Are you walking or driving?'

'I'm cycling,' he said. 'I don't drive.'

She looked amused. 'By circumstance or on principle?' She didn't wait for his answer and added, 'No wonder you look so healthy and handsome. Would you like to put your bicycle in the boot? Save you having to pick it up later.' Miraculously and efficiently she produced a plastic rope and they tied his bicycle securely.

In the car he examined her profile surreptitiously. She must have been a good-looking woman in her day. Still had the traces of it. He had an unexpected pang of regret that he hadn't known her then and that he was ten years younger than her now. A good-looking woman of independent means who could play chess, she was quite a catch. 'You're married?' she asked pleasantly.

'No,' he said, and looked sideways to see if she was pleased. There was no sign of any reaction. He wondered if she would ask him next if he was straight. He sighed.

'No need to sound so miserable about it,' she said. 'You've probably had a lucky escape. It's not a bed of roses.'

Again he shot a sideways look at her. There was no mistaking the angry bitterness of her expression. 'I suppose it all depends on your mate,' he said. 'Some couples seem happy enough. I know a few who have made a great success of marriage. I often envy them. It's lonely being single.'

'It's lonely being married, too,' she said. 'That's the worst loneliness of all. Never get married just to avoid bring lonely. Believe me, that's good advice.'

The confession and the advice surprised him. He warmed to her.

'You're a very good sport,' she continued. 'I know it hasn't been easy for you to be beaten by a newcomer, a woman. I can imagine what the others must say.'

He hesitated and then blurted out the oldest member's suggestion about looking for her weakness. He could have kicked himself. He had thrown away his possible advantage. He had made himself look like a fool and he had probably antagonised her as well.

'He may be right,' she said coolly. 'Try it and see. Of course he doesn't like me and it's easy to understand why. He was one of my husband's old drinking cronies. But he gave it up. It killed Frank. Perhaps Charlie blames me for the way Frank lived and died. Perhaps I should be blamed. I loved him for a short while. I hated him for a great many years. I think I'm glad he's dead. Even if I am not glad I'm not going to waste the rest of my life blaming myself for the waste of his. God knows I've wasted enough already. I shall never love anyone again. I don't think I am capable of it any more. And if you imagine that by revealing myself to you I've given you some clues to my personality which might help you in our next encounter, well, good luck to you.'

He couldn't help laughing at her last throwaway remark and after a moment she began to laugh as well. Over coffee they smiled at each other. She was still smiling when she locked the gates, the doors, at home.

Her friends watched the growth of the romance with disbelief. The oldest member could not hide his disgust. Bob and Edna played chess in her drawing-room now and she beat him less often.

'Why do you throw away your queen?' he once asked.

'I never throw it away,' she answered. 'I surrender it. It's an important difference.'

'I think it's a mistake,' he said. 'I know you love sneaking up with your bishop to give the belt of the crozier but if you meet a really strong player you won't survive the loss of a queen.'

'Most of the games I've lost so far,' she said, 'have been because I held on to my queen. I've entered for the next

Open. We'll see how it works then. Most people get careless after the sacrifice of a queen. When you're careless you make fatal mistakes. I never make mistakes.'

'Never?' he asked, thinking about Frank.

'Not any longer.' She looked coldly at him. 'I never make mistakes now.' A shiver, unaccountably, ran up his spine.

Bob didn't enter for the Open. He shrugged at the oldest member's dismay.

'I want to help Edna,' he said. 'She's terribly keen. And I've had my day.'

'You're a fool,' the oldest member said. 'A fool. She has you there.' He cupped the palm of his hand.

Bob shook his head. 'You're a bitter old man and you have a chip on your shoulder about Edna simply because you knew Frank.'

'Well, I admit I might be wrong about Frank. He was a no-good drifter always, even before he met her. Charming, but a bit of a waster. Yet there is something about her. Something peculiar. I can't put my finger on it. I feel if I shook hands with her that hers would be cold and clammy. Like a fish. Cold-blooded.'

Bob got angry then. 'Leave her alone,' he said. 'What the hell do you know about her?'

'She's ten years older than you,' the oldest member called after him as he turned away. 'I know that about her.'

Bob could not be sure afterwards if it wasn't merely disgust at Charlie's spite that made him propose to Edna the same evening. But he was certain of his own sense of reprieve, as if he had been snatched from the edge of a precipice, when she said, 'It's very kind of you to ask me, Bob, but no, thank you just the same. At least, not just yet. Perhaps later. But then, later I will be even older and that will be too late for both of us. Let's try and forget all about it.

I can cope with single loneliness, but not the other kind, ever again – and I wouldn't be any good for you either.'

He hadn't the courage, or perhaps the dishonesty, to plead with her. He thought she gave him a rather cynical look as if she hadn't expected any better of him. Damn that old devil, he thought angrily. He has messed everything up because of his spleen. He should retire to chew over his chess problems beside the fire and leave my private affairs alone. Next time I see him I'll tell him so.

To Edna Bob said, 'Age is relative, like everything else.'

'Relative to what?' she asked. 'Are you going to suggest we go space travelling, or that I go space travelling so that you will catch up on me? We're stuck on this planet for the time being and I don't mind ageing. In some ways I feel younger now than ever. I can thank you in part for it. Anyway, it's not so much that I'm too old for you as that you're too young for me.'

Irrationally then, he felt cheated out of some rich experience by her rejection, an immature, adolescent, forty-year-old bachelor, his last chance for growth taken from him.

The Open lasted for two days. As was expected, Edna did well. For her final game she met a seventeen-year-old who had nothing to lose and everything to gain. Cheerfully extrovert, he was encouraged by a gang of youthful supporters. Edna was not her usual cool self. His brash youth seemed to unnerve her. She sat at the board edgily, fingers playing a staccato tune on the table. He was not the kind of young man she was likely to meet in the normal course of events and he was very obviously not impressed or intimidated by her aristocratic air. His self-confidence was devastating. Worse than that was his enormous good humour. He treated the occasion with little respect.

Even Charlie was so irritated by his levity that he gave

outspoken support to Edna. 'Use that queen. Why do you think it's there? This fellow is good. What's more, he doesn't care about anything which makes him even more dangerous. It's almost as if he had no morals.'

'Perhaps that's his weakness,' she laughed, grateful for Charlie's apparent change of heart.

'His strength. His strength,' Charlie growled.

Edna and the seventeen-year-old sat face to face over the board, opposites in everything, age, sex, background, experience. The opening moves were made swiftly and without much reflection. With the exchange of the first pawns and the advance of the pieces, a little puff of tension hovered over the table. Edna, playing the disadvantaged black, exchanged a knight for a bishop and looked up to find Charlie glaring at her. She yawned delicately, patting her half-open mouth with a tender hand.

He turned away to mutter to Bob, 'That's all a performance. She is as nervous as a kitten. He'll make mincemeat of her and serve her right.'

'I think she has lost ground,' Bob agreed. 'He'll make her eat her mistakes. Underneath his blithe air he's very aggressive. But who knows? Maybe there's hidden aggression in Edna.'

'Now you're talking,' Charlie snorted. 'She's the most aggressive woman I have ever met. It's bottled up but it's there. Could be it's why she won't use her queen. Too much power. A Pandora's box for her. It would release too much. And what would she do with it? What would women do if we let them have power, tell me that? None of us would be safe. Bad enough they should be playing chess without them winning. She's met her match here. A young fellow who doesn't give a tinker's curse for her airs and graces.'

'You're talking in riddles,' Bob said. 'It's only a game.'

'You've been playing chess for over twenty-five years and you can say that! No wonder she swiped you. Chess is everything. Life and death, good and evil. Even the Devil plays chess, as you should know. He says check when a man falls into sin and unless he can cover the check by repentance, the Devil says mate and carries him off to hell from whence there is no escape.' The last phrase was uttered in a tone of melodramatic gloom. Charlie looked cynically diabolical and put two horn-like fingers mockingly on his crown before turning back to the game.

Edna was sitting back on her chair, her eyes closed. The young man nonchalantly wiped the back of his hand across his nose and yawned.

At the sound of the exhaled breath, Edna leaned over suddenly and said, 'Oh, I'm so sorry. Is it my move?'

His hand came down decisively and he played QR-Kt 1. She looked at her clock and then up at Charlie. He thought he caught a slight smile and he leaned over her opponent's shoulder to examine the board.

'Do you mind?' the young man said. 'You'll spoil my concentration.' The petulant tone was as unexpected as the admission and Charlie stared hard again at the board as he was ushered firmly back by a steward. He went off to find Bob who was smoking solitarily in another room, looking thoughtful and probably worried.

'You're right,' Charlie said. 'It is only a game. And winner takes all.'

A loud burst of cheering came from the hall. Charlie dashed back, followed by Bob, to find the young man being congratulated by the crowd, and Edna sitting quietly with the same smile on her face.

'What in the name of God did you do?' Charlie rasped the words in fury. 'You had him. You knew you had him.'

'It's only a game,' she said. 'Games are for children.'

'You offered your queen,' Charlie guessed, 'and he ignored it. I knew you'd come a cropper with your queen some day. What a waste.'

She spread her hands and said mildly, 'We all make mistakes.'

Bob took one hand protectively in his. He was smiling. 'It is only a game. Come and have a drink with me.'

'That would be very nice', she said, returning his smile and allowing him to lead her away, a proprietary arm now around her shoulder.

Charlie started to go after them. Then he stopped. 'Well,' he sighed. 'So that's it. And so checkmate to you too, old girl.'

Ruth

A picture of Ruth standing in a cornfield hung over the kitchen door. Long ago a battered Sacred Heart badge had acted as talisman. 'Guard this house' had been part of their evening prayer. Now, the picture of Ruth, cut from a child's Bible, framed in black, covered the crack in the plaster.

At the kitchen table the two women seemed to dream over their coffee. They floated contentedly, each one cocooned in a haze of forgetfulness. An onlooker might have supposed them to be drugtakers of a more deliberate kind, smoking pot or sniffing cocaine to induce the same euphoria.

The younger of the women pondered on the picture they must have made. For a brief second she stepped in imagination, outside her skin, to observe the scene. A tableau of mother and daughter. She was conscious of a prickling at the back of her neck and retreated to full self-possession. A second's extension might induce trance or precipitate death. For a moment it seemed just that easy.

'It's peaceful here, a relief to get away from the children for a few hours.'

'You should do it more often.'

'It's not easy.'

'Ah well. You know best.'

The mother's words were breathed out on a sigh. Like an echo, Eithne also sighed. They shared the strange habit of holding their breath for too long, as if afraid of disturbing some delicate balance, as if they always walked on a cobweb tightrope which might shatter at a rough exclamation and plunge them into awareness. When eventually they exhaled, they sounded bored or despairing. But one could not hold one's breath for ever. Purpled skin and certain asphyxiation the result. The brain was last to be deprived of oxygen, hanging on to it desperately to the bitter end. Poor brain.

'I read a most extraordinary thing yesterday,' her mother remarked. 'Some nineteenth-century Frenchman, an obscure philosopher, quoting Darwin to the effect that women's brains were smaller than men's and consequently could not be expected to conclude thought processes as effectively as men. He added that Parisian women had the disadvantage of having large feet. He appeared to be quite serious. Do you see the connection?'

'Perhaps it's the missing link. Parisian women's large feet and universal woman's small brains.'

They smiled at the joke. Eithne said, 'I think you picked my brains that time.'

'Did I? Are you sure it wasn't the other way round?' Eithne wasn't sure. She could never decide if it was one powerful impulse shooting across to the other that created the contact, an electrical charge, or if one spy invaded the other's territory. Her first husband had also been telepathic. At times it was inconvenient, especially when they shared dreams. But he was dead a long time, almost twelve years.

'Perhaps it was a mistake marrying a widower.'

Her mother's words floated across the table. They were not offensive. Still, she wished them unsaid.

'Two families are a lot for one woman,' the voice continued calmly. 'One family is a lot for one woman.'

'He's a good man. And they're good children.'

'Good? Good? A relative word.'

'Please don't.'

'Very well then. I won't.'

At the bottom of her cup the coffee sediments settled. She inhaled their fragrance. Peter, her stepson, had hair the same colour, coffee brown.

'Just before you came in,' her mother went on, 'I was sitting here thinking about the time when you were a baby, before the others were born. I was twenty-five then. I sat here, with my eyes closed, remembering the day I climbed the rickety stairs to the new dressmaker's flat. I went into the wrong room. An old, white-haired woman lay in bed. I cried for her when I went outside, she so old, I so young, she with her thin white hair, I with my thick golden hair. Your father once held a sovereign against my hair to compare the colour. Just as I opened my eyes the thought came to me – I suppose

I'm like that old creature now – and there you were, standing, smiling at me. You came in very quietly.'

'You are funny,' Eithne said lovingly.

'My mother used to say that to me too.'

'It's a long time since even I was in my twenties.'

'And your hair was never as bright as mine. None of you had hair like mine.'

It was not a reproach or a boast. It was said neither with regret nor complacency. It was simply the truth.

Golden sunshine poured through the window. The yellow coffee mugs beamed it back. On the clothes line outside pink underwear fluttered. On the lawn underneath a thrush picked a foolhardy worm. Scenario for spring. But there were clouds and sudden squally showers.

Her mother poured more coffee.

'Young Peter's at a difficult age. Look out for squalls.'

'He called me an old nag yesterday.'

'Hag, nag or bag. It has to be one of them.'

It was said knowledgeably. What wisdom, what treasures of experience were locked in that knowledge. If only it could all be released to float around in the ether so that everyone might benefit – not just the studious and the eager to learn, but the indifferent and the callous. Knowledge and wisdom would filter through by osmosis, unable to escape. There was, after all, only a quantum of knowledge in the biosphere and it had to be rehashed constantly, like yesterday's roast. How could you explain that to a stepson who might reply, 'You aren't really my mother. Your knowledge and mine don't even have the same chemical base.' She wouldn't dare contradict his mixture of matter and abstraction. He could pluck words out of the air as if he were a conjuror performing for a credulous audience. His sentences quivered with the startled consciousness of birds. Then he let them fly off, careless of their freedom.

'At that age,' her mother continued relentlessly, 'a boy needs freedom. You have to let him off.'

Had she been let off, long ago when she was a child and her mother still a golden girl? They had shared more joyous celebration then. The pleasant ease with which they sipped their coffee had been rehearsed more vibrantly forty years earlier with a glass of milk or lemonade. The colours of memory were different. All those other days were golden, all of them extravagant. They had moved through seasons of happiness, making daisy chains by the river in summer, picking blackberries in September, chanting 'I saw the sea first' in May, as they cycled over the brow of the hill or sped down to the delights of sand and waves. Were there no warning cries? No shouts of 'Be careful'? She could not recall any. Not even for torn summer dresses. She could scarcely remember the dressmaker.

'The dressmaker was very poor.' Her mother's voice was reflective, with an uncharacteristic touch of sadness. Yet was it uncharacteristic? Crowding into her memory were faint echoes of melancholy, trailing comments of wistfulness which seemed to tinge the golden haze with grey.

'Did you know her well?'

'No. But she was wonderful at turning clothes.'

'Turning clothes? What do you mean?'

'Have you forgotten the Foxford tweeds? When you grew out of your coats Miss Martin unpicked all the seams, turned them and restitched them for one of the younger children. Those French seams were tedious. I often pitied her but she was glad of the work and I was glad to have it done. Her eyesight was fading and she had to crouch over the cloth. She always sat by the window so that she could get the last glimmer of daylight.'

The bony hands were what Eithne suddenly remembered.

The bony hands plied the needle, not deftly and elegantly but painfully, clumsily as if the needle had to be forced into the cloth against its will, as if every stitch unpicked shrieked in rebellion and wailed again when locked into the resisting cloth.

'The stitches tore the cloth and the cloth suffocated the clothes.'

'You remember her saying that? I didn't think you noticed. Poor Miss Martin. She had a very sad life.'

'You always said that.'

'It was the truth.'

Eithne warmed her hands around the mug of coffee. Its heat eased the twinges of arthritis in her fingers.

Later, driving home, she made a detour through the narrow backstreets of town to avoid the traffic-jammed main streets. Every day the bulldozers were at work, tearing down the old houses and shops to make way for brighter and better buildings. For months, even years, the gaunt remains exposed themselves to the sky. Chimney-breasts and mantelpieces clung for survival to the remaining walls before crashing into dust. For weeks on end, patterned wallpapers were displayed, violated by the weather until, like tattered flags, they too fell.

The tattered flags were another memory as she drove across the bridge. Under its parapets the river struggled against corsets of stone and mud, its restricted energy pitiable, the threat of that same energy, unchannelled, ever present. Her grandmother wore high whaleboned corsets. Placed across the chair in her bedroom they retained her shape as her body kept the imprint of their bondage. As a child, viewing them with alarm, she had hoped for such a suitable compromise, one which her mother had less successfully made.

'Dissipation and waste,' Grandmother had said once, scornfully, when Eithne's mother had talked of lost opportunities, of faded visions, of her wish that she might have been something else. If – if – if. If only.

'You do what you must.' For Grandmother it had been duty, conscientiously even lovingly performed. Certainly the tree planting and the tending of animals had never seemed a chore. But one never knew with Grandmother. She had learned to live with the constraints of her time and had rebelled only at the age of eighty-four when she denied she had ever married or ever borne children. Calmly disclaiming responsibility for the lives she had created, she lived her last few years insisting that she was Winifred Morgan, spinster. It was hard to know if she had ever loved the man whose bed she had shared for fifty years. Could any woman love any man for so long? Could anyone love anyone for so long? A few years of treasured freedom, which, unaccustomed, soured to loneliness before death was a high price to pay for – what? For not being Miss Martin with her bony fingers?

Passing the boathouse she looked down the boatslip and glimpsed a canoe being launched by two youths. Every day a challenger fought the river, plotted and planned its courses, devised ways of outwitting its tidal tricks, its strong undercurrents. Occasionally there were casualties, bobbing bodies grasping at an oar as they swept under the parapet before being rescued farther up. Now and again a bloated body drifted to the bank or lodged in one of the reedy islands. An inquest was held and a bland verdict pronounced.

Considering the inadequacies of such verdicts she did not allow for the indifference of two girls sauntering across the road. Heart lurching she braked. The tyres protested noisily at her cruelty. The girls glared. As she passed she had a glimpse of tight, denim-clad bottoms and unrestrained denim tops. She wondered what she might symbolise for them. Neat costume-clad car driver versus blue-jeaned liberated pedestrian. Were their symbols any less oppressive than hers, her mother's, her grandmother's?

By one o'clock she had reached home. The reassuringly familiar smell of casseroled meat and vegetables reminded her to thank God for science and automatic ovens. By ten past one she was ready for the first arrival. By half past one all seven were fed or feeding. The two youngest quarrelled and gossiped. The three middles read, their books propped against sauce bottles and milk jug. She tried feeble protest and was smiled at innocently and ignored. The two eldest, her stepchildren Peter and Alison, seemed to drown in their own thoughts, polite but remote.

Watching them as she tended their needs she was filled with love for them all, a painful, tender, protective love. It reached out to them, anxiously yearning to fight their battles with them or for them. Surely they would sense it? Surely one of them would lift their gaze to hers, would respond with a small sign?

The sauce bottle fell with a clatter and cracked a side plate There were 'ooh's of alarm and reproval from the youngest, silent disapproval from the elders. The middles read on and fed on. She removed the cracked plate and righted the sauce bottle.

'Why don't you dye your hair like Mrs Diffley?' Maureen asked. 'It would make you much younger-looking and no one would ever know.'

Her shock at the question was quickly covered. 'I'd know, so what use would it be?'

'You are funny,' Maureen said lovingly.

Warmth spread through her veins. Even her toes tingled. Her inner eye, like a concealed lens, caught them, suspended in time, photographed for ever on the screen of her memory. Their voices receded and faded. This fact of their existence was the supreme consolation. For one second they were poised, all of them, at the very centre of time, in the core of the universe. Everything else revolved around them. Their existence illuminated the dark corners of her soul. Separate and distinct as they were, she became their unifying force, their common bond. Other achievements were as nothing compared with this. God-like, self-satisfied, she lingered.

The fading voices advanced to become small cries of alarm. Her head jerked violently and she became aware of seven pairs of eyes fixed anxiously on her.

'I was just day-dreaming. Did I startle you?'

'You looked sick.' The youngest rushed to hug her. 'Are you all right?'

'You looked' – Peter paused for the right word – 'disorientated.'

'Disoriented,' she corrected. 'It is the destiny of mothers.'

'You are only my stepmother,' he reminded her, cruelly polite, rejecting excuses.

She had an urge to slap his face, very hard.

'You shouldn't say "only",' Alison reproved him. 'I never think of you as "only" or even "step".' She looked kindly at Eithne.

'You're only a silly girl,' Peter said scornfully.

'And you're a male chauvinist pig, junior grade.'

'Enough,' Eithne said sternly. 'You'll be late back.'

'School is sick,' Thomas said sadly. 'I hate it. Can I take a half day off?' He whined a little.

'Crybaby,' Peter jeered. 'Mama's pet.'

Thomas lashed out with his feet. Peter sidestepped smartly, grinning at his own adroitness and at his brother's rage.

Boys are cruel, Eithne thought, cruel little beasts.

'Get off to school,' she cried impetuously. 'All of you. Shoo. Shoo.' She flapped a tea towel at them.

The young ones laughed and scuttled off, blowing kisses to her as they went. The middles followed, a little anxiously. Peter and Alison cycled, Peter thrusting his handlebars slightly ahead of Alison. They left the drive, Alison pretending not to notice, pressing harder on her pedals. They would pass and re-pass each other many times before they reached the crossroads where they parted for their separate schools.

Her head ached slightly, the creases between her brows becoming furrowed. For no good reason she was exhausted and regretted the wasted morning. Mother was never lonely after all, and needed no visits from dutiful daughters. You need them, her inner voice was insistent. You need to be reminded of your own existence. You also were born. Once, a long time ago, you inherited the earth too.

The greasy dinner plates stared menacingly at her from the table. To have to wash them again was like permitting more torture. Waste, waste, waste, she cried aloud. Dissipation and waste. Flashing in quick succession came images of the dressmaker with the bony fingers, her mother, white-haired, staring at her reflection, white-haired, propped up in a strange bed, the two girls straddling the road defiantly, the river threshing, the houses crumbling all around and somewhere, in the distance, a field of bright corn and Ruth, alien, weeping amid it.

Day at the Sea

When the brothers were children, their mother held out the promise of a day at the sea as a great attainable reward. When the darkness of her anger enveloped them, she withdrew the promise, only to restore it with her forgiveness. In latter years they agreed her anger had been necessary, remembering what wild youths they had been, although the mother protested that they had been the solace of her widowhood, the light of her eyes, better than twenty daughters in their gentleness, and equal to ten sons in their strength and diligence. Without them, wild as they thought they were, the farm would have wilted and died. Instead, it grew with them, a few acres here and a few more there, until it straggled in little parcels of land through the parish. It became so scattered that much of their time was spent in getting to the various portions. Sundays and Holy Days were all the one. In their best clothes then, they walked their fields, and it was sufficient holiday to be able to walk, watching for encroaching thistles and ragwort, detecting the first sign of rush in low-lying patches, seeking for gaps in the thick, well-laid hedges. It was seldom that an animal of theirs strayed into a neighbour's land. And it was seldom too that the brothers quarrelled with the farmers whose land bounded theirs. Whatever wildness they had shown in their youth was tamed by the demands of their land and their animals. They had no time for so-called pleasures, and if they ever had any inclination to court a woman, they stifled it out of consideration for their mother. 'It wouldn't be fair,' they said. 'It wouldn't work. Two women in a kitchen.' And she did not protest too hard. Occasionally, she might say as a sop to her conscience, 'Why don't you get a girl of your own and let me retire to the hob?' and they would laugh indulgently at her. 'Plenty of time yet,' they said. Later it became 'Who'd be bothered with us?' or 'The best of them are gone.' And she was content enough.

Only one thing bothered her. She had never after all managed to bring them to the sea. As she grew old it became an irritant to her. No matter how they reassured her, she sighed over the betrayed promise. 'I meant you to go. I always meant it. But we never seemed to have the time.' Where did all the time go, she wondered. Where did all those lovely years vanish? What were they doing? She sighed for the wonders they had missed. Her talk became less of stock and land and more of her lost girlhood. 'We would haul the sea wrack up in bags,' she told them, 'when the ass was working in the bog. As good manure for those stony fields as ever you saw. But what do you know of hardship?' And she grumbled a little. 'You were reared soft.'

They laughed, teasing her. 'Oh we had it easy all right,' eyeing each other at the humour of it.

'But what do you know of wonders who have never seen the sea? I want you to see it before I die.'

'Don't talk of dying,' they said, horrified. 'You were never a day sick in your life.'

'I'm eighty-one years old,' she reminded them, 'and I'm getting tired. I think I'll not get up today.'

The elder of the two asked a neighbour to drive for the doctor, that the mother was taken bad. When he came, he remarked sardonically that he wished he could be as fit as that when he reached her age. 'What's wrong with her?' they asked.

'She's old. She's old,' he said, as if that explained it.

'Old?' They were surprised. 'Is she sick?'

'Ah, her parts are wearing out a bit,' he explained. 'She has a touch of high blood pressure. A touch of bronchitis. Nothing to worry about.' He left a prescription and hurried off to visit a really sick patient, grumbling about the wasted time.

'That fellow!' the mother said scornfully. 'I wouldn't let him dose a sick hen. Throw that old bit of paper away. How much did he charge?' She blessed herself in outrage when they told her. 'Easy come, easy go. The likes of him would have it. I suppose he goes to the sea every year of his life.' She plucked at the sheets while they stood looking at her, overcome by the sudden realisation of her age, her mortality. They saw that she was withering as if the years she had cheated for so long had outwitted her in one great leap of destruction.

'My tide is ebbing,' she said. 'The great tides of home used to suck the sand up as they went.' They sat down, one on each side of her bed, listening as they had done so often before. 'In the winter the sea tore up the land, greedy. Up on the headland you could stay safely and watch it hurl itself, pounding away. The great claws of it reaching for us. The whiteness of its edges. Thick, thick, foaming lace. And the greenness of it. Like the eyes of a cat. In summer it smiled. Blue on yellow sands. Or grey as a pigeon's back on misty days. Quiet then. Quiet but waiting. I want you to see the sea boys. I want you to see it before I die. Will you not go to please me?'

Her hands crept over the bed cover and rested, each one on one of theirs. 'We'll go tomorrow,' the elder brother said. He said it quickly, because he wanted no time for thinking over it in case he changed his mind. Her pleasure was a little reward to him, although it hardly compensated for the vexation of knowing that a day at the sea meant a lost day, putting him irretrievably on the debit side of time in the busiest month of the summer. A lifetime had passed since he thought with longing of the sea, a lifetime in which all his urges had been controlled as tightly as the horse pulling his plough. Desire was an alien force in him. The quickening desire for a woman had been killed as soon as it was conceived by the warnings of clerics and the taboos of his time. Of sins of the flesh he knew nothing, because he turned away from sly remarks or double talk. He and the brother had drowned whatever longings they might have had in the drinking bouts of their early youth. 'A terror to the world,' their contemporaries remembered them, adding, lest they be misjudged, that two decenter men never lived. Tales survived of lost days when they vanished from the farm, leaving the mother to milk and scour and churn. When, prodigal, they returned, they were received without welcome or accusation and were never asked to account for the missing days. No one knew why they stopped drinking. Everyone knew that others who had started in the same way had ended up as alcoholics, or at least, permanent, heavy drinkers. But the brothers stopped short in their early twenties and never drank again. It was said that the reason they worked so hard was that they were forever trying to recapture the time they had squandered.

Arrangements for the proposed trip had to be made at once. A substitute milker was found and a car and driver hired for the day. A neighbour promised to keep an eye on the old woman. Another agreed to bring the churnfuls of milk to the creamery. 'Well, after all,' said the younger brother, 'one day out of so many is easy to spare.'

'Only loafers waste time,' the other said. 'But for the old lady we'll do it.' He half hoped the day would be wet.

But it was not wet. Grinning hugely the sun shot up in the early morning, splashing the fields with brilliance. The mother knew by the elder brother's face that he was not pleased. 'Don't go if it's only to soothe me,' she said. 'I don't want you to go just for the sake of my whim. But I'll not deny it would cheer me if you went. All my people were dead or emigrated before I left and I've never been back. And now I can't think why I never went back. I can't even remember how I came to leave it, or why I married your father. I'm old and doddery and I tied you to myself and to this place because I knew of no other way to live. Maybe I did wrong.'

'You didn't tie us,' he said patiently. 'And you did no wrong. It will be nice to see the sea after all, and the place where you were a girl.'

'I expect it's all changed,' she said. 'All modern now. Maybe no thatch left on any house.'

'Maybe. Maybe not,' he said and bent to kiss her lightly on the forehead.

'You're a good boy,' she whispered when he was gone, her eyes watering. 'God help you, you're both good boys.'

They turned their backs on their fields, the elder brother reluctantly, the younger brother with an easier mind. He did not feel the same urge to keep apace of time. 'It will all be there when we come back,' he thought, 'and it will be all there when we are gone forever.' He bore the brother's dogged insistence on work without rancour, acting as the junior partner in everything. There was no doubt in his mind that they had both been saved from the wretchedness of a hostel in London or Liverpool only by their unfailing labour. But he could relax without feeling guilty or without having to justify himself. He did not look forward to the day's outing. It was a thing that had to be done. It was a fitting gesture to the old woman whose memories were so ancient yet still fresh, and whose past had now usurped the present's importance.

The driver was both knowledgeable and inquisitive. They accepted his information with polite interest but gave back nothing in answer to his probing. His questions, however subtly framed, were discarded as being of no value. 'I've two odd bods here,' he thought, cheerfully forgiving them their silence. He took them over the mountain where the little houses shrank into the immensity of the space around them. The brothers, looking out on the sloping, rocky fields, thought of the work that had cleared them of stone and water to bring them to their little greenness. Behind their silence they hid the wonder they felt at the vastness of rock around them. When they reached the burren country and were swallowed up into the grey stretches of stone, they stared in amazement at the strange handiwork of nature. The driver pointed out Holy Well and the prehistoric tomb, and the younger brother had a fleeting thought of the ghosts who might haunt such places. A row of ruined cottages, oases of green in their undisturbed growth of trees and hedges, a castle, gaunt, indifferent as a man too used to neglect, a sudden rolling valley startling in its richness, more rocks, mountains of rocks, and then there was the sea.

It unfolded below them with such vividness that the younger brother felt his breath hold. He was filled with a strange sense of wonder. No sensation he had ever known could compare with it. A hunger he had never known began to possess him. As they descended the steep road and levelled out above the water, he wanted to stop the car and stare his fill in peace. The company of the other men was a hindrance to his enjoyment and he felt irked that he could not be alone to stem his hunger. But it was more like thirst. All his tissues seemed dehydrated. He longed to plunge straight into the sea for relief. The road cut through the mountain which fell below them into the water. Spray hit off the rocks, rebounding in white torrents. Ahead the road curved to encircle the beach, yellow under the sun.

'There we are,' the driver pointed. 'That's the place you wanted. Killbeg.' He stopped beside a petrol station and public house. They declined his offer of a pint and got out, stretching their cramped legs.

'It's quiet,' the elder brother said. 'Quiet.'

'I can hear the sea,' the younger man said.

It was possible even to feel the sound, a dull thundering mingling with his heart beats. They followed a track to the ruin which they were told had been the mother's house. There were two other ruins beside it, all of them roofless and in that state of dilapidation as common as blackberries on western roads. Their abandonment showed in the empty hearths through which the sky could be seen and in the little squares, once bedrooms, which flanked the central living space. The brothers stood there dutifully, paying tribute, embarrassed at this intrusion into the mother's past.

'It must have been a fine house in its day,' the younger brother said bravely. 'Small but solid.'

'Windy,' said the other. 'Exposed.' He drew his shoulders up to his neck and stared through the window space at the sea stretching itself below them. It was a long way down. The only fence to protect the unwary was made of slabs of the local stone buried upright along the edge. 'Well, we've seen it.' He moved out determinedly. 'We've seen it all.'

'Now that we're here,' said the other, 'we might as well walk down to the beach. The old lady will ask if we've been.'

'We could get half a day's meadowing cut if we went home now.'

'What's the hurry? She'll be disappointed if we don't spend the full day here.'

'What's the good of it? It's a waste of time.'

'Time.' The younger brother sighed exasperatedly. 'What's time?' And he was aware for a moment of a new concept of life. Lurking somewhere, if he could only find it, was an untouched vision. His mind strained to reach it. And it was gone.

'There are too many people on the beach.' The older brother began to get angry. 'A right pair of eejits we'll look there.'

'You only look what you feel.' The younger brother too was angry. Why was it he always had to give in? He would not capitulate today. He would not hand over this one day to the brother's miserly hoard of hours. He pretended it was filial duty, compassion for the old woman bundled in the bed, waiting, counting the minutes until they came back, anticipating their account of the day. 'What did you see?' she would cry. 'What way did you go? Did you meet anyone? Did you speak with anyone?', drawing out of their slow speech the nuggets of information to treasure and gloat over. He wished for the craft of word spinning, or the gift of a painter's brush so that he might hold for her as well as for himself the glory of this day. He determined not to relinquish even a moment of it. He walked towards the track leading down to the beach and a few minutes later heard the movement of his brother behind him.

The tide had turned. They walked in their leather boots and dark suits, stiffly collared, black against the colours of sea, sky and sand. The younger brother stared again at the breakers, curling, rolling, tumbling in towards them, then pulling back, dragged by the force of the twisting earth, sucking up the sand. It was true what his mother had said. The great tides of home sucked the sand as they went. Around him families sunbathed in semi-nakedness. He tried to look away but his eyes were drawn back again to the carefree bodies. He stooped suddenly and untied his boots. His brother looked in disbelief and scorn as the boots were thrown on a rock and he daringly rolled up his trousers. The white, hairy shanks glimmered below the dark blue serge. 'God save us,' the elder brother muttered and turned his head to blot out the embarrassing sight. The wet sand, he noticed, had strange patterns on it. There were little crevices in it with rivulets of water left behind by the sea. He was reminded of a chicken scurrying to catch up with its mother. But this was a cruel mother, devouring and laying waste at will. It swallowed up sailor and innocent child alike. He looked again at the patterns near his feet, and cried out in delight to his brother, 'Look here. Wheat. It's like wheat.'

The younger brother looked at the branching patterns. They *were* like wheat. There were the stems and the heavy seeding heads, all impressed in the sand and appearing to move because of the water rippling in them. 'It's strange all right,' he nodded, smiling, and moved off to poke at rock pools and stare in wonder at the creatures inside. The brother followed, pleased with his discovery and a little comforted. They looked into the same pool and saw two different worlds. One saw a miniature fantasy land, luminous and beautiful, where sea urchin, crab, periwinkle, sea anemone lived enchanted lives. The other saw snails and shells and weeds. He thought of the weed creeping into his wheat, and the snails that fell into the milk at night when the brother left the lid off.

They sat in the shade of a rock and began to eat their sandwiches. The elder brother's feet were cramped in his boots, the younger brother's wriggled, massaging the sand voluptuously. Around them, flesh worshipped the sun, the dedication of each worshipper revealed in the depth of the tan achieved. A fat white woman wallowed in the water, allowing the breakers to knock her over, while she shrieked in delight. 'They've no shame,' the older brother groaned, shuddering at the sight of great thighs and breasts barely encased by the swimsuit. The younger brother did not answer. He was shooting looks from under his eyelids at better proportioned and better coloured bodies. The air vibrated with exuberance, echoing shouts of joy and thundering waves. The sea itself was caught up in pagan delight. A dog ran up and down the beach barking, and the waves reached great frothy, frolicking paws back to him. 'This is the life,' the younger brother said, undoing his tie and removing his jacket. The other sat foolish in his dignity, black and stiff, rigid as the rock behind him, beginning to perspire in the heat. He wanted to say 'We'll go home now,' but the words would not come. For some reason he could not understand their roles were reversed. Here he had to follow the rule of his brother. Here was no place for his authority. This alien landscape cut away the order he had built into his life, the discipline he had forced on himself. The sea beat at his ears, primeval memories threatening to destroy him. A man could not fence those noisy acres or buy a patch to enlarge his holding. Too long ago his tissues had known that salty water. Earth in his nails now, earthy his skin. He felt the sterility of sand under his fingers. It had no substance. Its cleanness was unnerving, like the neurotic hygiene of a house-proud woman. He closed his eyes, suffering the day, enduring the salty heat.

There were other hazards to be faced before the day was over. Somehow, he could not tell how, the brother got into conversation with a fisherman from the smallest and nearest of the three islands lying off shore. And somehow the elder brother found himself clutching the sides of a currach as it rode the sea while the others in the boat laughed and talked. The young brother groped for remnants of his school Irish and came out triumphantly with 'Cé 'chaoi bhfuil tú?' They roared with laughter. 'Cé 'chaoi bhfuil tú féin?' they shouted, clapping him on the back.

Like an exile returned he beamed at them, seizing on every vaguely intelligible word, hanging on to each gesture and exclamation as if the secrets of his life might be revealed in them, laughing at everything, at the sky brighter than he ever remembered it, at the porpoises somersaulting around them, at the sea cradling him, wooing him, swinging him up into a peak of ecstasy. Drunk with joy he tasted every second of the hours as if they were the liquor-laden drops of his youth.

Inevitably the day's end had to be celebrated with the drink he had so long forsworn. To the brother watching the flamboyant lift of the younger man's elbow in the public house it was a fittingly miserable end to a miserable occasion. Sober and bitter he watched the brother become the raconteur of the night, applauded by strangers with a familiarity that made his blood curdle. He withdrew into the shadows while the room filled with the spillover from Lisdoonvarna, and the crowd, already satiated by a week of crucifyingly Irish music and dancing, song and drink, cheered for more. He looked at the middle-aged women mocking their maturity with a skittishness that revolted him. Black-edged eyes set in painted, tan faces flickered in the haze of smoke. And over it all the fiddle screeched and the accordion bellowed and outside the sea grumbled. A wasted day, he thought, a wasted hell of a day, and he cursed his brother and the foolish old woman and himself and pined for his quiet fields.

The taxi driver was amused. 'By God, he had a day and a half,' he said when they threw the rollicking brother into the back seat. 'I'd say he packed a lot into this day.'

'You could say that,' the older brother said. A little pity stirred in him.

It was destroyed with the driver's next sentence. 'He'll have one hell of a hangover tomorrow.'

Another day gone, he thought. Not only would he have to make up for this day, but he would have to carry the whole of the next one on his back and perhaps half the day after. It would surely take a day and a half for the brother to recover.

'It will all be there when we get back,' mumbled the body in the back seat. 'Not to worry. It won't go away. It will all wait. And let it wait.' The burst of energy and defiance needed to get the last sentence out was too much for him.

He snored for the whole of the journey home.

He awoke next morning at his usual time. He met the older brother's accusing silence with a silence of his own, challenging, assertive. He milked the cows painfully, one hand clutching his head. He drove to the creamery where his bloodshot eyes and purple-flecked skin drew some teasing. 'You must have got great sea air.' 'You have a fine tan.' 'I suppose you were swimming all day.' He ignored them. The old woman drew from them what she could. To their little words she added words of her own, embroidering their bare vocabulary so that the day they had spent began to take shape in her mind. She coaxed descriptions out of them, hinting with adjective and adverb, and pooled their sentences until she made a great treasury of experience to enrich her emptying hours. Their few words gave life to her memories so that they sprang back, invigorated. From her bed she stared through the window at fields and hedges and saw the great seas and the stone walls of her youth. The elder brother was relieved when the younger brother did not drink again. He forgot the day. He smiled at his swaying, silky green wheat and he felt a happiness he had not known for a long time. Sometimes he whistled at his work and he made overtures to the brother as if he had to make up to him for something. The potato fields had white blossoms on green undulating leaves. The calves pucked and played in the paddock. The younger brother carried on as usual, taking his share of the burden, listening and agreeing. But sometimes he stood staring at nothing, which was a thing he had never done before.